DEAD

Simon Shaw trained at the Bristol Old Vic
Theatre School and became a professional actor
in 1979. He has worked in rep, fringe, TV and in
the West End. His two previous Philip Fletcher
novels, *Murder Out of Tune* and *Bloody
Instructions*, were selected as books of the year
in the *Spectator*. His second novel, *Killer
Cinderella*, won the 'Last Laugh Award', given
by the Crime Writers' Association for the
funniest crime novel of the year. Simon Shaw
lives in London.

DEAD FOR A DUCAT

by

Simon Shaw

GOLLANCZ CRIME

First published in Great Britain 1992
by Victor Gollancz Ltd

First VG Crime edition published 1993
by Victor Gollancz
A Cassell imprint
Villiers House, 41/47 Strand, London WC2N 5JE

A catalogue record for this book is
available from the British Library

ISBN 0 575 05535 9

Printed and bound in Great Britain
by Cox & Wyman Ltd, Reading

For David Rintoul who told me a joke,
and for Rupert Graves who thinks he might
have been in it

. . . Let it work;
For 'tis the sport to have the enginer
Hoist with his own petar: and it shall go hard
But I will delve one yard below their mines,
And blow them at the moon.

Hamlet, III, iv

I

Waking up was the worst part of the day. A moment of blankness followed by dulled but unremitting awareness: the parched tongue and the sirocco breath rattling the throat; the inevitable tap-tap on the temples; the screwed-up dampness of the sheets; the remembrance that the bed was empty; the room was empty; the life empty. She wasn't there this morning, either.

Philip Fletcher opened a bloodshot eye and stared at the sunlight violating the cracks in the curtains.

'Good morning to the world,' he said in a dry whisper, 'and next . . .'

And next? Who did he have to say good morning to, next?

'Oh, fuck off, world!'

The blood rushed from his head as he staggered out of bed. He could feel it coursing through his veins, mixing somewhere down below in a sour cocktail with the residue of last night's binge. His stomach felt nauseous; his bladder ached; his liver had called in the shop stewards. He'd better get to the bathroom fast.

The fluorescent light stilettoed his retina. In a half-blind haze he managed to claw open the medicine cabinet, wrestle off the Panadol lid and set the Alka Seltzer fizzing in his tooth-brush mug. He emptied his bladder with appalled resignation and then, feeling thoroughly enervated, sat down heavily on the side of the bath. He stared grimly at himself in the mirror.

'What bloody man is that?'

He looked like something out of an Oxfam poster. Those weren't bags under his eyes, they were black plastic bin-liners. Where his cheeks had once been there were bottomless pits. Were those lank strands on his head hair or part of a misplaced toilet-brush? His skin looked like condemned blancmange.

He drank the Alka Seltzer, filled the cup again with metallic-tasting water and gulped it down. The Panadol were already in there, somewhere, taking their slow age to infiltrate the lead-lined stomach and swim their way against the post-alcoholic tide to soothe those raw and distant nerve-ends. He was going to feel buggered for another half hour at least.

'Oh God . . . why?'

He feebly clasped the edge of the sink and pulled himself up. He let the water run until it was cold, then soaked his flannel and wiped his face and neck. At least not all sensation was dead: there was a tingle. But nothing to write home about.

'I 'gin to be aweary of the sun,' he muttered into the mirror, and groaned. 'Stop quoting from that bloody play, will you?'

He stumbled out of the bathroom and stomped crossly into the kitchen. He tried to pull open a fresh foil pack of coffee, looked in vain for a sharp knife, then tried again with his teeth, to no avail. At least there was some water in the kettle, he wouldn't have to disturb the piles of crockery in the sink. He managed to find the jar of Gold Blend more or less where he thought he'd remembered leaving it; which was a minor bloody cause for celebration.

'This is a bloody mess. What day is it? Where's Mrs Thing got to?'

Mrs Thing only came in once a week, it was true, but surely he couldn't have created this Augean disaster area in only a sennight? The bin was bursting, the floor was filthy. There was broken glass in the corner and he had bare feet. Perhaps Mrs Thing was displeased with him and had resigned. No, no *perhaps* about it: he was way down on her list of favourite people; in fact, anchored firmly to the bottom. It had not always been thus. In the days when he had been neat and tidy it had been her wont to pronounce him her favourite. Surely some residual sympathy from those days lingered? She wouldn't just walk out on him without a word, would she?

The boiling kettle interrupted his fruitless mental anabasis. He wasted half a minute in the futile search for a clean cup, then bowed to the inevitable and went in search of a less than gangrenous one amidst the detritus in the sink. He found a chipped mug with the handle missing. Said it all, really.

He took his coffee next door, sat on the arm of the off-white sofa (getting more off by the day) and tucked his feet up under a cushion. His feet were cold. The rest of him wasn't warm. His pyjamas were damp and uncomfortable. Although the thermostat was up, it was the middle of bloody December. With any luck he'd catch pneumonia and die.

Bloody December . . . was that it? It wasn't sodding Christmas already, was it? Festive cards with indecipherable signatures had been arriving for weeks. Needless to say, they'd gone straight into the bin. Perhaps the world and Mrs Thing were on holiday, which would explain a lot.

The phone rang. Or rather, it didn't so much ring as make a modern mechanical buzzing noise, like an electric fart.

'Oh, piss off!' said Philip uselessly.

Ring-ring, it went. Buzz-buzz. Fart-fart. If the answerphone hadn't cut in by now it must mean he'd forgotten to leave the bloody thing on. What time was it, anyway? If the phone hadn't been ringing he could have used it to call up the speaking clock. Was there a clock in the room? Besides the one on the mantel-piece, which he hadn't remembered to wind up for three months? Would his watch be on the bedside table? Who knew? Who cared? He shrugged and took a sip of his coffee. It was disgusting. It wasn't like that in the ads. Wearily he lifted the phone.

'Yes?' he growled. He had meant to bark, but a growl was the most he could manage.

'Philip, it's John here.'

John? Who did he know called John? There was some agent fellow of the name who had sometimes called him in the dim and distant past. Could it be him?

'Hello, John there,' he murmured indifferently.

'Are you all right, Philip? You don't sound all there.'

'Bit early for me, love,' he said with casual off-the-shoulder theatricality.

'Bit early?' John laughed good-naturedly. 'Late last night, were we?'

As he spoke Philip noticed the video in the corner. The timer's green digits read 12.29. From the apparent general over-availability of sunlight it was unlikely to presage the imminent striking of half past midnight.

'Philip,' this John fellow was continuing, 'I've got something for you. Kenneth Kilmaine wants to see you. He'd like to meet you tonight.'

'Yes? Oh, good . . .'

Who the fuck was Kenneth Kilmaine?

'He says terribly sorry to butt in so near Christmas and all that' – ah-ha! – 'but he's desperate to meet you. I'm afraid I only got a fax, I don't have any details, but his secretary's promised to call me back and I'll speak to you later. It sounds like a pretty major film, Philip.'

'Mm. Jolly good.'

'Philip?'

There was a long pause. John had sounded hesitant. Philip tried another sip of his coffee and found it still revolting. He noticed an abandoned half-bottle of Scotch on the side-board.

'Er, Philip?'

'Yes,' he answered with a yawn. 'It's still little old me.' He leant across for the bottle.

'Philip, I don't want to be, well, intrusive, but . . . it is the season of good cheer, I know, but you will go easy on the drink tonight, won't you?'

Philip held the half-bottle upside-down over his coffee. A few drops plopped in.

'My dear, I'm not a complete alcoholic,' he answered morosely, thinking – not for bloody want of trying. He put the coffee to his lips again and failed to detect any improvement. John gave an embarrassed laugh.

'No, no, of course you're not, but . . . but it is three months since you got back from America and there hasn't been a dicky-bird. I've been doing my damnedest too, I promise you that.'

'Bad time of year, old thing. Bloody panto season.'

'Yes, I know, but . . . but this is something else. They wouldn't even see you for that thing at Central. And you know who they gave it to? Dick Jones. I ask you!'

Philip frowned. He seemed to remember that he had once thought of murdering Dick Jones. Pity he hadn't.

'I can't help it if they've got no judgement,' he said darkly.

'I'm afraid it may be more than a question of judgement, Philip. I think the court case did you a lot of harm.'

'Oh, that . . . oh, yes . . .'

He didn't want to talk about the court case. Nor, fortunately, did John, who repeated hurriedly that he would call back with the details later on and said goodbye. The line went dead.

'And merry bleeding Christmas to you,' said Philip, replacing the receiver thoughtfully. He rubbed his still sore head with a slow circular motion. He was sure there was a full bottle of whisky somewhere.

He went to run a bath, then came back and commenced a search. There were enough empty bottles – he counted five in all – but none in the preferred state. Were there any upstairs? He looked gingerly at the iron spiral staircase in the corner which led up to his 'study' and the spare room. Climbing those narrow treacherous steps (installed by the previous owner, a screaming interior designer) made him feel dizzy when he was hale and hearty. It was odds on he'd fall and break his neck if he tried to negotiate them in his present state. How badly did he want that drink?

'Bit early, isn't it?' he told himself. 'It's only the morning.'

'It's not, you know,' he answered aloud. 'It's nearly lunch-time.'

'That's academic. When was the last time you ate lunch? Isn't there anything in the fridge . . . ?'

He had a look. There was. An almost full bottle of Stolichnaya. It had been almost full for a year and a day now. He didn't like vodka. He had bought it for Kate.

He banged the fridge door shut. The thought of tasting vodka made him feel slightly ill. Was that a good sign? Or was he beyond redemption? Wasn't the bath about to overflow?

He scuttled out of the kitchen and into the bathroom and grabbed at the taps dramatically. The sudden expenditure of effort left him gasping for breath. He caught his eye in the half-steamed mirror.

'Not you again . . .'

He stuck out his tongue, which was yellow and unwholesome.

'Look at yourself!'

He looked. Not a pretty sight. Ready for the funeral baked meats.

'If sack and sugar be a fault, God help the wicked!'

'Get a grip on yourself before it's too late!'

'Too late already. You heard what he said about the court case. Inebriated actor charged with endangering life and limb on a jumbo jet, not to mention molesting a stewardess, punching a steward and resisting arrest at Heathrow. Tabloids had a field day. "Flopped Shakespearian star in drunken mid-Atlantic punch-up." Oh, reputation! Reputation! Reputation!'

'It's the flopped bit that really hurt, isn't it?'

'The bastards!'

He clutched his head in his hands. His headache was coming back. If it had ever gone away. Good thing he hadn't found any more whisky. He sank back against the bath.

'Water, water everywhere, and not a drop to drink.'

He felt so weak he could hardly support himself. He wanted to fall on to the floor and curl into a foetal heap.

'You're pretty far gone, old thing, aren't you?'

He slipped out of his sweat-stiffening pyjamas and lowered himself into the bath. It felt good, the heat, the steam. He wet his flannel and draped it over his head, shielding his eyes from the ugly fluorescent shine. He lay back dozily, and tried to imagine himself floating.

The water lapped gently at his chin. It was pleasant and embryonic to float. The laboured wheezing of his breath grew softer. Unbidden images flashed across his brain.

'A shocking and disgraceful exhibition of drunken and disorderly conduct from one in the public eye who should have known better.'

That was the judge. Thin-faced, almost lipless. Someone whose idea of a binge was topping up his amontillado before dinner.

'Shut up, you fucking old bore.'

He had been wanting to say that all the time in court. Instead, he had had to button his lip and concentrate hard on looking humble and repentant, than which nothing came less naturally to him.

'My client has been under severe strain,' his defence counsel had pleaded by way of mitigation. 'He has not only had to suffer a professional crisis brought on by the failure of his Macbeth on Broadway, but at the same time he has had to endure constant media harassment and intrusion into his private life following the much-publicised break-up of his relationship with Miss Katherine Webster.'

The humiliation in court had been even worse than his treatment by the tabloids. At least he could choose not to read the papers; he had had to endure the processes of legal dissection in public. What did it have to do with any of them, either the slating the critics had given him or his personal troubles?

'They do not excuse his deplorable conduct.'

The judge again.

'Oh, stick your wig up your arse, duckie!'

It would have been worth saying that just to see the old bore's expression. If he were capable of expression . . . colourless personality, reedy voice; what could the casting department have been thinking of?

'Philip, you're impossible!'

He sat up suddenly, creating a swell of water that splashed on to the floor. Her voice, it had sounded so close. He listened, as if for the sound of the key turning in the lock (the key she still had), her steps on the bare boards by the door.

'Kate?'

No, she was only in his head, of course. He knew perfectly well where she really was, thousands of miles away, in Hollywood, making movies. Where he had wanted to be. Where he had expected to be in the wake of his glorious triumph on the New York stage . . .

Inglorious catastrophe: closed after a fortnight; not a record but a humiliation none the less. It had only lasted that long because he'd had the producer over a barrel, but not even a gun to the head could have forced her beyond those two weeks.

'Do your worst, honey,' Martha had said. 'I can't run on forty per cent houses. You can't buck the critics in this town.'

Buck them? He'd have done more than that to the little shits if he'd had his way.

Tedious and unoriginal, uninspiring, dull, mediocre, insipid ... those were the good reviews. The accusatory adjectives stretched out to the crack of doom. They had gone for him hammer and tongs, no quarter given, no prisoners taken, red in tooth and claw. And then they'd twisted the knife and really made it hurt.

'What makes the production almost bearable is the Lady Macbeth of Kate Webster, the last-minute replacement for the better-known Lindsay Leonard, who quit the company over "artistic differences" (one sees her point). Ms Webster is a young actress of extraordinary power and versatility, an unknown, but not, I predict, for very long . . .'

They loved doing that, critics: tell one actor he's lousy, then beat him over the head with how good they think another one is.

'Philip, don't take it so personally.'

'Kate, for Christ's sake, shut up!'

He had almost hit her then, could have almost bloody strangled her. That her sympathy was genuine only made it worse; a woman killing him with kindness.

The only saving grace was that it had happened in America. Had it been in London, the English tabloids would scarcely have passed up the opportunity to gloat, but he was small beer in America. And destined to remain so. They'd got him on the way back anyway.

'Philip, they want me to go to Hollywood! For a screen test!'

Oh, God . . .

The water was tickling his nose. He was sinking millimetre by millimetre, as if willing himself to drown. That was an illusion. Why should he have had the courage for death when he didn't have enough to face up to life? He peeled the flannel off his face and tossed it with disgust towards his feet. He pulled the plug out with his toe. He no longer had strength to groan aloud.

Oh, God.

He stood dripping on to the bath-mat, watching his body shiver in the mirror. He was hunched, round-shouldered, febrile and etiolated. He was pathetic.

'You stupid, selfish, arrogant, destructive, drunken bastard!'

A flicker of a glint bestirred in his sallow eye.

'Oh, please! *Talented* bastard . . .'

He needed to be at his own ear, an inversion of Caesar's slave, to remind himself from time to time how good he was. If he didn't, no one else would. And if he overstated the case sometimes it was scarce surprising. His ego had been subjected to grievous assault and battery of late.

'Kate, I'm sorry.'

'Too late now, you prick.'

'I know, but I'm sorry anyway. It wasn't jealousy —'

'Ha!'

'All right, I mean it wasn't just jealousy . . . I was playing James Mason in *A Star Is Born*. Corny, I know, but at least my heart's in the wrong place. I'd brought you this far, you see. When Lindsay packed off I'd insisted on you for Mrs Macbeth against everyone's judgement, including your own. I was right though, wasn't I? Too bloody right. At exactly the same moment as I crashed fatally into a brick wall you overtook me and accelerated into the fast lane. Of course I was jealous, but what made it intolerable was the certainty I'd lost you. You riding into the sunset with your whole young life ahead of you (sorry about the crap script, I didn't write it), me left playing the bit-part opposite Johnny Walker. I couldn't have kept up. You wouldn't have wanted to be saddled with an old failed soak.'

'True, but you didn't have to behave like quite such a dickhead, did you?'

'Can't help it, love. It's not even acting.'

'O what a noble mind is here o'erthrown!'

'My thoughts exactly.'

'One who the vile blows and buffets of the world —'

'Not that bloody play again!'

'Then one like the base Indian –'

'Shut up!'

That was easily done: just press the lips together and keep them tight. Watch them whiten in the mirror. His forehead was wet, was it water or the sweat of concentration? The lines, unbidden, were buzzing round his head.

> . . . Of one not easily jealous, but, being wrought,
> Perplex'd in the extreme; of one whose hand,
> Like the base Indian, threw a pearl away
> Richer than all his tribe . . .

The lips slackened. Automatically they framed the end of the speech.

'I think we should declare a moratorium on that play too, luvvie.'

''Tis true. 'Tis pity. And pity 'tis –'

'And on that one too. On every one. Oh, God! Oh, no . . .'

He threw a towel over his head to shut out the world and felt his way back to the bedroom. When he removed the towel the first thing he saw was the Gordon Craig lithograph she had given him for his birthday. He put the towel back on. He should move house. Everywhere he looked there were memories. And when he looked inside too, only they were worse. He needed a drink. There wasn't any. He wanted a cigarette. The packet by the bed was empty, even the butts in the ashtray smoked down to the filter and irretrievable even by the desperate needy. He had to get out of here.

He rubbed his body down with the towel and went to the cupboard in search of clean clothes. Predictably, it was a waste of time. He had about as much chance of finding the Dead Sea Scrolls as a clean shirt. There were two pairs of clean underpants, though the elastic had gone in one and there were so many holes in the other that at first he mistook it for a string vest. Definitely not a day on which to get run over . . . There was a pair of clean socks too, though that had Father Christmases and fir trees embroidered on it and its presence in his cupboard was a complete mystery. But beggars, it has been justly observed, are so very rarely spoilt for choice. He put on the Christmas socks and the unelastic pants, and a suspiciously nylony yellow polo-neck top which he seemed to remember receiving one birthday from his Aunt Marjorie, and his only-slightly-stained but comfortable green corduroy trousers. He looked like an anaemic parrot. He reckoned that he had about reached the limits of slovenliness, and that he had no option in the continued absence of Mrs Thing but to try and remember how the washing-machine worked. He had known once, in the old impoverished Thing-less days. He had even been an allegedly dab hand with an iron. Hannah had always said he would have made someone a lovely wife.

He put on his long black coat and a scarf to cover his tired plumage. After wasting five minutes he found his keys in his coat pocket. Thoroughly bad-tempered, and with his headache rising, he stormed (or perhaps drizzled) out of the house.

The shock of fresh air made him gasp; it was like diving into a cold swimming-pool. He had to stop walking after a few paces and lean against the railings, he was so dizzy. Nausea enveloped him. For half a minute he thought he might be sick.

It passed and he walked on. He did feel a little like Boris Karloff stepping out of the mummy's tomb, but once his lungs had adjusted to the unaccustomed oxygen-rich atmosphere, something akin to a spring came into his gait. This third cousin twice-removed of jauntiness even tempted him to whistle as he crossed Highbury Fields.

There was a queue in the off-licence. Football fans. Philip disdained to notice them. The proximity to a major sporting venue was the one disadvantage of the area in his view. He loathed football with the kind of passionate intensity he usually reserved for all critics, most directors and those fellow thesps who quite manifestly didn't deserve to be where they were and certainly wouldn't be if only he had been offered the parts first, as he would have been if only all the producers in the world had had more than three brain cells to share between —

'Good morning, Mr Fletcher, and what can I get you today?'

The football fans had moved on, no doubt swilling lagers and gorging pasties to the accompaniment of their insidious moronic chants.

'Oh, um, morning, Jim. Twenty Rothmans and a bottle of Grouse, please.'

'Ah, the usual.'

The usual? Philip's return of the genial smile was thin. He tucked the whisky under his arm and had the first cigarette out of the foil and into his mouth before the door had swung shut behind him. The first drug-laden inhalation made his head swim again.

Halfway across the Fields he transferred the bottle to his other arm. His fingers lingered for a moment over the screw-top. He was tempted. A few whiffs of nicotine had been enough to douse the ache in his lungs; just a sip would soothe the rest of him. Only the shreds of self-respect stayed his hand. He hadn't sunk to the wino stage yet. He could wait till he got home. He walked faster.

He slowed down. What was he doing? Was he some kind of alcoholic?

'Yes, I think I probably am . . .'

He stopped. He was on the edge of the grass now, almost home. A laughing group of football supporters went by, decked in their red and white scarves. They were boisterous, but not drunk; not a can of lager in sight. Who was he to look down his nose at them? Not that it was anything personal: he looked down his nose at everybody.

He held up his free hand. It was almost steady, and the slight tremor there was could have come from tiredness. Who was he trying to kid? What did it matter? It mattered a lot. He couldn't carry on like this for ever. In fact, he could carry on like this for very little longer: the figures on his bank statements were suffering from terminal anorexia, and there was a crippling tax bill coming up next month, and that chunk of VAT, and then there was the sodding mortgage, and –

'God, I need a drink!'

He hated thinking about money, worrying about money – it

was the same thing. It got his pulse up, made him feel ill; made him feel like a drink. Just one, he had to go easy. What John had said about the drunkenness thing was worrying. So worrying he needed a drink to take his mind off it. John had practically said he was unemployable. Surely he'd been exaggerating? It was hardly as if he was the first actor to have made an exhibition of himself in public; he wasn't even the first to have been thrown off an aircraft. In fact, it was almost part of the job description. For a certain kind of actor, anyway. Not his kind. He had a reputation for quiet professionalism. He had had . . . The silence over the last three months was suspicious. This Kenneth Kilmaine person was the first producer who'd even so much as checked on his availability.

'Who the hell is Kenneth Kilmaine, anyway?'

He'd never heard of him. John had said he was going to phone back with details, maybe there'd be a message on his machine. He hurried across the road.

He stopped for a moment in the communal hall to get his breath back. It was then that he noticed the fresh pile of letters on the table. The blue airmail envelope on top was addressed to him.

He had to sit down on the chair beside the table. His legs felt very weak. For a few moments he just sat staring at the wall, then he lowered his eyes with calm deliberation and read the address on the back of the envelope. He had known anyway; a Californian postmark, and an elegant familiar hand. She always addressed her letters with the italicised script she had learnt at her convent. She always used the Mont Blanc pen he had given her.

He didn't open the letter. He put it in his pocket. He hadn't opened the whisky and he hadn't opened the letter. Profoundly impressed by his own self-control, he slowly mounted the stairs to his flat.

He inserted and turned the Yale key. He hadn't bothered with the deadlock. The door swung open easily and he stepped into his living-room.

A burglar was standing by the sofa.

2

Philip and the burglar stared at each other like a pair of deep-frozen bunnies.

The burglar was very small, and very young. He wore jeans, trainers, a bomber jacket and a red and white Arsenal scarf. He was black, had prominent cheekbones and a wide face, and huge round open eyes. He was holding Philip's video-recorder in one hand and a couple of tapes in the other.

''kin 'ell!' said the burglar, taking a twitchy step towards the bedroom.

'Stop!' demanded Philip, extending a hand in a gesture meant to convey magisterial sternness. Unfortunately he used the wrong hand, and succeeded merely in conveying the fact that he was the possessor of a bottle of Famous Grouse. 'Stop!' he repeated dramatically, though the burglar had advanced no further. He searched his mind desperately for inspiration: 'In the name of the law!'

Mention of 'the law', he realised afterwards, was probably a mistake. A look of panic flared across the burglar's face. He did a little convulsive side-shuffle – which Philip instinctively shadowed – then sprinted for the bedroom door.

In view of the fact that Philip was standing by the bedroom door, it appeared to him an odd choice of direction. Feeling close to panic himself, he raised his hands automatically to shield his face and noticed that he still had the whisky bottle in one of them. He hit the burglar over the head with it.

The bottle glanced off the burglar's skull and smashed into the door-frame. There was an explosion of glass and whisky, a diamanté amber shower which spattered across the burglar's back as he fell face down upon the floor, his belly cantilevered by the oblong box of the video-recorder. Philip stood mesmerised by the sound of fragmenting crystal and the sheer spontaneous violence of the blow. The germ of an old sinking feeling refamiliarised itself with the pit of his stomach.

Oh, shit! he thought. I've been here before . . .

The burglar lay immobile on the carpet, the back of his head and jacket sprinkled liberally with glass shards. The reek of whisky made Philip dizzy. He felt his knees about to give way and sank into a pre-emptive crouch.

Reluctantly he touched the burglar's head. The hair was soaked. Whisky, he presumed, until he saw the blood on his fingertips. The boy's eyes were closed, he didn't appear to be breathing. Carefully Philip picked up a large piece of glass, the base of the bottle, and placed it against the lips. He could detect no breathy mist. It was hardly scientific, but . . . perhaps his portable shaving mirror was still in the bathroom cabinet?

It wasn't, of course. He stood gawping uselessly at the open cabinet, incipient horrors lapping at the edges of his otherwise numbed brain. As if finding an intruder in his flat wasn't bad enough, why did he have to go and kill him afterwards? What was he going to tell the police? Self-defence? The boy couldn't have been more than fifteen, sixteen. What would the courts make of it? Old drunken Fletcher in the dock again; double Christmas celebrations for the headline writers. Why had Fate made him choose alcohol as an offensive weapon? Again?

He closed his eyes and saw another room, another body. The pungent whisky fumes tickled his memory; another stop on his private mental Circle Line. But no, he hadn't killed Gordon Wilde with the bottle. The bottle (champagne in any case) had merely stunned him; he had given the *coup de grâce* with a more solid blunt instrument. Perhaps he really had only caught the boy a glancing blow.

He turned the cold-water tap on full and soaked his flannel. He also filled up his tooth-brush mug and ran out with both to the bedroom. He emptied the mug over the burglar's head.

A twitch! A palpable twitch! Philip whooped as he laid the flannel across the bloody scalp. He grabbed the boy by the wrists and dragged him out of the doorway into the bedroom proper, the rush of adrenalin lending strength to his enfeebled body. He pulled a cushion off the bed and placed it carefully under the boy's head. He went back to the bathroom and refilled the mug.

The second cupful of water provoked more than a twitch. The boy groaned and fluttered his eyelids like a Rank starlet. Philip knelt astride him and lightly slapped his cheeks. The boy opened his eyes.

'Are you all right?' Philip enquired softly, laying a gentle hand on the boy's forehead to feel his temperature.

'Fuck off, you pervert!'

The boy bucked convulsively under him. Philip straightened with indignation. 'What are you insinuating?' he demanded coldly.

The boy looked at him weirdly, slithered up and down eelishly for a moment or two, and then kneed him in the balls.

Philip collapsed in groin-clutching agony. The boy pulled himself out from under him and clambered on to the bed, across which he attempted to crawl towards the open window. Despite the pain Philip grabbed at an ankle, caught it and held on. The boy kicked him in the arm and still he held on. He detached his free hand from nursing duty in the pelvic area and reached for the black metal bedside lamp, which he clasped by the stem and raised above his head.

'Kick me again and I'll break your knee-caps.'

He didn't make the mistake of raising his voice, or allowing himself to sound as angry as he felt. He said it deadpan, with glaciers in his eyes. When the boy glanced over his shoulder and saw them he went very still.

Philip got up and walked to the foot of the bed, equidistant between the boy, the window, the door. He threw some clothes off the chair and sat down. He balanced the lamp in his hands and stared the boy out. After a few seconds the boy looked away.

'What you gonna do to me?' he asked miserably.

'It's not up to me to do anything. That's a matter for the police.'

The boy looked at him sharply, anger and defiance in his eyes.

'I gotta few things to tell the Bill myself!' he declared, touching his scalp and giving a theatrical wince. 'You can't go round bashing people over the 'ead. It ain't right!'

Philip felt compelled to raise an eyebrow. 'If that's meant as an ethical rebuke I should venture to suggest that coming from you it perhaps lacks force,' he observed mildly.

'You what?' the miscreant protested uncouthly. His nostrils twitched and he sniffed elaborately. 'What'd you 'it me wiv, anyway?' He sniffed the knot in his Arsenal scarf and his wide eyes popped even wider. 'I can't go home stinkin' of booze! Me uncle'll kill me!'

'I'm glad at least that someone in your family is possessed of sound moral principles,' replied Philip curtly. Now that the adrenalin flow had ceased he was begining to feel irritated. He was further discomfited by the realisation that the drink which he had so craved was no longer on the immediate agenda. Not unless he was prepared to wring out the Arsenal scarf, a prospect which failed to appeal.

'You what?' the reprobate demanded. His globular eyes being incapable of further expansion, he curled his upper lip in an expression of incredulity before adding, 'You're weird, mate . . .'

'I would advise you to desist from insolence,' said Philip smartly. 'My patience is sorely tried already.'

The juvenile housebreaker placed a forefinger against his temple and turned it in a rapid clockwise/counter-clockwise manner suggestive of a deficiency in Philip's mental processes. Philip failed to find this amusing.

'What's your name?' he demanded, tight-lipped.

'Why should I tell you?' the boy responded with a jeer.

Philip stood up and slapped the base of the black metal lamp against his palm. 'Because if you don't I'll beat the shit out of you.'

The boy considered this for a moment. He shrugged.

'Fair enough. My name's George Washington.'

'Right, that does it!'

Philip marched round smartly to the side of the bed and primed his weapon.

'What you doin'?' the boy yelled, flinging out both hands to shield himself. ''S my name, honest!'

Desperately he pulled a black imitation-leather wallet out of his pocket and thrust it in Philip's face.

'Look!'

Philip took the wallet and flipped it open one-handed. There was a driving licence behind a plastic window.

'You're older than you look,' Philip remarked.

'I'm seventeen.'

'Precisely . . .' Philip studied the address. He gave a little snort. 'Lansbury House, eh?'

''S off Highbury Grove.'

'I know, I know. We're ex-neighbours.' Philip tossed back the wallet and sat down at the foot of the bed. 'So, George Cornelius Washington. How did you come to be christened with such exotic singularity?'

'You what?'

'You do know there was an historical character of the same name, I take it?'

'Yeah.'

'Do you know who he was?'

'Some bloke.'

'Is that all you know? That he was "some bloke"?'

'I didn't come 'ere for no history lesson!'

'No, you came here to rob me. It seems to me that historical ignorance is probably the least of your educational deficiencies. Are you still at school?'

'No.'

'Do you have a job?'

'No. Why you asking me all these questions?'

'Curiosity. It isn't every day one meets a real live burglar face to face. And I have what might be called a quasi-professional interest. How long have you been housebreaking?'

'Why should I answer your questions?'

'Because if you do I may let you go.'

'What?' George Cornelius Washington's eyes narrowed. Philip could almost hear him thinking aloud, looking for the catch. 'What you wanna let me go for?'

'I haven't yet guaranteed that I will. Nor, should I elect to do so, would I feel compelled to offer you an explanation. However, I am prepared to admit to a general reluctance to involve myself unnecessarily with the instruments of law and order.'

'Do you talk like this all the time?'

'I've already had occasion to speak to you about impertinence. Take this as a final warning. I propose that I shall ask the questions and you answer them. How did you break in here?'

'I didn't break nothing. The window's open.'

'This window? We're on the second floor. How did you get up?'

'The drainpipe.'

'How depressingly unoriginal. Weren't you deterred by the burglar alarm?'

'No. If the window was open it probably weren't on anyway.'

'I see. But how did you know I weren't – I wasn't in?'

'I rung the bell.'

'I might not have heard it.'

'I couldn't help it if you're deaf, could I! You gotta take some risks.'

'Yes . . . but what if the alarm had been on?'

'Nobody've paid no notice.'

'But if it had been on you could have disconnected it?'

'Might have.'

'Don't avoid the question. Can you or can you not disable a burglar alarm?'

'All right. Yeah.'

'Any burglar alarm?'

'Depends on the model. This one, yeah. Piece of piss.'

'Where did you acquire such specialist knowledge?'

'You what?'

'Where did you learn your trade?'

'In the nick.'

'Borstal?'

'Yeah.'

'I'm glad to know they don't keep you entirely idle at the taxpayers' expense. Will you show me how?'

'You what?'

'I should like you to demonstrate to me the procedure for disabling a burglar alarm.'

'What you wanna know that for?'

'It might come in handy one day. Is that what you were inside for?'

'No. Twoccing.'

'What's that?'

'Taking without owner's consent. Motors.'

'Ah, a genuine Renaissance villain. Did you break in here on the spur of the moment or did you, as they say, case the joint first?'

'No, I'm on me way to the football.'

'Ah, yes. The Arsenal. I can't say I'm a football lover myself.'

'Me neither. Poxy bloody game. I hate it.'

'You don't say . . .'

Philip paused a moment to collect his thoughts. He examined keenly the face of George Cornelius Washington. He saw a physiognomy which under other circumstances he might have described as possessing a natural – and quite winning – openness. He reflected briefly to himself upon the vagaries of human nature, recrossed his legs and laughed.

'There may be more to you than meets the eye, young man. I'm afraid that I cannot desist from asking the obvious question: if you hate football so much – and here at least we may find common ground – why do you go?'

'To get out the 'ouse. Me uncle thinks it keeps me outta trouble.'

'Mm. It sounds as if perhaps your uncle doesn't know you very well. Do you live with him?'

'Yeah. And me aunt.'

'Are your parents alive?'

'Yeah, but me mum wouldn't have me no more. Said she

couldn't handle me. So me uncle said I could come and live up 'ere. Keep an eye on me.'

'Clearly more of a full-time job than he bargained for. And have you been in trouble with the police lately?'

'No, I ain't done nothing. Me uncle said he'd kill me if I got nicked again.'

'A threat you were obviously prepared to live with. Why did you choose today to become a recidivist?'

'You what?'

'You really must stop using that phrase, it's extremely irritating. I want to know why you picked today to re-embark upon your life of crime. And why you picked on me.'

'Dunno. Just looked over when I was in the road and saw the window open. Looked like a piece of piss.'

'Another inelegant phrase you would do well to dispense with. Please would you be so good as to turn out your pockets.'

'You what?'

'If you say that again I will not be responsible for my actions. I said, turn out your pockets. I want to see what you've got of mine tucked away in there.'

Reluctantly the boy put his hands into his deep jacket pockets and withdrew therefrom the mantelpiece clock which didn't work and two videotapes in their slip-cases.

''S all I got. Honest.'

'Not the most convincing protestation you could have made . . . Pass me over the videotapes, please.'

The tapes were tossed casually to the foot of the bed. Philip picked up the nearest one and read his own neat label grimly.

'You little bastard.'

'What?'

'I said, you little bastard.'

Philip seized the stem of the metal lamp and stood up angrily. The burglar cringed.

'I ain't done nothin'!' he whined.

'Nothing!' Philip spluttered, so angry he could hardly speak. He thrust the tape into the boy's face.

'Read the label, you little bugger.'

The little bugger read the label.

'So what?' he said, attempting a show of bravado but too frightened and bewildered to be able to manage it.

'So what?' repeated Philip, indignant and sarcastic all at once. 'You can read that – "*Sir Walter Raleigh*, episodes 1–2" – and dare to remain unmoved? Thou whoreson little tidy Bartholomew boar-pig! Which other one did you lay your grubby little paws on?'

Philip snatched the other tape off the bed and scanned the sleeve. It slipped back on to the duvet through nerveless fingers.

'Episodes 5 and 6!' he whispered, aghast. 'You took 5 and 6, without bothering with episodes 3 and 4? Is there no end to your perfidy? One of the finest performances in the annals of British television and you have the gall to steal the sandwich and leave the filling behind! Away, you scullion! You rampallion! You fustilarian! Have you no soul, wretch?'

'Please, mister, I – '

'Oh, Spartan dog! Fie, for shame!'

'I don't – '

'Shut up!'

Philip's most tremendous bass explosion reverberated round the bedroom walls. It might have been sufficient to quell the Volscians; it was more than enough to turn the slender form of George Cornelius Washington to jellied silence.

'Stay exactly where you are,' said Philip, icily.

He walked over to the door and picked the video-recorder up off the floor. It was sticky with whisky but there were no visible signs of damage. He carried it over to the wall facing the bed and plugged it in, connecting the cable to his small portable TV, which was on top of the dresser. He turned on both machines and inserted the first tape. He sat back down on the end of the bed, making sure that his visitor had a clear view of the screen.

'Watch and – just possibly – learn.'

The programme began. He hadn't seen it for a while, and although the tape was only three years old he was surprised initially at how young he looked, even in the first scene where he was playing the old Raleigh in a grey wig and beard. Perhaps it was the shape of his face, which had been plumper three years ago, or the waistband, which had been tighter. At the end of the first scene the story went into flashback and he appeared as Raleigh in his twenties. Now, with thick dark hair and beard and a cunningly contrived youthful complexion, he didn't look a bit like himself. He watched the way he skipped into frame in doublet and hose, a boyish gallant about to take the court of Good Queen Bess by storm. He really did look twentysomething – how on earth had he managed it? Partly it must have been clever editing and filming (there were hardly any close-ups), but it was a damned fine piece of acting for all that. He'd been forty-four years old when he'd done that. Only three years back, but he knew that he couldn't have done it now. It would have been a sobering prospect, were he not so bloody sober already.

'Is that you, then?' asked the burglar, his voice tinged with amazement and respect.

'Mm . . .'

Philip was beginning to feel twitchy again. The shock of his encounter with the criminal element currently disposed on his bed had been a blow to the system. His various dysfunctions had been temporarily suspended; now normal service was about to be resumed. He lit a cigarette and noticed a trembling in his hand.

'Got a fag?' asked George Washington jauntily.

'Yes, thanks.'

The telephone rang. Philip reached for the remote control and turned down the television. He stood up slowly, feeling the ache in his limbs, the post-alcoholic exhaustion which recent excitements had only temporarily suspended.

'You'll have to excuse me,' he murmured drily. He picked up the cordless phone from the bedside table and carried it next door, not that he expected the call to be personal.

'Are you all right?' John Quennell enquired. 'You're sounding a little off-colour.'

Off-colour? No, he was a pretty even shade of beige.

'Kenneth Kilmaine would like you to come to his office. It's in Dean Street, he'll send a car. Will six o'clock be all right?'

'God, yes,' answered Philip, to whom time had never seemed more immaterial.

'Good. I'm afraid the secretary's a bit Essex, still couldn't get much sense out of her, but apparently the movie's called *Midnight Rider* and Kilmaine wants to see you for Geoffrey, which is the major supporting role. Sorry I can't be more helpful, but she didn't have either a script or a breakdown. I gather Kilmaine's only just flown in, it's all a bit chaotic.'

'Flown in from where?'

'The States, I think.'

'So he's American, is he? I have to confess I've never heard of him.'

'Um, well, to tell you the truth I don't know much more myself. Name faintly rings a bell, I seem to have heard it in connection with a few projects over the years, but nothing major. This sounds kosher, though, he's obviously got decent backing. I did hear something about *Midnight Rider* on the grapevine a few months back, but I thought it had folded. In fact I did put your name forward at the time, but I never heard anything, though you know how long it takes — '

'Well, better late than never, eh, John? No doubt I'll find out more tonight. I'll call you tomorrow.'

'Please do. I'll be at home.'

Philip went back into the bedroom. His visitor was still watching the TV.

'I wasn't sure you'd still be here,' Philip drawled, with a nod towards the window. He went to the cupboard and had another look at his clothes. He still didn't have a clean shirt in which to meet Kenneth Kilmaine.

'When was this on, then?' the burglar asked. 'I don't remember this.'

'Oh, a few years back . . .' Philip watched the scene for a minute; he had forgotten this bit and couldn't remember what came next. 'I thought you'd have turned over to *Ninja Turtles*, or something.'

'What? No, I'm watching this. I'm really enjoying it.'

Philip stared at him suspiciously.

'I never met a real actor before,' the boy continued eagerly. 'You're really good, you know that?'

Actually Philip did, but it was always nice to be told. He softened.

'Jolly nice of you to say so. Thanks.'

No clean shirts in the wardrobe, no clean anything. Reluctantly Philip peered into his bulging laundry bag. Fastidiously he scooped out a handful of soiled garments.

'Excuse me a moment, I've got to put some washing on. You, er, you want to carry on watching this, do you?'

'Oh, yeah, if that's all right with you. I don't want to be no trouble.'

'Oh, no, you're not, no trouble at all. Why don't you give me your scarf – I might as well wash that too.'

'Oh, right. Cheers.'

He took off his whisky-sodden Arsenal scarf and passed it over. Philip added it to the pile in his arms.

'Don't want to get you into hot water with your uncle,' he said pleasantly.

He carried the bundle into the kitchen, stuffed it into the washing-machine, crossed his fingers and opened the cupboard next to it. There was some washing powder. With a silent Hallelujah for the Christmas miracle he depressed a button or two and let the washing cycle commence. He returned to the bedroom and watched the rest of Episode 1 with his guest.

Hardly were the credits rolling than Episode 2 was requested. Ever the complaisant host, Philip let the tape run on. He set up the ironing-board and, the drying cycle concluded, managed to press a dark blue shirt into some kind of shape. The light blue, which he would have preferred, had unfortunately turned a pinkish shade due to the running of the football scarf.

'Had enough?' Philip asked at the end of Episode 2.

'How much else you got?'

Another four times fifty minutes' worth: Philip loaded Episode 3. Shortly thereafter he nodded off, and when he woke up again they were halfway through Episode 4. He went to the bathroom to wash, put on his fresh shirt and a relatively creaseless dark suit and gave his best black shoes a wipe with instant polish. Then he checked to see if his keys were still in his coat pocket. They were. And so was the letter with a California postmark.

Somehow, over the pounding in his head, he heard the doorbell ring.

3

Philip turned the letter over in his hands, again. Again and again: the sweat of his palm had smudged the ink; it was looking dog-eared already. Why didn't he just open the bloody thing, get it over with? There was no point – the back of the minicab was too dark, the street-lamps dim and far between. He leaned forward and tapped the driver on the shoulder.

'Excuse me!' He spoke clearly and slowly. 'Would you mind pulling over for a moment, please?'

The driver veered suddenly towards the kerb and braked without signalling. Car horns blared behind them. The driver swore in a pan-Aramaic language with which Philip was un-familiar.

'Thank you very much,' he said patiently. 'Please wait here.'

Philip got out. They were only at the bottom of Upper Street but he was already glad of the chance to stretch his legs. When Kenneth Kilmaine had said that he was sending round a car, Philip had fondly imagined a limousine, or perhaps even a Rolls Royce, naturally with uniformed chauffeur. The possibility of a mildewed rust-bucket the size of a supermarket trolley driven by a monoglot terrorist on his night off had not occurred to him. George Cornelius Washington had not been impressed.

'Ain'tcha gonna offer me a lift home, then?' he had demanded, when he had been able to stop laughing.

Philip had suggested a proximal orifice up which he could stick that one. George had not pressed the point. Philip had last seen him disappearing over the Fields in the twilight gloom, when he had allowed himself to feel a savage twitch of annoyance at the provocative jauntiness of the young man's mien. The thought that it wasn't too late to call the rozzers and turn the little bastard in flashed briefly across his mind before he banished it to the unworthy lower depths.

Philip slammed the door of the cab a little too hard (any harder and it might have detached itself from its rusty hinges) and walked over to the nearest street-lamp. He held the letter up to the light. Still he hesitated.

'Come on, you bloody fool,' he said angrily.

He needed bolstering up. He needed a drink. He lit a cigarette, took deep lungfuls and felt himself calm down. He peered hard at the writing on the envelope.

What did it contain? Had she poured out her heart to him? Was she begging his forgiveness, begging to return? A scene flashed across his inner eye, her on her knees, imploring, he patriarchal and stern with profile turned and unblinking eye fixed on the horizon. They were both in Regency costume; somehow he knew the scene would play better in period.

'Get a grip!' he told himself curtly. 'You can't stand here all night, it's bloody freezing.'

The waking dream fled. He turned the envelope over and tucked his thumb under the ungummed corner.

'*Morituri te salutant . . .*'

He slit open the envelope and looked inside.

It was a Christmas card.

It was a Madonna and Child, Italian Renaissance, traditional and vaguely familiar. He stared at it, somewhat bemused.

'Well, what did you expect? Fucking elves?'

Was there a letter enclosed, or had she just written inside? He opened up the card impatiently.

The left side was blank. In the middle of the right was the message 'Merry Christmas' in flowery script. Beneath it was written in her round, familiar hand: 'All the best for Christmas and the New Year – love, Kate'.

'I don't – '

His head spun and his eyes swam out of focus. The blue ink letters danced mockingly before him. He let out a long keening moan: 'I don't believe it!'

There was a sob in his voice; he felt the wrench in his heart.

For a moment it was touch and go which would prevail, pity or rage. Rage won by a short head.

'Fucking – slag – bitch!'

Fury had made him incoherent. Sentences or phrases were beyond him, the best he could manage was disconnected abuse. Still, it was better than nothing. He kicked the lamp-post, much too hard, and almost cried with the pain.

'Stu – blo – fu – shi – bug –'

Now he couldn't even get the good old Anglo-Saxon expletives out. Phoneme abuse didn't sound the same. He clenched his teeth and emitted a Baskervilleish howl of pure animal anger. He ripped the Christmas card and the envelope to pieces, flung the pieces at the pavement and jumped up and down on them.

'Merry Christmas!' said a passer-by chirpily.

'Up your arse!' rasped Philip, who was not in the mood for an exchange of festive pieties. He staggered back to the cab, yanked open the door and threw himself across the back seat.

'Get the hell out of here! Drive!'

He saw the driver staring at him in the mirror suspiciously.

'Don't just sit there gawping, man! Step on it!'

The man started the engine and the car trickled into the traffic stream. Almost immediately it pulled up at a red light and Philip found himself the object of scrutiny again.

'Anything the matter?' he demanded testily.

'You one angry feller,' the man said thickly. He turned round in his seat to face Philip and a headlamp illumined his features. He had the unshaved swarthy look of a spaghetti westerner.

'The light is green,' observed Philip coolly.

They drove on until the next red light, the junction of Pentonville Road. Philip wound down the window and threw out his cigarette stub.

'Bloody woman!'

The driver turned round eagerly in his seat.

'Is woman, I knew it!'

'Just drive the fucking car, will you?'

The lights changed and they moved off again. Philip lit another cigarette. His pulse was still racing.

'Shit, I don't believe it . . .'

How could he have believed it? It was incredible. He'd been carrying the bloody envelope around with him the whole afternoon and after all that, what should it contain? He almost wished he hadn't torn it up. He would have liked to have looked at it again, to confirm the unconfirmable. Merry Christmas. Was that all? Merry-she-had-to-be-bloody-joking-what? He leant forward and rested his hands against the back of the passenger seat, gripping the upholstery hard. They were slowing down again, Rosebery Avenue and Farringdon Road. He puffed on his cigarette.

'Do you know what that bloody woman did to me?' he demanded through the corner of his mouth.

The driver glanced over his shoulder expectantly. Philip removed the cigarette and enunciated very clearly: 'She sent me a bloody Christmas card.'

The driver stared at him blankly for a few moments, clearly unwilling to digest the enormity of the offence. At length he nodded sagely: 'What a bitch!'

Philip slumped back into his seat. He felt terrible. What could he do? He wanted to go home, shut the curtains, drink a pint of whisky, hide under the bed. But he had to be at his best tonight, not his worst. That was a grim joke. He closed his eyes and tried to think of nothing. He chain-smoked. The minutes passed and his feeling of claustrophobia became unbearable.

When he next opened his eyes and registered his surroundings they were coming into Cambridge Circus. As the façade of the Palace Theatre hove into view the driver slowed down and started to peer hard through his windscreen.

'Is round here somewhere, Dean Street, I think,' he declared uncertainly.

They were at another red light. Philip grabbed suddenly at the door.

'Near enough for me, old man, I'll walk from here.'

Philip flung open the door and squeezed himself out. The driver made an incomprehensible protest. Philip waved at him through the window.

'It's all right, we're a bit early. Need a walk anyway. Thanks very much.'

He slammed the door for the last time and hurriedly crossed the Charing Cross Road. It was true, he was a bit early, and a brisk walk would get his circulation going again, clear his head. He went into Old Compton Street.

'Want to see a show, darling?' a girl in a blonde wig which didn't match her eyebrows asked from a doorway.

'Not tonight, thanks,' answered Philip politely.

The girl smiled and he smiled back. Invitations like that didn't embarrass him. He loved Soho, the garishness, the tackiness, the shoddily packaged degeneracy. He felt at ease in the company of prostitutes and shysters. Some of them were his best friends.

He was coming to a familiar corner. He slowed down, glanced at his watch. He had nearly a quarter of an hour, plenty of time. It wasn't as if he was going out of his way, and – no, he didn't really need to talk himself into it. He went through the frosted-glass door.

The pub was nearly empty. A quick glance along the occupied bar stools told him there was no one he knew. He eased himself down, a five-pound note at the ready.

'Double Scotch and a Pils, please,' he said to the barman, though whether 'barman' was quite accurate was a moot point: this one was wearing purple mascara and carmine lipstick.

Philip picked up the Scotch, tipped back his head and let the brown corrosive fluid strip his throat. He gasped with pleasure.

'Another, please.'

'Don't I know you?' the barman lisped, returning with the refill.

'Maybe.' Philip measured the second drink more studiously – two swigs instead of one. God, it was good. 'Been in once or twice with Seymour Loseby.'

'Seymour Loseby!' declared a fruity Irish voice incredulously from the corner. 'Is she yet living?'

'And another, please,' said Philip to the barman. He turned round on his stool. The man in the corner had got up and was coming towards him.

'Well, if it isn't Philip Fletcher. The last heterosexual in London.'

'Hello, Brendan. Want a drink?'

'No, this one's on me.' He dropped some change on to the counter. 'Get me a voddy, will you, Alice?'

Brendan O'Malley settled himself on to a stool. A big lopsided grin sprang up on his coarse red face.

'You're looking well,' said Philip.

'You look like shit yourself.'

'I've always felt you were a loss to the Diplomatic Corps, Brendan. Funnily enough, I was looking at old Walter Raleigh today. I'd forgotten how ludicrous you looked in that beard.'

'Ah, my dear friend Gonorrhoea.'

Brendan had played the part of Gondomar, the Spanish ambassador.

'Happy days,' said Philip, knocking back his drink. 'Same again, please, and a vodka for him.'

'Steady on, dear, I haven't finished this one yet.' He looked at Philip quizzically. 'Don't remember you drinking at this pace before.'

'Hallelujah, I've seen the light.'

'Well, glory be!'

He felt a kind of incandescence spreading out from within him. The first drink of the day had been too long delayed, there was ground to be made up, interest to be paid. The warming spirit filled him out, gave life to the anaemic husk that was his body. Why, Philip's himself again . . .

'If I had a thousand sons,' Brendan began sonorously, quoting Falstaff but staring into his drink with Romeo's eyes, 'the first principle I would teach them should be, to forswear thin potations.'

'If you ever had one son, Brendan, it would be a matter of considerable surprise.'

'You're a devil of a hair-splitter, Fletcher. What you doing for Christmas?'

'Fuck all.'

'A man after my own heart.'

'When is it anyway?'

'Monday, Tuesday?'

'Who knows?'

'Who cares?'

'Let's drink to that.'

'Amen.'

Down the hatch, and the devil take the hindmost. Better go steady but, then again, he could handle it. He could take his drink, no lily-livered pup he. No liver left to speak of at all.

'Working?' he asked.

'Nevermore, quoth the raven. Who'd employ an old soak like me? Yourself?'

'Maybe. Ever heard of Kenneth Kilmaine?'

'Is that a mick name? Avoid him like the plague.'

'I think he's American. He's a film producer.'

'Avoid him anyway. If I had a pound for every man I've ever met who claimed to be a film producer I'd buy you another drink. I'll buy you another drink anyway.'

'Frightfully decent of you, old man.'

'Will you stop sounding like such a Brit, Fletcher? Jesus, Alice, will you look at those glasses? A man could die of thirst round here! Shame again!'

'Shame again? Shome mistake, shurely?'

Philip took more than a minute to stop laughing. What a release, and what a relief! He should have been getting out more, it was silly to stay at home hogging the bottle. A shared drink was a beneficial and beneficent experience.

'Laugh and the world laughs with you!' he said.

'Freeloading bastards!'

'Mud in your eye!'

Philip knocked back his drink. Another glass, another empty. This was just what the doctor ordered. His life had been too much in the stop–start mode of late; now he could sense it flowing again. He climbed down from his stool.

'Must pay a visit to the Gents. Back soon. Set 'em up, Alice.'

He left more money on the table and sauntered off. Brendan called out something to him and he waved back gaily. He went crashing through the door of the Gents, lost his footing and fell flat on his face. He lay splayed out on the unsavoury-smelling floor, too stunned to move. After the passage of an immeasurable period of time he felt helping hands securing a grip under his armpits. He heard Brendan's voice: 'What I said was, "Mind the step."'

Brendan hauled him up to face the mirror. 'Christ, you look even worse than before. Here.' Brendan handed him his handkerchief. Philip used it to staunch the flow of blood from his nose.

'Going to have a nice shiner there, my friend,' Brendan remarked encouragingly.

There was an ominous swelling round his eye. He had fallen so suddenly that he hadn't even had time to fling forward a protective arm. His face looked well squashed.

'Oh, my God . . . is there any blood on my shirt?'

There was a bit. He should have worn the pink-stained shirt after all.

'Button your jacket up, it won't show. And hold your head back, man, it'll stop the bleeding.'

'All right, but – oh, my God! What's the time?'

He squinted feverishly at his watch. It was ten past six.

'I'm late! Oh, God! Oh, no! Oh, shit!'

He skidded round the malodorous little room like a deranged clockwork thing. He started to go out, then his bladder reminded him of why he'd come in in the first place. He headed for the door again, then caught a glimpse of himself in the mirror and scooted for the sink. He filled his cupped hands with cold water and feverishly washed his bloodstained visage. He soaked the handkerchief and held it close to his nose.

'Got to run!' he said breathlessly. 'Thanks for the drinks. Thanks for the hankie. See you soon.'

'Your flies are undone,' Brendan remarked as Philip disappeared in a dervish whirl.

He ran out of the pub and up towards Dean Street, pulling at his zip. He'd written the number in his diary before coming out, he checked it quickly on the run, found he was at the wrong end, pushed on faster. His lungs protested, shooting pains jabbed at his chest. He realised that he was not in tip-top physical condition.

He pulled himself up gasping outside a whitewashed building with big plate-glass doors. He leapt up the steps and scanned the name-plates on the wall. The top one read *KenKil Productions*. Pausing only to reflect on the limitlessness of human ingenuity, he flung open the glass doors and staggered on through.

He caught his breath back on the way up. Fortunately there was a mirror in the lift, he was able to wipe off a bit more blood, pull his lapels across to conceal the stains, straighten his tie, pat his hair into shape. He stared dumbly at his watch. Fifteen minutes late! He couldn't believe it. What sloppiness! What stupidity! He felt light-headed. Perhaps he'd had one too many, but no, he'd needed that for inner fortification. He could handle his booze anyway, no problem. He wasn't late because he'd stopped off for a drink; he'd just stayed there a bit too long.

The lift stopped on the third floor and he stepped out into a thinly carpeted corridor. A door marked with the KenKil logo was in front of him. He went up to it smartly, knocked and went on in.

He found himself in a large, brightly lit office. There were the usual desks, chairs, computer and typing equipment, but no sign of life. There was another door, slightly ajar, set in the far wall. He went over, pushed it open and walked on through.

He found himself in a second office which contained another desk and a large black leather sofa. A man of about Philip's age and a rather younger woman were sitting on the sofa. The man had his hand up the woman's skirt.

'Who the – '

The man and the woman sprang apart. Both their faces were erubescent. So was Philip's.

'Oh, I'm terribly sorry,' he said, just about overcoming his confusion.

'Don't you ever knock?' the man spluttered.

Philip looked at him in a puzzled way. He was aware that his brain wasn't functioning particularly well at the moment, he felt a bit hazy, a bit fuzzy round the edges; his reactions were terribly slow.

'Um, sometimes . . .' he answered vaguely.

He didn't feel very comfortable in this room. He decided to leave it. He went back out into the other office and closed the door behind him.

'Mm, that's torn it,' he remarked to himself.

He presumed that the man on the sofa had been Kenneth Kilmaine. This was his office, there was no doubt about that. What should he do now?

'Go back to the pub?'

The idea had much to commend it. He thought that he was probably about half-drunk, and half was nothing neither way: what he really needed was to go and get well and truly plastered. On the other hand, he was supposed to be here for a job interview. But why bother? He was hardly likely to get it now, was he?

'Oh, what the hell. In for a penny, in for a ducat . . .'

He knocked on the door. After a few moments it was opened with some violence.

'Yes?' demanded the man aggressively.

He was quite a small man, neat and wiry, with little pointed ears like a fox and furtive, mobile eyes to match. Philip smiled pleasantly.

'Good evening. I'm Flillip Pletcher.'

Or something like that. Perhaps he had had one too many after all.

'I mean, Philip Fletcher,' he repeated hastily.

The man stared at him blankly for a moment, then gave such an enormous grin that it seemed to split his face in two. His teeth were uniform and dazzlingly white.

'Phil, how you doing? Come on in!'

He grabbed Philip's hand and yanked him inside. The girl was now sitting at the desk, the pencil in her hand posed unconvincingly over the notebook on her lap. She was tall and blonde and in her early twenties. The pout looked fixed.

'Shaz, this is Phil. Say hello, Shaz.'

'Hello, Phil,' she said dully, keeping her eyes on the pad.

'Take a pew, Phil.'

The sofa was indicated. Philip sat down on it and Kilmaine perched himself on the edge of the desk.

'I'm sorry I was late, Mr Kilmaine, I — '

'Ken, please! Everyone calls me Ken, even my ex-wife. Ha ha ha ha!'

Ken threw back his head and roared, giving Philip another view of his magnificent teeth. He reached across and tweaked the girl's ear affectionately.

'Hey, Shaz, how's about a drink for old Phil here, huh?'

She put down her pad self-consciously and walked over to the glass door. Ken kept his eyes firmly on her plump buttocks. Philip did the same, out of politeness. When she had gone through to the other office Ken winked at him.

'Not bad, eh? 38–26-36. Never much good at the old maths myself, but I could develop a head for figures like that, if you know what I mean, ha ha! ... Sorry about the little misunderstanding just now, Phil. To tell you the truth we'd rather given up on you, and we had some secretarial work to catch up on.'

Putting the dic back into dictation, Philip supposed. He smiled indulgently. Ken's grin remained as fixed as before. Had his muscles got stuck? Philip wondered. The result of over-enthusiasm from his plastic surgeon? There was more than a hint of plasticity about him, from the starched clean collar to the even tan, from the immaculate teeth to the neat line of the too-perfect black toupee. Philip always found men of his own age with the jowls of a twenty-year-old disconcerting.

'So, Phil, how's tricks?'

He had a very odd accent. Philip couldn't place it.

'Oh, um ... thanks ...'

He was saved from his own inconsequential murmurings by the reappearance of Shaz bearing a drinks tray. She bent towards him, offering both an assortment of bottles and a generous view of her cleavage.

'See anything you fancy?' chortled Ken, his voice suddenly pure cockney.

'Oh, I see!' Philip remarked to himself, as he helped himself to a stiff three fingers of malt whisky. That was it: the accent was

45

a put-on, fake mid-Atlantic. Although the tan and the hairpiece might carry Californian labels, underneath it all Ken was no more than common-or-garden Brit with variable vowels. Probably over there they thought he sounded like Jeremy Irons.

'A man who appreciates his Glenmorangie! I think I can do business with you, Phil.'

'That's not how you pronounce it, actually.'

'Eh?'

'It's Glen*mor*angie – sounds like orangery.'

'Really? I didn't know that.'

'Well, now you do. Cheers.'

Shaz had brought Ken the tray and he was mixing himself a rather smaller Scotch with water. When he was done he gave her bottom a lingering fondle.

'Better get on with your filing, honey. Me and Phil have got some man's talking to do. See you later. Oh – and wear the garter-belt!'

'Get away!' said Shaz in answer to his suggestive chortling. She wiggled her way back to the outer office, her little black dress so tight and her heels so precarious that she moved like a jointless Barbie-doll, an impression reinforced by the bundles of peroxide hair and the doll-like blank eyes. Now that he thought about it, Philip seemed to remember from conversations with a friend's small daughter that Barbie had a boyfriend called Ken. Had this man been the model? He was about the right age. And his teeth were good enough. Shaz closed the glass door behind her.

'Bet the only filing she does is to her nails,' bantered Ken.

The smile Philip returned was his thinnest yet. He was finding Ken's continuous grinning a touch wearisome, and he recalled almost with affection the spontaneous anger which had greeted his first clumsy entrance.

'So then, Phil – '

'It's Philip.'

The snap in his voice was sharp. Ken looked momentarily nonplussed.

'It's Philip, my name's Philip.'

He had Ken's undivided attention. He needed it, because he

was only capable of speaking slowly. He needed time to concentrate and get the words out, and Ken was like some energetic little terrier, snapping about and not giving him time to settle. He continued at his own pace: 'Phil is too casual, too careless, it's . . . it's not me. I don't want to appear pedantic, old boy, but I should like to make this point as one of two preconditions for getting this relationship off on the right footing.'

'What's the other?'

'That you refill my glass this instant. For some extraordinary reason it appears to be empty.'

He tittered to himself. Ken came over to fill his glass, bobbing and grinning like Mister Punch. Philip felt an almost irresistible urge to boff him on the nose, but he did manage to resist it. It wouldn't have created a good impression, he thought.

'Frankly, my dear, I don't give a damn.'

'I'm sorry?'

'Oh, nothing . . .'

Why had he said that out loud? He hadn't meant to. Perhaps he was drunker than he thought he was, he should stop now.

'Nasty bruise you've got coming on there,' Ken remarked.

Philip touched his swelling eye. He bridled defensively.

'I'm not drunk, you know.'

'Sorry?'

'I said I'm not drunk. I just didn't see the step. I'd have fallen over anyway, even if I'd been sober. And anyway I was sober. Just coincidence it was in the pub. I'm not drunk, you know.'

'Oh, I know, I didn't say you were!'

'I know that, I know that, but . . .'

He stared very hard at the floor. He'd forgotten what he was going to say. He was feeling very weary. Would it be all right if he put his feet up and had a lie-down on the sofa? he wondered.

'Well, Phi-lip . . .' Ken pronounced the two syllables very deliberately. 'And what's your agent told you about our little project?'

'Oh . . .' Philip waved his hand vaguely. 'Fuck all. The usual.'

'Ha ha! Yeah, sometimes I wonder what they're for myself. You do know it's a movie?'

'Oh yeah, and – just remembered – you want me for Geoffrey.'

'The judge. That's right.'

'Judge? D'you say judge? You fucking serious?'

Philip gave a belligerent snort. Ken looked momentarily taken aback, but then he pressed on eagerly: 'Oh, yes, I'm serious, Phi-lip, I am very, very ser-i-ous indeed!'

Ken began to pace excitedly about the room. Philip kicked off his shoes and leaned back on the sofa.

'Yes, siree, am I serious . . . Been looking around for someone to fit the bill for months now, the exact right person, and I'm sure you're my man, the final piece of the jigsaw. You do that historical stuff pretty well, don't you?'

''Storical, is it?'

'Yup. Set in the good old seven – or is it the eighteenth century? Dunno, always get 'em mixed up. You're the judge who's after Dick.'

'The hell I am.'

'No, Dick, the hero. This is the story of the legendary Dick Turpin, highwayman and folk hero. We see him as the Robin Hood of his day.'

'You mean like Kevin Costner?'

'That is a suggestion which I refute utterly. The fact that there are similarities in the script is entirely coincidental and, if I may say so, inevitable anyway. After all, great minds think alike and there is no such thing as an original idea, as we well know. I know there are people out there who will snipe at us and say that it bears a certain resemblance to other movies not a million miles from the one you have just mentioned, but that's just envy, and the fact that it is a period swashbuckler set in rural England about an outlaw stealing from the rich and giving to the poor doesn't mean it owes anything at all to any other film whatsoever irrespective of whether or not they grossed hundreds of millions of dollars at the box office, if you take my meaning.'

'I'm not wearing tights.'

'You don't have to. Judges don't wear tights, just wigs.'

'Like yours?'

'What?'

Philip had just enough control over himself to let that one pass.

'Who's the . . .' he started to ask, then forgot what it was he was asking.

'The director?' Ken suggested.

'That's the one.'

'He's pretty hot . . .' Ken paused for dramatic effect. 'We managed to get Schlesinger.'

'Oh . . .' Philip was surprised. He was also impressed. He took a sip of his drink. 'That is pretty hot. John Szlnger, eh?'

'Well . . .' Ken stretched the word out. He indicated Philip's glass. 'Looks like you could do with a refill, my friend.'

He brought the bottle over. Philip thought about refusing for a moment, but he didn't. He only wished his stomach wasn't so empty. When was the last time he'd eaten? He knitted his brow with concentration.

'John Slizeneger, eh . . .' It was a difficult name to pronounce. Philip frowned. 'John, anyway, I got that bit.'

'Ah, yes.' Ken laughed along with him. 'Actually, it's Wayne Schlesinger.'

'Huh?'

'I'm talking about Wayne Schlesinger. He's our director, not the other one.'

'Wayne Slizen – who the fuck's he?'

'Oh, he's very good, very good indeed, you'll love him. Done some fantastic work. Do you remember a movie called *Aliens Stole My Surfboard*?'

Philip looked completely blank.

'Well, that was one of Wayne's,' Ken continued. 'A real cult hit of the seventies, I'm surprised you don't know it.'

'Well, I don't. What else's he done?'

'Some great stuff. He even did some of the early episodes of *Desire*, which is a hell of a coincidence because we've got Shelley Lamour for the female lead.'

'Who?'

'Shelley Lamour! You know, Montana Madigan in *Desire*.'

'*Desire*?'

'Yes, *Desire*, the classic TV soap. Everyone's seen *Desire*!'

'That the one about the shipping tycoon whose wife's having an affair with his son who turns out to be the real son of his worst enemy, whose daughter had a lesbian affair with his wife?'

'See, I knew you'd know it! Well, Shelley Lamour is playing Celestia, your daughter.'

'Geoffrey's got a daughter?'

'You betcha. She's the romantic interest.'

'What, for me?'

'No, no, it's not that kind of film. Dick's after her.'

'And is she after Dick?'

'Yup.'

'Sounds like that sort of film to me. Who's Montana playing?'

'That's the name of Shelley's character in *Desire*, Montana Madigan.'

'Then who's Celestia?'

'I think you're getting confused.'

'Too right . . . Where's the script?'

Ken gave him a pantomime wink and walked over to the corner, where stood a small black safe. With a flourish he bent down and manipulated the combination lock.

Philip watched distractedly as he clicked on the numbers. That's funny, he thought, I know that combination. He laughed. 'Oh, I get it,' he muttered under his breath. '38–26–36. Hope you don't change your secretaries too often. Ha bloody ha!'

'What's that?' Ken asked, his head buried in the safe.

'Um, nothing,' Philip answered.

Ken pulled out a stapled wad of paper.

'Here it is,' he pronounced reverently. 'The Holy Grail.'

Like many people in the film industry, Ken had a mild tendency towards hyperbole.

'Who wrote it?' asked Philip.

A look of immense self-satisfaction settled on Ken's face. It has to be said that he hadn't looked especially displeased with himself before.

'We managed to get Goldman.'

'What, William Goldman? *Butch Cassidy and the Sundance Kid*?'

'Well . . . No, Harvey Goldman, actually.'

'Who?'

'Harve, Harve Goldman. He's a really well-respected writer, one of the tops in Hollywood.'

'Did he write *Desire*, by any chance?'

'No, no, Harve's strictly a movie writer. Did you ever see *Robo Psycho 2*?'

'Didn't see *Sobo Rycho 1*.'

'Well, Harve collaborated on that. Got nominated for Best Special Effects, you know, at the Bucharest Film Festival.'

'What, the script got nominated?'

'Well, no, the movie.'

Philip was relieved to hear that. He had had visions of the script exploding. He was having other visions too. Although he realised that his perceptions were a little hazy, he still didn't like the look of them. He got to his feet, with some difficulty.

'Ken, old thing, thanks awfully for the drink, but I think I'd better be getting along now.'

'But I haven't told you about the script yet!'

'Thanks, but . . . no thanks, I'm sure it's very good, but it's not really up my street.'

'But you can't do this to me! I've been searching months for the right actor to play the part, and it's you. I'm sorry, but I'm not going to let you go that easily. I haven't even told you about Dick. We've got Sleat for Dick!'

'You got what?'

'Sleat. You know, SLEAT!'

He repeated the name so loudly that Philip instinctively retreated. He fell back on to the sofa.

'Steady on . . .'

'You must know who Sleat is, everyone knows Sleat. Three Top Ten hits last year alone. He's done the most fantastic sound-track for us, it's gonna be mega.'

Philip gazed at him in complete horror.

'Are you trying to tell me he's some kind of . . . pop singer?'

'Of course he is! The lead singer of Arms for Oblivion, the hottest young band in the English-speaking world, and anywhere else for that matter. You've got to have heard of them.'

Philip was too shell-shocked to reply. If there was one thing in the world worse than pop music, it was pop singers who thought they could act.

'I'm sorry, but . . .' His voice trailed off. He tried once more to get up. 'I've got to go.'

'But Phi-lip, I haven't even made you an offer!'

Phi-lip didn't want to hear about an offer. He wanted to get up smartly and walk out, but he seemed incapable of getting off the sofa. He had reached the leaden stage of drunkenness, where all objects appeared monolithic and movement required an impossible degree of co-ordination and concentration. Furthermore, he was feeling distinctly queasy.

'Sorry, I don't discuss money,' he said. 'Talk to my agent.'

'I'm offering you a hundred grand.'

'Eh?' He stopped even trying to move. He wondered if he'd heard correctly. 'A hun — pounds?'

'Yup. Pounds sterling. You know the ones, with a picture of the world's favourite corgi owner on the back. One hundred thousand of them. Plus third billing after Sleat and Shelley, plus your name above the title – it's a major part, the judge, the Sheriff of Nottingham character, which isn't to say that it bears any resemblance to any other films, that's just a convenient way of putting it. Plus any and all fringe benefits you ask for and we can work out to our mutual satisfaction, plus two-and-a-half per cent of net profits. There's my offer, and it's on the table. All we ask of you is eight weeks of your precious time, starting a fortnight tomorrow. What do you say?'

Philip was too amazed to say anything. A hundred thousand pounds for eight weeks' work? He wasn't worth half that, it was incredible! What in heaven's name was going on? This was the most peculiar interview, he'd never known another like it. He knew he was pissed as a fart, why hadn't he been thrown out on his ear?

'But . . . why do you want me?'

Ken swapped his habitual grin for a look of Lassie-like earnest devotion.

'Because you're the best, Phi-lip. As soon as I saw your tapes

I knew you were our man. Shelley said so and Wayne and Harve too, everyone's saying it. I've never been surer of anything in my life, you're what's needed to make this a really class movie, you're the missing link.'

Philip wasn't quite sure how to take this. He had never been compared to a hypothetical neo-Neanderthal before, though he could think of quite a few actors who ought to have been. He was lost for words.

'But . . .'

A hundred thousand pounds. The offer of a share of net was worthless, the creative accountants would see to that, but five noughts! He could clear all his debts, stick two fingers up at the taxman, do something about that millstone of a mortgage. He could . . . he could fill his room to the ceiling with best malt whisky. He could buy a bloody distillery. He finished his drink.

'Oh, God!'

His head was swimming. Was it shock or alcohol? He fell back into the sofa and closed his eyes. Ken was walking about the room, wittering away in his quickfire fashion.

'. . . and that's where the idea came from, I just suddenly thought, hell, why not go back to good old blighty! Have idea, will travel. Lot of finance about in Europe, you know, but if you want to crack the American market you've got to speak the right lingo and that is where everyone in England is just failing to cash in, Phi-lip my friend. It's not just that you're sitting on a gold-mine, you know – you're speaking it!'

Philip couldn't be bothered to concentrate. It was like listening to a double-glazing salesman. He felt his mind slip away, heard the words merge into a meaningless buzz of sound. He wished he hadn't drunk so much. He wished he wasn't so damned tired. Why was his life such a mess?

'Phi-lip!'

He started. Ken was standing over him, shaking his shoulders.

'What the –'

Ken was slapping him gently on the cheeks.

'Wakey, wakey, Phi-lip. Time to go beddy-byes!'

Then why did you wake me? Philip thought. He must have

dozed off, he'd been comfortable on the sofa. Now he felt uncomfortable and disoriented.

'Shaz? Come and give me a hand, will you?'

The Barbie-doll secretary had reappeared. She was on one side of him (Ken was on the other), helping him up. A potent perfume stirred his hibernating instincts and he leant towards her musky warmth.

'See anything you fancy?' he said to Ken with a wink. He bent his lips to Shaz's ample bosom and blew a raspberry between her cleavage. She squealed. 'I don't think that's very funny!' she protested angrily.

Philip did. He almost doubled up with laughter. The laughter caught in his throat. Nauseous feelings rippled through him and he stayed down, hunched over the floor, staring at Ken's expensive shiny crocodile shoes.

'Come on, old feller, let's get you to a cab,' said Ken, and thumped him heartily on the back.

Philip vomited copiously over Ken's shoes.

Oh dear, he thought to himself, just before sinking back on to the sofa and passing out, it hasn't been what you'd call a good day . . .

4

When John Quennell phoned the next morning – a Sunday, which in itself was enough to confirm the time was out of joint – Philip at first refused to believe him.

'But Kilmaine is really sold on you,' Quennell insisted. 'You must have made a fantastic impression. The deal is amazing . . .'

Philip wasn't listening. He'd already heard about the deal. It was all too ridiculous to be taken seriously. He made a few grunting noises and got Quennell off the phone as quickly as possible. He then went and lay in his bath for an hour and a half. It would have been longer, for he felt so terrible that he never wanted to move again, but then somebody started to ring the doorbell, and was so insistent that finally he had to rouse himself just to silence the horrible loud buzzing noise that was making his head explode. He went downstairs and found a messenger with an envelope and a Christmas-wrapped package that looked like a bottle. The envelope contained the script, and another envelope in which he found a Christmas card, a New Year calendar and a diary, all stamped with the KenKil logo, two red capital Ks intertwined, one back to front.

He sat in his living-room and stared blankly at the 130 or so pages of script. His head hurt, he just didn't understand any of this. He knew that he had behaved more disgracefully than at any time in his life, that he had been more irresponsible, more slovenly, more unemployable than in the worst scenes of his nightmares, those dreams all actors know and fear when their imaginations leave them dry on stage in alien productions where they never remember their lines. He had no recollection at all of how he'd got home the previous night, and it was probably just as well. He wanted to blot out those few strands of memory which alcohol had left unblasted. He wanted to bury his head in the earth until shame had wilted him away.

But he'd got the job. Was there no justice? What was the catch? He tried to read the script, but his eyes wouldn't focus. What had Quennell said on the phone? They really were going to pay him a fortune. He unwrapped the package that looked like a bottle. It was a bottle, a litre of best malt whisky to which was attached a greetings card stamped with the ubiquitous KenKil logo.

He was almost sick again looking at it, but there was nothing left in his stomach to expel. He felt utterly empty, as if he had puked away his soul.

He felt empty, and sick, and ashamed, and lonely, and thoroughly miserable. He remembered the time of year and wondered if it was too late to buy his aunt a present. A little while later he turned on the radio and happened to hear the choir of Kings singing a carol. He sat in his chair and wept buckets.

Later he went to the kitchen and poured the whole bottle of whisky down the sink.

23 December. God, I must be bored. Why else would I write in this stupid bloody diary? What a tacky little object, cheap paper bound in plastic with a silly little pencil which has broken already. I hate diaries. I've never kept a diary in my life. Look what happens to people who do. No, let's not get into that. Let discretion be the better part of a prison-free existence. What's the point of this rambling? Something to do, I suppose. A kind of routine. I should have goals. I'd better get myself sorted out. What goals? Don't drink today. Give yourself a chance. Try and eat.

24 December. Shops are all open. Just as well, nothing in the house. Walked down to the Angel, knackered but did me good. Went back to bed. Watched TV. Ate a banana. Ecstasy? My pulse as yours doth temperately keep time.

25 December. Happy Christmas, Philip.

26 December. Had some wine yesterday, celebrate

Christmas. Ho ho. Half a glass of Chablis. It was corked, disgusting. Cooked an omelette. Did the washing. Hoovered the bedroom. Almost died of excitement.

27 December. Shaz the secretary bird rang me today, covering me instantly with confusion. I can't remember – did I throw up over her as well or was it just Ken? At any rate she sounded a little frosty. She said the contract was coming tomorrow, and Ken wanted to know, what did I think of the script? I lied badly. Couldn't say I hadn't even read the bloody thing, could I? She also said something about a party-cum-press conference next week at Ken's place in the country, said she'd be sending details. Yippee. Ken also wanted to know, had I got the whisky? I said thank him for the diary.

I went for a swim.

28 December. A woman whose name I didn't catch – Brummie, genus mechanical, sub-species lesser spotted wardrobe mistress – rang to ask me for measurements. Wasn't concentrating, started mumbling, then understood cause of silent bafflement at the other end was my having given Shaz the secretary's vital statistics. 38–26–36, can't seem to get them out of my head. Cringing apologies hastily given. Oh, *my* measurements – ha ha ha! Suppose in a way it's a good sign, brain getting back on to normal track, libido about to resurface after long hibernation. I can never remember my hat and glove size. Told her to ring Quennell, let him do something for a change.

29 December. Swam again. Five lengths. Big deal. Five more than I could have managed last week. I was shaking when I walked home. Told myself I was cold. Like hell. I started to go into the off-licence automatically. This is awful. Doth it not show vilely in me to desire small beer? I lay in bed all afternoon and sulked.

But I didn't drink. The cold sweats racked me, I was shivering, I kept dozing off and waking after mini-nightmares, my throat parched, my nerves screaming. Nothing to soothe them. I didn't drink. I suffered.

I didn't know I had the stuff of martyrs in me. A bloody hero.

30 December. Today I watched a pop video. This does not mean that I am a certifiable lunatic, it merely indicates curiosity. I have never before watched a pop video. Now I know why. I rented it from round the corner. On the slip-case it says the following:

'Warning: This product can give you a seriously good time'.

Beneath are photographs of four young men you would not want your sister to marry. According to the captions they are the Arms for Oblivion and the one who looks like a serial axe-murderer is Sleat himself.

Actually, I'm not sure if Sleat would be strong enough to wield an axe. He seems incredibly thin and straight, like a rake in unwashed denims. His face is pasty-white and his hair a surely artificial ginger-pink. In most shots he appears in sunglasses, but in a few you can see that he has aggressive piggy eyes. The look on his face is invariably surly. He wears one ring in his ear, and a very thin one through one nostril. I find him seriously peculiar, but I assume that people of my age are meant to.

I managed to last through about ten minutes of this video. I think I heard three, but maybe it was only two 'songs' during this time. Frankly, it was impossible to tell where one ended and another began.

I have often wondered what hell is like. I think it may be a room without doors and this video playing at full volume on continuous loop. As I'm obviously headed there I suppose I'd better get used to it now.

I have been trying to imagine what a hundred thousand pounds looks like. I think I will ask for it in fivers and keep it in the bath. I will wallow there like a hippopotamus in mud.

31 December. New Year's Eve. Not 10 January, as it says. I merely overran on my last entry. Would that time could be rearranged so neatly in real life, that one could skip at a whim the boring days. But on second thoughts I'd be skipping all the time ... Went to the baths today and swam twenty lengths. Not bad. There are better forms of physical exercise, but not on the menu at present. Walked to the video shop and back. Rented two episodes of *Desire* on one tape, from the Classic Soaps series. Tried to get *Psycho Robo 2* but was told there was a three-week waiting list. An acne-ridden juvenile delinquent in the shop looked up long enough from his Nintendo to vouchsafe me the opinion that it was mega-ace. Have decided that I will take his word for it.

Watched one episode of *Desire*. One's enough, I think. Plot incomprehensible, characters ludicrous, actors appalling. I wonder how much they got paid, the lucky bastards.

Shelley Lamour is something else. She may not be able to act (correction: she can't act) but with a body like that, does it matter? Are her breasts under separate contract? Even on video I couldn't take my eyes off her cleavage. How on earth is one meant to work opposite it (them) in the flesh? One would feel like Gulliver among the Brobdingnagian women. The only thing that's small about her is her voice, narrow-registered and squeaky, the accent pure fingerlickin' Southern Belle. Scarlett O'Hara meets Minnie Mouse. What on earth is she going to sound like as my daughter?

When the reviews of this film come out, I will hide in my bath and cover my head with the money.

1 January. Last night I stayed in. I turned on the television at midnight and waited for the men in kilts to appear, but none did. What has happened to the BBC? There were always men in kilts and women in long tartan dresses. I grew up with them, they are as much a part of the fabric of televisual life as the test card. Putting a bald Australian on is not the same thing at all.

I opened a quarter-bottle of champagne and drank half of it. I smoked two cigarettes. I've got down to about ten a day. I am thinking of writing to the Vatican to propose myself for beatification.

2 January. I read the script for the first time today.

3 January. Read the script for the second time. Tried to approach it afresh, from a new angle, give it another chance. It didn't take it.

I suppose worse scripts have been written. Every episode of *Desire*, for instance. I've just never been in one. How am I meant to learn this shit? I've scribbled a few rewrites in, but once I started I couldn't stop. The story is so idiotic it needs brutal amputation, not minor cosmetic surgery. This is it:

Our Dick, an honest farmer lad, lives with his homely widowed ma, his gentle virginal sister and a picturesque array of domestic animals in darkest Essex, an apparently mountainous region of England teeming with savage wildlife. Unfortunately Ma is ill (possibly the effect of the inhospitable terrain), so to raise money for an operation Sis has to go and work in the rowdy local village inn while Dick has to take their last remaining sheep to market. But Dick, unfortunately, appears to be a born accident waiting to happen, for no sooner has he had to come to the rescue of his flock by wrestling to the death with a wild bear (one of the famous Essex wild bears, I presume) than he has an unfortunate roadside encounter with the villain (the estimable Philip Fletcher) who, despite earnest entreaties from his gushingly winsome daughter (the magnificently endowed Miss Shelley Lamour) has poor Dick thrown into prison on a trumped-up charge of sheep-stealing, a capital offence. Finely judging the gravity of his situation, Dick escapes from the gallows at the very moment of execution (with some help from the enamoured Miss Lamour) and dodges the guards sent out to recapture him, the guards fulfilling all the necessary criteria for impersonating minor B-movie baddies, i.e., having no brains. Dick is just in time to rescue Sis from the evil advances of the villainous Fletcher, who is of course not merely bad but also extremely lecherous. (This bit might be fun.) Dick helps Sis escape intact and together they make for the hills (oh, those wild Essex hills!) where they fall in with a mysterious masked figure called The Captain, who takes our hero under his wing. Now poor Dick has no choice but to turn to crime to survive, not to mention pay his mother's mounting medical bills, and thus begins his celebrated career. No one is safe, not even the villainous judge (another splendidly judged appearance by the excellent Fletcher), who incarcerates his besotted daughter in York Castle and makes plans to marry her off to an aristocratic fop. Anyway, to cut a long story short (and if only someone would), Dick rides all night to York and bursts in on the wedding ceremony before the knot can be tied. Dick then single-handedly massacres the wedding guests, except for the judge (the splendid Fletcher once more) whom he takes with him as hostage, rowing him and his daughter across the moat to safety. Once safely on shore Dick gallantly agrees to release his loved one's pa (yup, me again), only for the dastardly villain to pull a knife on him. A furious fight ensues, at the end of which, in a magnificently rendered death scene, the judge finally shuffles off this mortal coil, ostensibly as a result of having a sword run through his gizzard, but in reality probably as a result of delayed cardiac arrest brought on by the shame of agreeing to appear in the movie. Dick then rides off into the sunset with Shelley Lamour over his saddle (he'd better take care she doesn't tip over), and they are reunited with Sis and Dick's friend The Captain to whom Sis is now engaged. Dick apologises for murdering Shelley's dad (me), she says don't mention it, he wasn't my dad really anyway, he was only my stepfather, Dick says, oh, that's all right then, stepfathers obviously don't count, so he and her and Sis and Captain all have a jolly double wedding under the greenwood tree fêted by assorted merry men and live happily ever after. THE END.

It would be laughably euphemistic to describe this fearful load of old tosh as a travesty. No brief synopsis can do justice to it, for however absurd the plot, it is more than matched by the dialogue, which is stuffed like a magpie's Christmas stocking with all manner of extraneous gobbledegook. And I am expected to say much the worst of it. I begin to have horrible suspicions concerning the casting of this role. Just how many actors turned it down before he got to me? I asked Ken and he said none. I think he doth protest too much. We spoke on the phone. I should have been contrite. After all, I hadn't spoken to him since redecorating his shoes from a great height, but I was too worked up for politeness. Indeed, I made some very disparaging remarks about the mental capacity of Mr Harvey Goldman. Ken was his usual Brylcreemed self. He said of course I could change my lines (if I couldn't, I said, I'd walk off the set) subject to the director's approval. And when, I queried, might that august functionary be available for consultation? He is arriving in London at the weekend and I can speak to him at this party-cum-press conference. Bloody wonderful. What am I supposed to do if we don't see eye to eye?

Why did I sign that contract? Because my eyes are bigger than my belly. Because my bath is bigger than my wallet.

The impression is growing that Mr Kenneth Kilmaine is something of an Arthur Daley figure. I have instructed Quennell to ensure that all payments are received in full and on the dot. I regret that we did not demand any money up front. I have further faxed Martha Kielmansegge in New York in the quest for information. What she doesn't know about what's what and who's who on the other side of the Atlantic isn't worth knowing. But I confess that I rather dread finding out what she may have to say . . .

4 January. Went into town today for a costume and wig fitting. Usual eighteenth-century gear, big boots and frilly shirts, tricorne hat and embroidered waistcoats. With any luck no one will recognise me underneath it all. While I was being fitted, a black American chap came in and introduced himself to everyone as Brad. Seemed very pleasant, had a nice chat. Thought he was a designer, asked him questions about the material. More blank looks. Eventually penny dropped. He is Bradley Pitman, an actor. Saw his name on the cast list but it didn't mean anything. He is playing the Captain, Dick's friend. I wonder where they got the idea of Dick having a black side-kick?

5 January. It rained all day. I stayed in by the window, watching it come down. Tried to read the script and felt immense self-sorrow. Consoled myself with dreaming of ill-gotten gains. Rain slowed to drizzle mid-afternoon. Scooted out to shops, on my way back who should I see but George Cornelius Washington, driving a blue car along Upper Street. Waved frantically, and I'm sure he saw me, but did he stop and offer me a lift?

The little bastard.

6 January. Start filming on Monday. Can't believe it. Oh horror, horror, horror. Am I up to it? I don't feel as bad as I did but I'm hardly a hundred per cent yet. God, I feel like a drink. But I've been so bloody good. Been training myself to go to bed early, the next few months are going to be pretty gruelling. I shan't have time to write in this diary any more. How serious a loss this will be to posterity remains to be seen.

7 January. What a peculiar morning I've had! I went for a swim and when I came back I found the front door was ajar and heard someone crashing about inside. Oh no, I thought, not *again* . . .

5

He stood in the open doorway, listening. The sounds were coming from the kitchen, dull thuds and clashings. The kitchen was full of knives, he looked around for a weapon of his own. Then he saw the alarm cabinet hanging open, the key dangling inside in the off position. Surely a burglar wouldn't have had time to find the key before it went off? He tiptoed over to the kitchen door and peeped inside. He laughed, like a relieved hyena.

'Why, Mrs Tomascevski, what a surprise!'

Mrs Thing looked up from the cupboard in which she had been nosing.

'Mr Fletcher I try to ring but no answer,' she said in her mournful B-movie accent. 'I am only back in country two days, not free to come Wednesdays usually.'

Mrs Thing and the English language were only fleetingly acquainted. Punctuation and she were complete strangers.

'Ah, yes, I'd forgotten you were going away. Well, it's very nice to see you now. I'm afraid it's all been a little chaotic in your absence.'

Though it was certainly a lot better than it had been. Mrs Thing finished replacing the contents of one cupboard and moved on to the next. Her manner was brisk and businesslike but he did not detect signs of unfriendliness. And she was never reticent about letting her disapproval be known.

'And how's Mr Tomascevski been keeping?'

'Not too bad thanks for asking Mr Fletcher again back is bad but Good Lord provide.'

Mr Tomascevski's back was always bad, and other parts of him were frequently out in sympathy. Philip had often wondered how much his hypochondria was affected by his wife's lugubriousness, and vice versa.

'Well, I'll get out of your way,' he said pleasantly.

'Mr Fletcher while you was out was man here for you.'

'Really? When?'

'Not long five minutes maybe ten was black man.'

The adjective was pronounced with heavily parenthesised disapproval. Mrs Thing was Poland's answer to Alf Garnett.

'Did he say what he wanted?'

'Said wanted you said urgent but I keep close door no trust this man I say go away he say come later back.'

'Ah. Well, at least he came by the door. If it's who I think it is, that's an improvement. His usual method of ingress is via the window.'

'What is you say?'

'Never mind. Excuse me, that's the phone, I'd better go and answer it.'

He went next door and carried the phone over to the window. While he spoke to his agent he scanned the street for a jaunty familiar face.

'I've been asking around a bit about old Ken Kilmaine, as you suggested,' said John Quennell.

'And what have you found out?'

'Yes, well, I don't know how to put this, but his past does seem to have been a little on the dodgy side.'

'Oh, yes?' Philip braced himself. 'It's not entirely unexpected, but tell me more.'

'Well, to put it delicately, he doesn't normally make the kind of films you'd want to take your granny to see. In fact he doesn't seem to have made any films at all in the last few years, but, er, hang on a sec, I've got a list of back-titles here somewhere; ah yes, here we are . . . there's *Night Of The Nymphomaniac Nurses*, then there's *Doctor Dildo*, and another called *Doctor Dildo and the Busty Bimbos*, a sequel, I presume . . .'

'Either that or an extension. Got a bit of a medical fixation, hasn't he?'

'I'm afraid it's not exactly Dr Kildare. I should emphasise that all these were some years ago, I gather he's been making an attempt to go legit and there are some other more recent titles which seem innocuous enough. He seems quite above-board these days. I'm sorry I didn't find any of this out earlier, but he's been pretty canny about covering his tracks.'

'I understand why. Well, it's too late to go all Disgusted of Tunbridge Wells, anyway. I'm under contract and that's that. Besides, I've never felt moral considerations were really an issue in the movie world. Everyone's so busy screwing everyone else anyway that you can hardly blame someone for filming it.'

'You're beginning to sound more like your usual self, Philip.'

'You mean my speech doesn't sound slurred?'

'Now, Philip — '

'It's all right, old chap, I can take a bit of plain speaking. I know I've had a problem, but I think I can say without fear of hubris that I'm on top of it now. Excuse me, John, there's somebody ringing my doorbell.' Philip clamped his hand over the receiver and called out, 'Mrs Tomascevski, could you see who that is, please?' He heard her talking into the intercom in the kitchen. He put the phone back to his ear. 'Sorry about that, John. The thing is, would you keep your antennae open – there's something not quite right about all this. The money — '

'Don't worry about the money, Philip. The contract's signed, he's got to pay you.'

'Yes, but we all know it's more than I'm worth.'

'Don't say that, Philip. If what you're saying about the script is true, then maybe he's thinking that you're the class act who's going to rescue his movie.'

'Yes, but – excuse me again, will you . . .'

He lowered the phone. Mrs Tomascevski had appeared in the kitchen door.

'Is same man before says name Vashington what I do?'

'Would you ask him to come up, please?'

Mrs Thing gave him the kind of outraged look she might have given had he invited her to a showing of *Dr Dildo and the Busty Bimbos*, but she went back into the kitchen and pressed the intercom buzzer.

'I have to go now,' he said to his agent. 'Please keep your eyes and ears open for anything about Ken Kilmaine.'

There was a knock on the door. Philip put down the phone and went to answer it. As he approached there was a second knock.

'You are an impatient young man, aren't you?' he commented as he opened the door. 'I've a bone to — '

He stopped in mid-sentence. The person on his doorstep was not who he had been expecting at all.

'Do I have the honour of addressing Mr Philip Fletcher?' the person boomed.

Philip nodded. The person was about his age, but there all similarities ended. He was very big and very burly, with coal-black skin and dark fierce eyes. His thick curly hair and beard were shot through with pepper-and-salt and he wore an impressive, dignified air. He also wore, along with the traditional plain black suit, a crisp white dog-collar.

'I am the Reverend Cornelius Washington. May I have a word with you, please?'

The voice spread from the diaphragm and rumbled magnificently. It was a voice an actor might kill for. Why, in Aleppo once —

'Yes, of course, come in,' said Philip smartly, overcoming his surprise. He ushered his visitor into the room and indicated the sofa. 'Can I offer you something to drink?'

The Rev. Washington narrowed his eyes. 'Alcohol is the devil's own work, Mr Fletcher. I never touch the stuff.'

'Yes, well, I was thinking more of a cup of coffee actually.'

The Rev. Washington shook his head sadly. 'Stimulants, Mr Fletcher, stimulants.'

'All right, well, we'll pass on that one then. Please tell me how I can help you, and please do take a seat.'

Philip had sat down himself in his armchair, but the Rev. Washington was still standing in the middle of the room. He made no move to sit. Philip thought that perhaps he found the idea of cushions morally corrupting and he decided not to press the point.

'I have come to speak to you about my nephew, George.'

'Ah, yes.'

'He claims he is known to you, Mr Fletcher. Is this true?'

'It is,' Philip answered uncomfortably, for there was something unmistakably magisterial about the Reverend's tones, and he had never felt comfortable in the company of magistrates.

'And how did you and George come to be acquainted?'

The question sounded suspiciously like an accusation. Philip answered carefully, though it did occur to him to wonder why he should be covering up for the apprentice housebreaker.

'Oh, it was a chance encounter as I recall. No doubt George will remember the details better than me . . .'

'He says that you invited him up here to watch a videotape.'

'Yes. Well, more or less.'

'My wife and I are very careful in what we allow young George to watch, Mr Fletcher, there is so much offensive material available even to the young and innocent. Is it true, then, that you are an actor?'

The word 'actor' was phrased in such a way as to suggest that the Rev. Washington considered it interchangeable with 'sinner'.

'I am,' replied Philip meekly, conscious that in his case the implication was just.

The Reverend once more shook his head sadly. 'It is not my world, Mr Fletcher, not my world at all. George is very young, very young and very impressionable. A boy, I think, of some promise.'

In the criminal sphere very much so, Philip thought. He gave a sweet smile of agreement.

'Mr Fletcher, I fear you have led young George astray.'

'I —'

The protest died in his throat. He could only stare dumbly at his guest, who was leaning his fists on the back of the sofa and peering at him as if over a pulpit.

'Mr Fletcher, you have been filling young George's head with ideas, dangerous ideas. An upright member of my congregation has generously offered the boy work in his grocery store, but George refuses to entertain notions of gainful employment. He has determined, Mr Fletcher, to become an actor. What do you have to say?'

'Not guilty?' suggested Philip.

The Reverend's eyes brimmed with dissatisfaction. 'This is no time for levity, Mr Fletcher.'

Wasn't it? Philip could feel distinctly the onset of delirium in his diaphragm. He couldn't help the broad smile which blossomed on his face, though which was the funnier he could not decide, the notion of himself as foul ambition's catalyst or the image of George taking the West End by storm. Taking the box office receipts, more like.

'We-ell,' Philip said at last, managing to rein in his hilarity. 'I can only assure you, sir, in all honesty, that neither did George confide any of this to me, nor, had he done so, would I in any wit or wise have encouraged him. In fact, it has been a rule of my life – one of the few, but I have followed it assiduously – actively to dissuade those young impressionables who have from time to time besought my advice regarding the pursuance of a career theatrical. Let us hope it is a fad. If so, it will soon wither if ignored. Attempting to sow tares in George's mind would, I think, prove counter-productive. In fact, in this particular vineyard, we may hope to see the talent long remain buried, if indeed – '

'There is no need to labour the analogy, Mr Fletcher, I understand you. But clearly you have some influence with the boy. I cannot let you stand idly by while he is sucked into the well of depravity and the den of corruption.'

'I'm afraid the Department of Health and Social Security would be his more likely destination. Why should you suppose I have any influence over him?'

'He has cited you as his referee, has he not?'

'Has he? Referee for what?'

'His application for drama school.'

'Oh.' Philip digested the news philosophically. 'Well, I'm obviously not equipped to referee at the Arsenal. None the less, I have to tell you that this comes as a complete surprise to me.'

'That may be, that may be . . .'

The Reverend Washington advanced upon him, it seemed with

menace. Philip shrank instinctively into his chair but the Reverend approached no nearer than the mantelpiece. It was near enough, though, to make his already impressive frame seem huger. The sense of his occupying the high ground was reinforced.

'Mr Fletcher, I can tell that you have the seeds of morality deep within you.'

'Have I?'

Philip's surprise was genuine.

'I accept now that you did not knowingly encourage the boy, but none the less it would seem that he has fixed on you as an example. He has strayed, and the shepherd is calling him to his flock. Will you help him, Mr Fletcher, will you help me? Will you heed the cry of the lost lamb, the voice crying out in the wilderness?'

It was a stirring rhetorical declaration, as magnificent and innately theatrical as Philip's first impressions had seemed to promise. He could not know what kind of services the Reverend presided over, but he doubted that they bore much resemblance to the mundane Home Counties Anglicanism which he remembered from his choirboy days. Indeed, so stirring was the oratory that he found himself on the point of suffering an alien and wild compulsion to leap to his feet, waving his arms about while crying ecstatically:

'Hallelujah! Glory be!'

But he managed to restrain himself.

'I do take your point,' he said instead. 'I'll have a word with him if you like.'

The Reverend's eyes softened. He seemed satisfied. He indicated that he was about to leave. 'Very good, Mr Fletcher, very good. It is no more than I hoped for. Between us we may make young George see the light.'

I'd put a lock on it first, Philip mused.

The Reverend paused at the door. 'I took the liberty of bringing the boy with me. He is downstairs waiting in the hall. May I send him up?'

'By all means.'

Philip shrugged. He was unsure quite how he had allowed himself to be cast in the unlikely role of youth counsellor, but the deed had clearly been done and he had somehow acquired responsibilities which it would be easier to discharge than to shirk. The Reverend smiled kindly at him and went out, leaving the front door ajar. Philip resettled himself in his armchair. Mrs Tomascevski stuck her head out of the kitchen.

'He gone?' she demanded, flaring her nostrils suspiciously as if divining a hostile scent. 'I like to hoover.'

'*Chacun à son goût*, Mrs Tomascevski. I'm afraid the hoovering will have to wait.'

There was a light rap on the door and George Cornelius Washington sauntered in unbidden. Mrs Tomascevski's nostrils expanded to bursting-point.

'You wanted a word?' enquired George carelessly.

An indignant spasm contorted Mrs T's face. She shot Philip an outraged glance before retreating into the kitchen, slamming the door shut behind her.

Philip eyed his young visitor coolly. 'No, not so much a word, more an explanation.'

George shrugged and sat on the arm of the sofa.

'Make yourself comfortable,' suggested Philip ironically.

George picked up his copy of the script of *Midnight Rider*. 'What's this then?'

'It's a film script, not that it's any of your business. I shall be working on it as of Monday.'

'Yeah? Can I be in it?'

'Certainly not.'

'Why not?'

Philip snorted. 'Because only actors appear in films. I am an actor, you are a criminal. Therefore I am employable, you are not. A simple syllogism, but one which encompasses the pertinent facts.'

'You what?'

'Don't start that again. Now, young man, I should like an explanation: what on earth has given you the idiotic idea that you might forsake a profession for which you seem prodigiously well suited in favour of one which demands qualities too numerous to list but all of which seem to me conspicuously absent in you? Furthermore, how dare you take my name in vain as an unsolicited and unwilling sponsor of your madcap scheme? And don't say "You what?". You know perfectly well what I'm talking about.'

'How do you know I ain't got qualities?'

'A suspicion based on observation and deduction.'

'You sound really stuck-up sometimes, you know that?'

'That may be true, but it's beside the point. Acting ability is something you're born with. A good drama school can teach technique, but it can't improve on something that isn't there. Even allowing that you were admitted to a drama school – and it's quite possible: as you are young, black and apparently disadvantaged you could appear to possess the requisite entry qualifications to the anxiously correct middle-class liberals who run such institutions – even allowing, as I say, for your admission, your presence in such a school for two years or so would yield no benefit and would furthermore constitute an intolerable drain on scarce resources to the already long-suffering taxpayer.'

'You trying to deprive me of my rights?'

'What of the rights of unborn audiences everywhere? Do they have none? Why should they be expected to subsidise what would amount to a criminal assault on the works of innocent unprotected authors?'

'You trying to tell me I'm crap or something?'

'Most admirably expressed with your usual concision.'

'How do you know?'

'As I said — '

George sprang up aggressively and adopted a challenging stance on the hearthrug. 'It ain't fair, you ain't giving me a chance, no one ever gives me a chance, it's the same old story, I just get dumped on the scrap-heap, then people go around complaining about me nicking things, well, it ain't surprising, is it? I mean, it's society that's to blame, innit, I mean it's a social — '

'Yes, yes, write to the *Guardian* if you want to, it's really not my concern. George, I'm afraid I really do believe that you're not cut out for the world of motley.'

'Yeah? Prove it!'

George's lip was trembling, his whole body aquiver. He seemed genuinely upset.

'Very well . . .' Philip paused to consider his options. How best to strangle at birth George's nascent delusions? While he was mulling over the possibilities the phone rang.

'You'll have to excuse me a moment,' he said.

It was one of the production assistants from the film, checking that he had received the invitation and map to Ken's party and the first week's shooting schedule. He had.

'A nice early start, I see.'

'I've arranged for you to be picked up at five o'clock on Monday morning. Do you want a car laid on for the party?'

'That would be . . .' Philip paused to consider. He recalled the rust-bucket which Kilmaine had sent round last time. 'I'm not sure, can I call you back on that one?'

Philip put down the phone. George was still standing by the sofa, glowering at him.

'You gonna prove I can't act then?' he demanded belligerently.

'In a moment . . .' Philip reached over to the bookcase by his armchair and picked out his Complete Works. He opened it at *Romeo and Juliet*.

'I saw you driving in Upper Street the other day in a blue car. You saw me too but chose to pretend you hadn't. Whose car was it?'

George bridled indignantly. 'Me uncle's. What you think, I nicked it?'

'Whatever would have given me that idea? Does your uncle often let you borrow his car?'

'Yeah, why shouldn't he?'

'Well, they say charity begins at home. I am in need of a chauffeur for tomorrow night. If you can borrow the car and take me – it's not far, just the other side of Uxbridge – then I am prepared to listen to you reading to me, after which I will give you my frank and unbiased professional opinion as to whether or not you possess any talent.'

''Ere! That's blackmail!'

'That's a highly selective interpretation. Do we have a deal?'

'That ain't fair!'

'I'd say it's preposterously generous on my part. Come on, I haven't got all day.'

'I'll have to ask.'

'And if you do, then I'm sure you will receive. I'll take that for a yes, then, and I shall hold you to your word. Now read this.'

'But soft, what light — '

'No, have a look at it first. Read it through to yourself, see if you understand it.'

Philip sat back in his armchair and watched George as he bent his head over the book, his brow knotted in furious concentration, his mouth popping open and shut as he murmured the words under his breath. Despite himself Philip found something rather endearing in the sight.

'Well, do you understand it?'

George shrugged nonchalantly. 'Piece of piss.'

'F. R. Leavis, eat your heart out . . .'

'Want me to read it now?'

'I can hardly wait.'

'But soft — '

'No, stand up first. You can't be passionate sitting down. And don't slouch. And don't look so miserable. And don't lean against the mantelpiece, stand squarely on your own two feet. Do you know what Kean used to ask aspiring young actors?'

'Who?'

'Never mind. He asked only one question, and it had nothing to do with talent. It was this – "Can you starve?" If you can't, then I'd suggest you start practising. Now get on with it.'

Philip leant back his head and closed his eyes, while the dulcet tones of an Arsenal fan reciting the Bard washed over him. Before turning over his full attention to his critical faculties he wondered to himself briefly why he was indulging in this ludicrous charitable exercise. He concluded that the probable cause was premature senility.

6

The party was scheduled to begin at eight o'clock and Philip, feeling like a rajah in his howdah in the back of the Rev. Washington's blue Ford, arrived on the dot, having been greatly entertained during the journey by George's descriptions of his uncle's ministry, which, it turned out, was based not in a church proper at all but in a nearby leisure centre. As Philip had suspected, the style of worship was not of the traditional variety; rather, the principal ingredients consisted of hand-clapping, swaying and much disconnected speaking in tongues. George himself was of the opinion that there was very little to choose between one of his uncle's services and Saturday afternoon at the Arsenal. Philip was almost convinced that he would have enjoyed the football better.

The Kilmaine residence, at the end of a long country lane in Iver, was surrounded by a high wall which appeared to contain a substantial acreage. A small queue of cars was formed outside the gate, through which Philip glimpsed a drive at the end of which stood a large Georgian house. Somebody was checking names off on a clipboard before allowing the cars through. Only when their turn came did Philip realise that the somebody was wearing fancy dress.

As George wound down the window, a masked figure in a black hat and cloak advanced on them. He thrust an antique pistol through the window and demanded, 'Stand and deliver!'

This challenge did not impress George. 'Deliver what, mate? What do you think I am, Securicor?'

George's spontaneous wit was enough to floor the pseudo-highwayman, who lowered his weapon uncertainly and consulted his clipboard. 'Er, name please,' he murmured.

'George.'

Philip leant forward and tapped him on the shoulder. 'I think he means me actually.' He gave his name. 'No need to take me in, George, I'll walk from here. I don't care what you do in the next hour, but for God's sake make sure you're back at nine, or no more Shakespeare lessons for you. Got it?'

'All right!' George answered impatiently.

Philip was both touched and amused that the threat seemed to carry weight. Actually, George's reading hadn't been that bad (though in truth it hadn't been that good either) once he had got over the habit of singing the verse like a football chant (George 1 Swan of Avon 0). There was even a possibility that deep down he might have a glimmer of a spark of talent. Perverse as it seemed to him, Philip had none the less quite enjoyed the role of drama coach.

He got out and walked up the drive, past the slow-moving line of cars waiting to deposit their passengers outside the front of the house. He took a short-cut across an oval patch of lawn.

Suddenly a great streak of light flashed across the grass and the revving of a car engine sounded loudly behind him. He turned, rather startled, and a horn blared. A huge metallic shape loomed out of the darkness.

He jumped to the side, half-blinded by the headlights, and a black limousine whooshed over where he had been standing and made a bee-line for the house. A car was just pulling away from the front steps, leaving room for the next in the queue to come forward, but the black limousine darted in off the grass and slewed round like something out of a bad action movie amidst a squeal of brakes and a crunch of gravel. Philip barked an indignant curse, then strode on rapidly in the wake of the limousine, between the faint twin tyre tracks glistening in the dew of the lawn.

The car had stopped outside a raised porch supported by pillars. As Philip approached a man got out of the front and opened the rear door.

'Excuse me — ' he began tartly, but nobody heard him.

A rake-thin figure appeared out of the back. The bright lights spilling from the open front door caught the frizzy points of his hair in a marmalade glow, the narrow pointed face beneath shining dully like freckled plaster. With shoulders hunched over long limbs he moved like a secretary bird up to the steps.

And people sprang from nowhere to surround him. Before he had reached the second step a gaggle of screaming girls was pecking at him. Photographers' flash-bulbs flickered like roman candles, and notepad-clutching reporters jostled for the empty spaces. From some obscure corner of the night materialised the Cheshire grin of walking, talking Ken Kilmaine: 'Let him breathe, ladies and gents. Clear a space for him there, boys.'

The boys he referred to were a couple more beefy highwaymen, who promptly poked their pistols into a few faces and elbowed out a clearing amidst the human mass. Ken signalled to one of the shrieking girls and the yells of deranged ecstasy were stemmed.

Philip, on the edge of the supplicants' circle, smiled wryly to himself. The girl to whom Ken had signalled was none other than the multi-talented Shaz. A political candidate would surely have paid dearly for Ken's stage-managing skills.

'This way, Sleat!'

'Here, can you give us a quote?'

The wraith-like pop star casually presented his profile to the off-side photographers and another aurora limned his head. Clearly the flashing lights did not discomfit him; he was wearing opaque dark glasses.

'How d'ya feel 'bout acting in yer first movie, then, Sleat?' called out a buck-toothed woman in the fine, bell-like tones of a TV yoof presenter.

'Yeah, give us the low-down,' chimed in another.

The great man lazily turned his head to encompass them all and shrugged.

'Er, it's like great, you know, I'm really looking forward to it!' he declared in an indeterminate Northern nasal whine.

Philip's heart, already somewhere down by his knees, sank further towards the loam.

'Have you had acting lessons?' demanded a more conventional-sounding reporter.

'Nah!' There was almost a flicker of emotion – annoyance – in the pale, unresponsive face. 'I'm a graduate of the University of Life, me, and that's got a real-and-kicking drama department of its own, you know. And I've got a Ph.D.'

'Thanks, Sleat!' said the buck-toothed woman as she scribbled enthusiastically. 'That's a mega-quote, that is.'

Sleat shrugged again. *Noblesse oblige*, his thinly smiling lips seemed to say.

'OK now, folks!' said Ken, clapping his hands for attention. 'You got enough pics for now, so let the man through and give him a break, you can ask your questions later.'

'Nah, it's all right,' protested Sleat indulgently. 'Let 'em ask away, Ken, I like my views to be known.'

Ken did not seem unequivocally thrilled to hear this, but with his protégé so unwilling to relinquish centre-stage he had little option but to step back with as good a grace, and as emollient a grin, as possible. There was a flurry of quick-fire questions.

'When's the single coming out, then?'

'What do the other band members think of it all?'

'What do you think of Shelley Lamour?'

'What attracted you to the part in the first place?'

Sleat raised his hands for silence. 'Whoa! Whoa! Give me a chance to answer there, guys. I think Shelley's terrific, I'm a great fan, we get on great. As for the single, you'd better give me a chance to write it first, and you'd better ask the band if you want to know what they think. What really attracted me to the character of Dick Turpin is that this guy's like from the wrong side of the tracks, you know, like he finds injustice everywhere he looks, like Robin Hood, and he has to stamp it out, but the really crucial thing is that it's the capitalist system that's driven him to crime, he has no alternative, which is why the ruling class finds him so dangerous, because he isn't afraid of their repression, 'cos he doesn't know his place like he's supposed to, and he really represents the people, he's an original working-class hero, and I think he's got this amazing, like, empathy with the natural world, because he lives wild and free, you see, so I think it's important we get away from the stereotypes and see him in terms of being an ecological role model, and that's what I think's really great, you know.'

From the blank looks that greeted this manifesto it was not clear that his audience did know. There was a pause before one called out, 'You mentioned Robin Hood —'

'Just a figure of speech,' interrupted Ken smoothly, pushing his way to Sleat's side and taking him by the elbow. 'Now, look everybody, I really don't see the point of us spending the whole night out here nattering away, when there's booze and buffet and Miss Shelley Lamour inside. So if you all come on down now I'll get the two stars to pose for you together and we can all partake of some liquid refreshment — 'nuff said?'

It was a persuasive argument. Ken steered Sleat into the house and the massed ranks of the media filed in after. Philip brought up the rear, a wiser and a sadder man.

He found himself in an elegantly proportioned hallway, whose centrepiece was an impressive marble staircase with ornate gilded banisters over which hung a large banner bearing the legend in red letters: 'STICK 'EM UP! DICK'S BACK'.

Stick what up Dick's back? Philip wondered.

Ken, Sleat and the crowd headed off through large open double doors to the right. As nobody seemed to be paying him the slightest attention, Philip peeled off discreetly left.

He found himself in a kitchen, where period serving lads and wenches were busy preparing food under the direction of a bossy, hatchet-faced woman who would have been a natural for Mrs Danvers. Philip hogged a corner and nibbled at some savoury snacks. He supposed that he ought to go on in and make his presence known, but the thought of socialising depressed him thoroughly. The thought of what probably lay in store for him over the next few months depressed him even more. Why was he here? He didn't think there'd be anybody he knew, and if the sample of assorted pop journalist types he had encountered outside was anything to go by, then the average age of the other guests was probably going to be no more than twelve. What on earth was he going to do with himself for the next hour or so? If George was still around, could he sneak out sooner?

A pretty young highwaywoman came in. At least Philip assumed she was meant to be a highwaywoman, though in her black boots and tights, frilly white shirt and mask she could have been mistaken for Dick Whittington's cat.

'You're Philip Fletcher, aren't you?'

The voice was soft and warm and, even to Philip's jaundiced ear, encouragingly friendly. He gave his best Colgate-casting smile and she pushed her mask back on to her dark curly hair, which made him grin that much more, for she was even prettier than he had supposed and the set of her almond eyes did indeed have the most feline – and alluring – quality.

'I'm Mandy Morgan,' she said, returning his smile with a touch of coyness. 'I'm an enormous fan of yours.'

'Oh, really?'

Perhaps the next hour wouldn't be so bad after all. Philip went through the motions of trying to look modest.

'Oh, yes!' she answered beamingly. 'I saw your Uncle Vanya at Chichester. I think you're wonderful!'

Well, that makes two of us, he thought, adding for his private benefit: you're not so bad yourself . . .

'Tell me, Mandy,' he said, giving her costume an appraising glance, 'what do you do when you're not robbing stage-coaches?'

'Good question,' she answered with a most becoming blush. 'Actually, I'm an actress.'

Her name had seemed vaguely familiar; now he recalled that he had seen it on the cast list.

'Of course!' He snapped his fingers at his own stupidity. 'Mandy Morgan – you're playing the sister.'

'That's right!' She was obviously pleased that he knew. 'I'm Cathy Turpin.'

Philip considered it a small mercy that Harvey Goldman hadn't christened the character Tracey.

'Good,' he said, 'oh, very good . . . we've got some scenes together.'

He recalled that one stage direction required him to rip off her bodice. At least he wouldn't have too much difficulty getting to grips with his motivation. It was all the other scenes that were going to be the problem.

'Do you know if our director is here by any chance?'

'I think so, but he's jet-lagged. Ken said he was having a lie-down upstairs.'

'What about Harvey?'

'You mean the writer?'

'Well, I wasn't referring to the big white rabbit.'

She turned bright crimson again and giggled. She had a very fresh, girlish quality. He didn't think she could have been any more than twenty, perhaps even younger.

'Done any films before?' he asked shrewdly.

She shook her head and looked suddenly serious. 'I'm so, so lucky, I can't tell you. I've only been acting for a year, all I've done is a bit of rep and a cough and a spit on telly.'

'You must have a good agent.'

'No. I mean – I've got one now, since getting the film, but I didn't have one then.'

'Sometimes knowing the right casting director is enough.'

'I'm afraid I don't even know who it is! Ken cast me. All I did was send in my photograph when I read about it in *PCR*. I still can't believe it's all happening!'

'Ah, I see,' said Philip, who thought he did, quite clearly. He felt a sudden pang of jealousy. He remembered the expansive leather sofa in Ken's office. How central an item of furniture was it in his casting sessions?

'Well, we can't stand here all night!' Mandy said with a laugh. 'I think we should go and find you a drink.'

She took him by the hand, which he didn't mind at all, and led him out into the hall. There was something very trusting about her, it made him feel strangely protective. That wasn't all he felt either, but it was the more unusual sensation.

'Quite a pad,' he remarked, genuinely impressed.

'You should see the rest of the house,' she answered.

She clearly had. He felt that pang again. Was she just a guest herself tonight or did she have an ancillary function? If she was Ken's bit on the side, then he was already hopelessly and wildly jealous. And he had never been much good at coping with jealousy.

'It is crowded, isn't it!' she said, squeezing his hand as they stopped outside the double doors through which the others had gone earlier. 'I can't see Harvey.'

The room was large and decorated in a manner not in keeping with its obvious Georgian origins. The ceiling was fluffed out with curly gilded bits of Victoriana, and an unlikely candelabra that hung down like an outsized pomegranate. This vast confection of crystal was at the centre of a spider's web of banners, all gaily flaunting the name of Dick. Streamers and balloons bobbed between them, while coloured spotlights bathed the scene in a lurid glow. Most of the people seemed to be crammed into one corner, where blood-red velvet curtains framed a vast bay window in front of which Sleat was posing for the photographers. Philip caught a glimpse of a little blonde head bobbing up and down beside the pop star.

'Is that Shelley Lamour?'

'That is she,' replied Mandy softly. 'Montana Madigan from TV's *Desire*, as it says on all the publicity. I'm afraid I mumble it in my sleep.'

'Mm, I'd like to hear that,' Philip mumbled himself.

The photographers rearranged themselves for another shot and now Philip caught a glimpse of the famous soap queen.

She was tiny, a blue-eyed, blonde-ringleted China doll, with rich sensual lips and eyelashes born to flutter. She was wearing a low-cut scarlet gown which was very revealing and, as was widely acknowledged, she had much to reveal. But strangely – like the decor around her – it didn't all quite match up. Something was lacking, probably the illusory skills of television production. The face was too little-girlish, the rest of her anything but. It was as if the head of Shirley Temple had been transplanted on to the body of Dolly Parton – a combination to rival the most fevered outpouring from the pen of that other Shelley, Mary.

Shelley Lamour pouted and posed, then pouted some more. The flash-bulbs must have been on overtime. One of the photographers sauntered up between shots and laid a casual hand on one of her bare shoulders.

'Could we have a shot of you in his arms, like — '

An enormous cowboy appeared suddenly from within the recesses of the bay window, like Hamlet from behind his arras, and grabbed the photographer roughly. 'Take your hands off of her, mister.'

The photographer did as he was bid (evidently a sensible man) and stared dumbly at the huge figure towering over him. Philip rather shared his amazement. Cowboys were not native to these parts, let alone one who was nearer seven feet than six in his white ten-gallon hat and probably not much narrower across his buckskin-covered chest.

'Interesting lines in fancy dress here tonight,' Philip remarked to Mandy.

'I wouldn't say that to his face, if I were you,' she replied seriously.

'I'm not sure if I could get up high enough in the first place . . .'

Shelley's pout had faded, to be replaced by an expression of mixed annoyance and resignation. She made as if to try and push the cowboy away, which to Philip invoked the image of an ant swatting an elephant. The egregious Ken appeared from nowhere in particular, gesturing in all directions like a deranged variety compere.

'OK everyone, I think you've got enough now, haven't you? It's meant to be party-time, folks, so how's about we all get ourselves a drink, all right, boys and girls?'

The photographers did not remonstrate; no doubt they were all intimidated by the cowboy's presence. Some of them continued to hang around Sleat, who seemed more than happy to lap up all the attention that was going, but everyone gave a wide berth to the cowboy, who came away from the window with Shelley tucked under his armpit, like a one-man rugby scrum shielding the ball.

'Who on earth is he?' Philip asked Mandy, when Little and Large were out of earshot.

'That's her husband, Marvin J. Loudwater the second.'

'I see. Well, I'll try not to confuse him with Marvin J. Loud-water the first. Should I have heard of either of them, by the way?'

'I think he's pretty big in Texas.'

'I'd say he's pretty big anywhere . . .'

She laughed. He liked that. She was still holding on to his hand and he liked that too.

'What about that drink, then?' he said.

They went over to one of the tables laden with goodies and were served with tumblers of orange juice on request. Philip continued to be amazed at his own self-control. Others around him, he noticed, had less cause for smugness, particularly those in the vicinity of the pop star and his entourage.

'Why, hi there, Philip!'

'Bradley, how do you do?'

Bradley Pitman, too, was dressed in highwayman's gear. Philip smiled at him pleasantly. 'Glad to see you already in costume. You obviously can't wait to get started.'

'Mm . . .' Bradley gave a wry smile. 'Should be quite a challenge.'

Philip returned his smile knowingly.

'Mandy's promised to introduce me to Harvey Goldman. Is he around?'

'I haven't seen him in here,' Mandy said.

'I think he was next door in the dining-room earlier,' Bradley offered, giving Philip a shrewd look. He murmured, 'Good luck.'

'Thanks.'

'I'm hoping to have a word with Ken myself.'

'Good luck.'

'Thanks . . .'

As if on cue, the man himself appeared, accompanied by a dignified, grey-haired gentleman in an expensive suit and a toothy teenage girl with spiky ginger hair.

'All right then, everyone?' Ken demanded (it would be superfluous to add 'grinning'). 'Phi-lip!' he continued, before anyone had the chance to reply. 'Great to see you, old man. You're keeping an eye on him, I hope, young Mand?'

Mandy gave one of her routine blushes. Philip felt his eyes narrow as Ken laid a hand on her shoulder and idly squeezed it. It was hard to tell if the gesture was meant to be proprietorial; Ken was just like that. He flapped his other hand at the grey-haired gentleman, introducing him as Mr Witt. 'But we're allowed to call him Anton. Everyone does – even his wife! Ha ha ha!'

It was Mr Witt's turn to blush. Ken carried on regardless, once he had stopped laughing at his own joke. 'And this is the apple of his eye, no less, his lovely daughter Heidi.'

'Actually, it is Helga,' said the toothy girl in a thick foreign accent.

'You've got to be nice to our Anton now,' Ken continued, ignoring her. 'He's our principal backer, without him we'd all be going nowhere fast!'

Mr Witt mumbled something in an equally dense accent. Ken, who seemed to possess the gift of being able to spread embarrassment effortlessly, practised it again now. 'Phi-lip here's also a man to keep in with, you know,' he said with one of his outsize winks. 'A man who knows his malt, my friend here, a real connoisseur. I don't know what he's got in his glass there, but odds on it rhymes with orangery, ha ha ha!'

Philip winced. Fortunately Ken was making to move on and no one else knew what he was talking about.

'Ken, can I have a word?' said Bradley.

'Later, old man, later,' said the grinning producer, taking Mr Witt by the arm. 'But you'll have to excuse us for now, boys and girls, only I've promised to introduce my main man here and his pulchritudinous progeny to our twinkling little stars. Coming, Anton?'

'But of course!' answered Mr Witt eagerly. 'I am eager to make Miss Lamour's acquaintance again. Most pleased to have met you, Mr Fletcher.'

Philip inclined his head graciously. Helga clutched at Ken's sleeve.

'And you are promising me I can obtain the autograph of Sleat?'

Ken nodded. She beamed.

'I haf all his albums, you know!'

'Great! Catch the rest of you later!'

Philip hoped not. Ken and the Witts headed off towards Sleat.

'Excuse me,' murmured Bradley grimly, 'but I think I'd better hang on in there.'

'Of course.' Philip turned to Mandy. 'And you're going to take me to meet the big white rabbit, aren't you?'

They went back out into the hall, squeezing their way through the oddly assorted crowd.

'This does seem to be a rather curious party,' Philip remarked, 'if it doesn't sound too rude to say so. Is it a social event or a press conference? What is it for and who are all these people?'

'I'm not really sure,' she said earnestly. 'Ken said something about wanting to let everyone know it was for real. I think he's had a lot of trouble getting it off the ground, you know.'

'Well, it's not the easiest thing in the world to get a film together. You, um, you know Ken quite well, then?'

'Not really. Here we are.'

She stopped outside a panelled mahogany door which she opened for him. He walked on in, little expecting to be grabbed roughly by an irate cowboy and pinned back against the wall, which to his very considerable surprise was exactly what happened.

'Your ears need cleaning out or something?' yelled the cowboy. 'I thought I told you to keep out of here, mister.'

Philip was far too stunned to be able to reply. As there was a massive hairy forearm pressing into his windpipe, he probably wouldn't have been able to speak anyway. The cowboy loomed over him like a terrifying fairytale ogre.

'Oh, Marve!' Shelley whined from somewhere over his vast shoulder. 'Will you cool it, honey?'

'This is Philip Fletcher,' Mandy shouted urgently. 'Please let go of him, Mr Loudwater.'

Shelley shrieked. Philip heard her tiny footsteps come pattering across the floor.

'Now, let him go this instant, Marve, d'ya hear? This ain't no pressman you've got by the throat there, honey, this is the famous Shakespeherian actor who's playing my poppa!'

The pressure on his throat was relaxed, and the cowboy backed off sullenly. Philip gasped for breath and Mandy offered a supporting arm. Shelley came bounding up on the other side.

'Why, are you all right there now?' She stamped her foot crossly. 'Marve! You done near gone and strangled the poor man. I want you to apologise this instant, d'ya hear?'

The cowboy shifted his weight uncomfortably. He coughed. 'I'm real sorry, Pop, but them critters have been a-hounding my baby and asking personal questions they ain't got no right to ask ever since we got here. I'm sorry about that there bear-hug I gave you just now, but you know how it is, huh? No hard feelings.'

Marve took his hand and tried to see how many bones he could crush in one go. Philip could not quite stifle a yelp.

'Why, he's looking real faint!' declared Shelley dramatically. 'Let's get him sitting down now.'

The two women helped him to the head of a large oak dining-table and sat him down. Philip was consumed by a violent coughing fit.

'I'll get you some water,' said Mandy anxiously, and rushed out of the door.

Shelley thumped his back. 'You feeling better now? Really, Marve, that ain't no way to treat a Shakespeherian actor is it now, honey? Why, what will Mr Fletcher think of our Southern hospitality?'

Marve mumbled something that might have been meant to sound apologetic.

'Now, is there anything more we can get you?' Shelley asked earnestly, turning back to Philip. 'Anything at all? You've only got to ask.'

'No, I don't want to . . .' Philip brought himself short. What was he doing being so damned polite and English? Who had been strangling whom, for Christ's sake? 'Yes!' he declared decisively. 'Actually I'd very much appreciate a large Scotch.'

After two weeks' abstention one wasn't going to kill him. In fact it might just save him; he was still shaking from Marve's assault.

'Honey, go get him a whisky now, d'ya hear? It's the least you can do for the poor man. And you can get me another glass of that little old vintage champagne while you're out there.'

After some more *sotto voce* murmurings of dissent Marve exited with bad grace, slamming the door hard behind him. Shelley smiled sweetly and fluttered her eyelashes.

'I do apologise for him, sugar,' she said, breathing softly over him and laying her hand on his. 'He means well but he can be real clumsy sometimes.'

'Ah, yes.'

Even though they were alone, he still thought it politic to disengage his hand; Marve was clearly the kind of man who would have given Othello a good name.

'We've been having a little trouble with them there journalists, as I'm sure you realised. Me and Marve, we was having a little spot of marital difficulties last year, you see, and he gets a mite over-sensitive when strangers come poking their noses in, you understand?'

'Ah, yes.'

'Why, I just love your accent! It's real cute, you know that?'

'Yes? Ah, thanks . . .'

Was she flirting with him or did she always sound like that? Philip felt himself blush.

'Why, sugar, you look all hot and bothered there still. Why don't we loosen you up a little . . .'

Suddenly her hands were at his tie, pulling the knot apart. He felt his blush deepen. She undid his top button, and then the one underneath, and then the one underneath that.

'Um, I think that's enough act — '

'My, what a hairy chest you've got, Mr Fletcher!'

Her fingers were inside his shirt, stroking his collar-bone. He gaped at her stupidly, too paralysed to react. She tossed her golden head of curls and giggled girlishly.

'Why, I just love a man that's hairy in all the right places, you know that?'

Suddenly the door was flung open with a loud crash and a dreaded Texan voice boomed, 'Got your whisky, Pop, and champagne for my little honey-pie.'

Philip jumped. Shelley coolly withdrew her hand and folded it into her other under the table. 'Why, I just love them little bubbles,' she drawled. 'Don't you?'

Philip smiled weakly. His smile froze as her hand brushed his knee under the table. She winked meaningfully at him.

'Here's your booze, then,' declared Marve heartily, smacking the glasses down.

Shelley inserted her forefinger under the rim of her glass and languidly ran her nail round the edge. She licked her lips and pointed her tongue at him.

There's more to this than meets the eye, Philip thought sagely to himself.

'Come on, then, Pop!' exclaimed Marve, indicating his whisky. 'Drink it down now, you hear?'

Philip lifted the whisky to his lips. It was neat, and the smell was pungent. He took a little sip and experienced a sensation of mixed pleasure and nausea. Under the table Shelley ran her hand along his thigh.

Philip spluttered whisky and saliva over the dining-table.

'Why, are you all right there, sugar?' Shelley asked, running round behind his chair to hit his back again. Philip fended her off.

'I'm fine, fine, thanks! Never felt better in my life, ha ha!'

Marve was staring at him suspiciously. It was a look to loosen the bowels of Superman.

'Excuse me, I've got to go to the bathroom,' Philip gabbled. He made for the door.

'That way, Pop,' growled Marve, pointing to another door on the other side of the room while still giving him that narrow-eyed gun-slinger's glare.

Philip was not about to argue the toss. He mumbled an incoherent thank-you and took himself off in the direction indicated.

'Look forward to working with you, sugar!' he heard Shelley call out just before he closed the door.

He found himself in a small hallway in which there was a functional staircase and two doors. One was glass-panelled and opened directly on to the garden (he could see some greenhouses on the lawn); the other was solid and led into a toilet. He went in and pulled the flush, which was very loud. Under cover of the plumbing he sneaked on tiptoe up the stairs.

He was at the back of the house, in a long, narrow corridor. He surmised that the door he could see at the other end must lead to the top of the main front staircase and he started to go that way, but hardly had he done so than a peculiar moaning noise made him stop.

He stopped and listened, and when the sound was repeated he moved to the door from behind which it had seemed to come. He could hear it distinctly now, a man's voice muttering incoherently, 'Oh God, I'm floating to Disneyland . . . stop the boat, I wanna get off . . .'

Philip hesitated. Whoever was behind the door, it was no business of his, but then again he was curious, and he rarely needed any more powerful stimulant than that. He knocked lightly on the door.

'Hello? Are you all right in there?'

There was silence on the other side, then he heard footsteps softly approaching.

'Hey, man!' a voice called out to him in a harsh whisper through the keyhole. 'Are you the keeper of the gate?'

'Am I the what?'

'The keeper of the black gate, the daemon. There's a lot of heavy shit going down tonight, man.'

'Is there? Well – '

'Hey, don't go away, man!' The door-handle was rattled from the other side. Philip noticed that there was a key on his side. It had obviously been turned. 'You gotta let me out. I've been locked in!'

'Not entirely surprising really, is it?'

'What's that you're saying?'

'Look, I'm sorry, you'll have to excuse — ' Philip stopped himself. A sudden horrible thought had struck him. 'I say, you're not Harvey Goldman by any chance, are you?'

'Harvey Goldman? The schmuck, you've gotta be kidding. I'm Wayne Schlesinger.'

'What!'

Philip twisted the key savagely to the right and flung open the door. There was an agonised yelp from inside.

'Who the hell did you say you were?' Philip demanded furiously.

Sitting on the floor in front of him, rubbing his head, was a lanky figure in striped red and white pyjamas. Philip saw a long bearded face beneath a bird's nest of thick black hair streaked white. A pair of owlish round eyes blinked at him from behind cheap plastic-framed spectacles.

'You sure caught me there, mister.' The man edged away suspiciously, still massaging his skull. 'You're not the Dungeonmaster of Doom, are you?'

Philip stared at him, horrified. 'Are you really trying to tell me you're . . . Wayne Schlesinger? The director of *Midnight Rider*?'

'Sure am. Say, have you got an E?'

'A what?'

'Or some coke? Anything, man. There's weird things going down tonight, I gotta have something to help me along.'

'A strait-jacket and a few thousand volts through the back of the head by the sound of it. What are you doing in here?'

'They put me in here, man, but I gotta rest anyway, gotta get my strength up, but Jeez, you ever tried sleeping on one of those things? It's like being in a Freudian womb-nightmare.'

He indicated over his shoulder where a massive black silk-covered water-bed filled half of the room. Above it hung an enormous portrait of Ken Kilmaine with his arm round a well-known American chat-show host.

'Can't say I have,' Philip answered neutrally, taking the opportunity to examine the other smaller portraits dotting the walls, all of which featured the same absurdly grinning visage. At least the photographer wouldn't have had to ask him to say cheese. He nodded his head appraisingly. 'So – this, I take it, is the master bedroom . . .'

The pyjama-clad figure on the floor stiffened.

'The Master? Where's the Master?'

'In my mind's eye, Horatio. You do realise we start filming tomorrow, I hope?'

'If they let us.'

'If who let us?'

'The minions of Doom. Say, have you ever been to Stonehenge? You know, I'm sure I had some tabs somewhere . . .'

Philip watched him crawl across the floor, his nose to the carpet, sniffing like a bloodhound. Bad feelings had been stirring within him for some time now; he sensed that they might be about to come to the boil.

'Very nice to have met you, Wayne,' he said grimly. 'You'll have to excuse me now . . .'

He left him searching through the pockets of his discarded clothing. Somebody was definitely going to have some explaining to do. He marched sternly away down the corridor.

At the top of the corridor was the door which he presumed would lead back to the main staircase. He went through confidently and was surprised to find himself in a sitting-room. A small, round, frog-like man was sitting in an armchair in the corner, watching some kind of sci-fi bloodbath on the TV.

'Excuse me, do you know where the front staircase is?' Philip asked loudly. He had to be loud; the TV was on full volume.

The frog-like man turned his pop-eyes on him. He blew out his puffy cheeks, gave the wispy pampas of his scalp a scratch, and shrugged. 'Gee, I can't say as I do . . .' he squeaked. He squinted at Philip. As he had some kind of a tic in his left eye, Philip found this mildly disconcerting. The man picked a remote-control device off the arm of his chair and lowered the volume. 'Say, haven't I seen you on TV?'

'Not in anything like that,' Philip answered coolly, indicating the TV. The frog-man prickled.

'And what do you think's wrong with it, mister?'

'Oh, nothing, it's just not my cup of tea.'

'Ha! Cup of tea! Is that all you English ever think about?'

'As a matter of fact, that's not such a bad idea. Excuse me, I've got to be going . . .' There were two doors leading off from the room roughly in the direction he wanted to go. He advanced on the nearest. 'Nice to have met you, Mr — '

'Goldman, Harvey Goldman.'

'Oh, shit . . .'

Philip's hand fell back limply from the door-knob. He sank with resignation into the nearest chair.

'Actually, I wanted a word with you, Mr Goldman. I'm Philip Fletcher.'

'Oh yeah, I thought so!'

'Mr Goldman — '

'Harve. Please call me Harve, everyone does.'

'Even your wife?'

'Huh? No, I'm not married, actually.'

As he looked like a failed auditionee for *Creature From The Black Lagoon*, this was perhaps not surprising.

'What did you want a word about?' Harve asked.

'The script. There were just a couple of minor historical points I wanted to clear up. In the scene — '

'It's all been thoroughly researched,' Harve cut in quickly, sitting forward on the edge of his chair. 'All thoroughly researched. I read two whole reference books cover to cover before I even wrote a word!'

Which two reference books, though? Philip wondered. *Ken Hom's Chinese Cookery* and *Baedeker's Guide to Albania*?

'Oh, I don't doubt it,' he said smoothly, slipping in an easy placatory smile. Harve did not smile back. He continued, 'This character I'm playing, the judge — '

'Judge Jeffreys.'

'Yes, that's my first point. As you are no doubt aware, there was an historical character of the same name — '

'That's where I got the idea from. There I was looking for like a real life eighteenth-century role-model for bad guys, and up he jumps, zap! out of the page I was reading at the time. That's what I just love about your English history, there's so much of it!'

'Well you don't have to put it all in at once.'

'Huh?'

'You see, by the time Dick Turpin was around the real Judge Jeffreys had been dead for about thirty or forty years; I think you've got the wrong century.'

'Hey, give me a break, will you?' Harve snapped. 'What the hell difference does a couple of years make, huh? As Bismarck said, that's just a matter of dates.'

'I think it was Talleyrand actually, but . . .'

'You trying to tell me my job, mister?' Harve demanded through gritted teeth.

Well somebody ought to, Philip almost answered back.

Suddenly the door behind him was flung open and a familiar shaggy figure in red and white pyjamas burst in. When he saw Harvey Goldman he did a tremendous double-take.

'By Crom! The High Priest himself!'

'For Christ's sake, Wayne!' Harve squealed. 'I am not the High Priest of Doom!'

Wayne put the back of his hand to his mouth and whispered to Philip, 'Do not under any circumstances buy a used car from that man.'

'I won't,' Philip promised. Wayne stiffened.

'They're back! Help!'

Outside in the corridor Philip heard Mandy's voice calling his name. Wayne winked at him.

'Race you to the matter-transmitter!'

He rushed out through one of the other doors. Harve snarled, 'Gee, that guy's a head-case.'

'Takes one to know one,' Philip said, hardly bothering to lower his voice.

Mandy came in from the corridor. She was holding a glass of water.

'Philip! I've been looking for you everywhere. Who was that funny man in pyjamas?'

'It's a long story . . .'

There was an almighty crash from outside.

'What's going on out there?' Mandy demanded, pointing to the door by which Wayne had just exited.

Philip rose reluctantly. 'Let's go and see, shall we?'

They went out together and found themselves on the landing by the top of the main staircase. Wayne had just knocked over a large plant and shattered the pot. He was attempting to climb up on to the banister.

'Oh God no!' Ken Kilmaine shouted as he ran up the stairs. There was a swell of bemused murmurings from below as more people came out to investigate the noise. 'Wayne, get down, please get down!'

Wayne was waving his arms frantically for balance. 'Look everybody!' he yelled. 'I can fly!'

'Oh Wayne, no . . .'

Ken's cry was drowned out by a scream of panic below. As he breasted the top of the stairs he lunged desperately at a pyjama-leg but his hands clawed empty air. Wayne sprang from the banister towards the ceiling, seemed to hang for a moment with his arms and legs splayed like a fluoride mobile, then plummeted to the ground in as conclusive a demonstration of Newtonian physics as any Philip had witnessed. Mandy hid her head in his chest. He gave her hair a comforting stroke.

Wayne must have caught a banner and some streamers as he fell, for he lay entangled in a mess of bunting. A dozen or so partygoers milled around him uncertainly. He was lying flat on his back, staring blankly at the ceiling.

'Man,' Philip heard him groan thickly, 'what a bummer!'

'Ambulance!' someone shouted down below, and the cry was taken up all around – 'Call an ambulance!'

'Oh God, no . . .' groaned Ken. 'Who the hell let him out?'

'I'm afraid it must have been me,' Philip answered.

'You?' Ken turned on him angrily. 'I think you'd better explain yourself.'

'Oh really?'

Ken was livid with fury; not even a hint of a pretence of a smile lingered. Philip was impressed. He detached himself from Mandy and leant casually against the banister rail, fixing Ken's eye. He spoke with icy calm: 'I was rather hoping for an explanation or two myself. What exactly is going on here, Mr Kilmaine?'

7

Philip was called early but not used at all on the first day of filming, which was about par for the course – it never ceased to amaze him that the general public found the movie industry glamorous and exotic; most of the time it was about as exciting as indigestion. He spent all day in his caravan, catching up on his rudely interrupted sleep (the five o'clock alarm call had been a terrible shock) and talking to Denis, his dresser, who (it is hardly necessary to add) turned out to be as camp as a Bedouin mobile home; Philip had never met a dresser who wasn't. Before dawn on the second day, as Denis was once more helping him into his costume, the first assistant came to apologise for all the delays.

They were on location in Black Park, a convenient few miles down the road from Pinewood Studios, where some studio work was scheduled for the second month. Philip's trailer was right on the end of the row, at the edge of a large car park.

'I'm terribly sorry about yesterday,' said Terry, the first assistant. 'Teething problems, I'm afraid. You know how chaotic it can get sometimes.'

'With Wayne Schlesinger around it'll be more than sometimes,' Philip answered dubiously.

'Sit still!' said Denis sternly. 'I can't get at your hooks!'

Terry watched morosely as Denis did up the fastenings on Philip's jacket. He looked tired out already, which wasn't a good sign. Philip smiled sympathetically. 'Don't let it get you down, old friend.'

'Old friend' was overdoing it slightly, but they had worked together once fifteen years before on a television play, and many a showbiz friendship has been founded on less.

'Well, to tell you the truth, I am a bit down in the dumps,' said Terry quietly, responding to Philip's proffered intimacy. 'I've been at some badly organised shoots in my time but this takes the biscuit. They just don't make 'em like they used to. I haven't even got a shooting script.'

'You're kidding.'

'Would that I were. I know they don't storyboard properly any more, and call me old-fashioned if you will, but it would help to know what the hell's supposed to come next.'

'Doesn't Wayne?'

'Now you're the one who's kidding. Don't tell anyone I said so, but from what I've seen so far I'm not sure he knows the difference between a movie camera and an Instamatic. To tell you the truth, I don't know what to make of him.'

Philip eyed him shrewdly. 'If you want the truth of the matter, I'm afraid there's nothing to make. I think with our Wayne, what you see is what you get.'

'I see . . . so you think he really is a bit nutty?'

'He's a raging fruitcake, Terry. Ken Kilmaine insisted to me he'd be fine once the work got under way, but I don't believe a word of it and neither do you. I know you're only meant to be the assistant, but I think we're all going to be depending on you.'

'Mm, yes, I was afraid of that. Well, it won't be the first time it's happened, though never on this sort of scale. I'm sure we'll be all right on the night.'

Philip failed to find this totally reassuring.

'Cheer up!' said Denis when Terry had gone. 'It may never happen.'

'You obviously haven't seen the script . . .'

Gloom overtook him and his supply of small talk dried up as Denis helped him into his black leather boots and heavily brocaded black velvet coat.

'Mm!' said Denis appraisingly when he had finished. 'Love the booties. Dead butch!'

Half an hour later, fully made up and wearing his thick grey judge's wig, Philip received his call. With heavy heart he went outside where a minibus was waiting to take him to the location. Dawn was just breaking.

Black Park, which lies between Slough and Uxbridge, covers a substantial area. It is mostly woodland, but there is also a large open space and a lake, both of which were to feature in the filming. And not for the first time, it has to be said, for it is possibly the most heavily over-used location in the history of British film. It also has to be said that most of the films in which it has featured have been of the B-grade variety. The exercise in which they were currently engaged, Philip reflected, was unlikely to alter the gauge on the quality threshold.

The minibus bumped along the rutted track towards the park's interior, reminding Philip uncomfortably of the excessively greasy bacon sandwich which he had consumed for breakfast an hour ago.

They stopped, still amongst the trees, and spilled out on to a path around which the detritus of filming – lights, cameras, cables – was much in evidence. People with peculiar job titles – a gaffer here, a focus puller there – were milling about furiously but apparently aimlessly in all directions. Philip was pointed to a table under a tree around which steaming coffees were being poured. He took himself over to be out of the way.

'Beep! Beep!' said a voice behind him, over a squeal of unoiled wheels.

Philip stepped aside grimly as a heavily bandaged figure, his right leg stuck out in splints in front of him, whizzed past in a wheelchair.

'Morning, Dungeon-master!'

'Hello, Wayne,' Philip answered dully. He got himself a coffee and slumped into a vacant canvas chair, his head hunched into his shoulders.

'Hail, O minions of Doom!' Wayne called out to all and sundry as his wheelchair minder reversed him on to a pre-laid duckboard platform at the side of the path. No one answered.

'Is he trying to be funny?' the continuity girl asked one of the third assistants under her breath. The third assistant just shrugged. Terry went and told Wayne about the shot they were setting up.

'Sounds good to me,' Wayne pronounced, searching down

the sides of his wheelchair for something. 'Anyone seen my Walkman?'

If anyone had, they weren't owning up. Wayne didn't seem too bothered about losing it anyway. He was soon busily amusing himself by executing three-point turns in his wheelchair.

'Maybe he's some sort of a genius underneath,' the third assistant proposed after reflection, without however sounding terribly convinced by his own theory.

Philip knew that he was right not to be. A vague sense of impending catastrophe gnawed away inside him. He had had bad vibes about this project from the off, and Ken's evasions on the night of the party had not soothed him. The producer's confident exterior was looking less and less justified. Philip had a suspicion that he might have tried to cut half a dozen corners too many.

He watched the technicians at work while he sipped his coffee. It was comforting at least to see people who knew what they were doing. As if to ruffle him on cue, the big black shape of Sleat's limousine swung into view at the end of the path. A brightly coloured dune buggy followed.

The second assistant came stomping over to the coffee table. 'Where the hell's the animal minder?'

The third assistant scratched his head. 'I think he took his dog for a walk.'

'Well, go and find him. And find out where the hell the sheep have got to.'

Philip crossed his fingers. As if fate didn't need tempting already, they were about to breach one of the sternest of all commandments: they were going to work with the beasts of the field.

The limousine pulled up and a heavy in mirror sunglasses got out of the front to open the rear door. Sleat, also in reflector shades, squeezed himself out. The dune buggy stopped behind and Marve the cowboy unfurled his arboreal limbs from around and under the steering-wheel. He came round to the passenger side, plucked Shelley like a plastic doll from her seat and deposited her carefully on the ground.

'Watch for them there puddles, honey, don't want you getting your pretty little ankles all wet and muddy, now do we?'

'Why no, sugar, and not on my cutesy little gown neither.'

Philip waited for them to produce banjos and start slapping their thighs.

The other limousine door was opened and Ken Kilmaine emerged.

'Morning, boys and girls!' he said, dispensing his grin in all directions. 'Just came to check everything's OK.'

He came sauntering over to the coffee table. 'Everything all right here?'

'No,' Philip answered tersely.

'Great!' said Ken, not listening. Someone gave him a coffee and he took a hip-flask from his pocket, adding a nip of brandy to his styrofoam cup. He offered it to Philip.

'No, thanks.'

'Go on!' Ken said coaxingly. 'What the doctor ordered on a day like this.'

'Gave it up for Lent,' Philip answered.

Ken was about to say something when he noticed Wayne. 'Hey, everybody!' he said, laughing uncertainly. 'Why's Wayne wearing silver foil on his head?'

'Because of the aliens,' the third assistant explained.

'Huh?'

'He says he thinks they're trying to suck his brains up through a laser-beam.'

'A case of closing the stable door after the horse has bolted?' suggested Philip.

Ken pulled a patronising face. 'You creative types! I love it. Sleat, my man, how are you?'

The pop star came over, now flanked by a pair of heavies in the ubiquitous mirror glasses. He looked like a squirt of mustard between two beefburgers. 'Hi there,' he said lazily, unconsciously flapping his hands in a gesture that would have raised Denis's eyebrows.

'You remember Phi-lip, don't you, from the party?'

'Oh yeah. How you doing?'

They had not actually been introduced, but Philip told him that he was doing quite nicely, thank you. Ken wandered off to speak to Shelley, leaving the two of them alone. Alone, that is, if one discounted the heavies, which Philip was inclined to do: he doubted if human speech featured among their accomplishments anyway.

'Wicked gear,' said Sleat, casting an eye over his costume. 'Wore something like that on my Rainforest Tour.'

'Yes?' Philip didn't really know what to say. 'Um, shouldn't have thought you got much of an audience for your sort of thing in a rainforest.'

Sleat laughed indulgently. 'Wicked sense of humour, man. I like it.'

Philip looked at him uneasily. Faced by three expressionless sets of mirror-lensed eyes, he was beginning to feel uncomfortable. As he was sitting and they were all standing over him, the feeling was quickly exacerbated.

'Would you like a coffee?' Philip asked, trying to fill the awkward pause.

'Not out of one of those I wouldn't.' He indicated Philip's plastic cup. Philip was surprised. What did he usually drink out of, then? A dog bowl?

'That thing there,' said Sleat, wagging his finger at him sternly, 'is non-biodegradable ozone-hostile. You are committing an act of ecological terrorism.'

'You don't say . . .'

Feeling somewhat bemused, Philip semi-consciously reached for his cigarettes. Sleat gasped. 'I don't allow those things anywhere near me!' he yelled. 'Ken, come here!'

Ken skidded over, his most naturally mollifying look at the ready.

'Ken, no cancer-sticks. Tell him.'

'Ah, yes,' said Ken apologetically, turning to Philip. 'It's in his contract, I'm afraid, no tobacco products on set. He insisted.'

'Too right I insisted!' Sleat continued, his thin voice squeaky with indignation. 'My next gig is gonna be as part of the Rock against Passive Smoking Awareness Concert, and I intend to be still around for it. So don't start polluting my airspace, mister!'

With a toss of his freshly tied pony-tail the normally laconic chart-topper turned on his heels and flounced off in a huff, flanked by his personal praetorians. Ken gave Philip the benefit of one of his indulgent grins. 'Sorry about all that, artistic temperament, you know what I mean. Look, I've got to dash now, Phi-lip old boy, but anything you need, don't hesitate to give me a call.'

'Ken, I want to OK a few script changes, and Wayne —'

'As far as I'm concerned you've got *carte blanche*, Phi-lip, *carte blanche*. Anything you want to iron out, talk to Harve Goldman, he'll be along later. Must run, I've got a plane to catch. *Arrivederci*, toots!'

'Philip!' Terry called before he could remonstrate. 'Could we have you over here, please?'

While Ken jumped into the black limo Philip went to join Terry, who was with Shelley and the egregious Marve. They were led a little way down the path to a small clearing in which a rather flimsy period coach drawn by two white horses was standing. The driver, a burly stuntman and bit-part actor, was introduced as Bill Harris. 'But please call me Chopper,' he said pleasantly, in a voice like the young Arthur Mullard's.

He gave Philip a leg-up into the passenger seat, while Shelley was lifted in by Marve. Philip did wonder what the giant cowboy was doing on set but he decided that he was simply too big to be asked. He settled himself as well as he could on the narrow leather seat, which was not very well at all: the interior was cramped and uncomfortable, with barely enough room for two to sit side by side, as the script demanded.

'Gee, it's kinda squeezy here!' Shelley giggled. Marve, who had closed the door after her and was peering in suspiciously through the window, narrowed his eyes at Philip. 'Don't crowd her there, mister.'

Philip, whose confinement in the corner would have attracted the sympathy of sardines, could only raise a helpless eyebrow.

'Excuse us, Mr Loudwater,' Terry said as firmly as he dared

through the other window, 'but we've got to get on with our work now.'

Marve withdrew sullenly. Terry called to Chopper, 'All right up there? Good, can you get into position, please?'

The barely sprung coach began to move. Shelley shivered and grasped Philip's hand. 'Cold today, ain't it, sugar?'

He wasn't aware of it. A trickle of sweat ran down the side of his face. He mumbled something and withdrew his hand. Shelley leaned over and nibbled his ear. 'I think you're real cute,' she whispered, 'you know that?'

'Oh, um, thanks very much,' he mumbled, glancing furtively to left and right to make sure that Marve was no longer visible. 'Ah, look, I think we're about to start . . .'

But they weren't. The coach stopped suddenly, jolting them forward. They heard Chopper dismount from his seat.

'Sorry about that,' he apologised, poking his head through the window. 'I don't think we're starting quite yet, I think they're still rounding up the sheep. I fancy a fag.'

'Jeez,' Shelley whispered in Philip's ear again, 'he sure doesn't look gay, does he?'

Philip laughed nervously. He made a grab for the door-handle. 'Excuse me, Shelley. Hey, Chopper!' Philip jumped down from the coach, taking out his own cigarettes. 'Got a light?'

Chopper struck another match. They stood on the side of the path smoking.

'A word of warning, by the way,' said Philip when he had taken a deep drag. 'Don't light up in front of our star turn over there. He's a nicotine Nazi.'

'You're joking.'

'I'm afraid not. The sanctimonious little prick. Tell me, you're a younger man than me: I had always thought that pop stars were Bacchanalian degenerates interested solely in sex and drugs. Have I been labouring under a massive delusion all these years?'

'Dunno, mate. Kids these days are on a different planet.'

'Like our director. Well, we've certainly got all life-forms here, haven't we?'

They smoked out their cigarettes in peace, waiting for the call.

When it didn't come, Philip instantly lit another. He felt rather as he always did on National No Smoking Day, militantly bolshie.

'Looks like they're playing silly buggers up there,' Chopper remarked, nodding down the path to where they were setting up the shot. The animal handler was introducing an energetic little collie dog to Sleat. On the other side of a specially constructed little wooden bridge, where a stream ran under the path, his assistant was attempting to manoeuvre some recalcitrant sheep.

The animal handler gave Sleat some biscuits and he knelt down to try and gain the dog's affection. The dog didn't want to know, and who, thought Philip, could blame him? Although the pop star's hair colour had been toned down to a sort of septic blond there was still very little that was averagely human about him. Philip could appreciate that in a doggy's eyes the offer of a stroke from those awkward bony fingers would be less than compelling. The doggy began to look around him for more entertaining distractions.

'What's this scene all about, then?' Chopper asked, taking a copy of the script out of the inside of his jacket. 'I was just told I had to drive you, but now they've told me I've got some lines to say.'

'You can have a few of mine if you like. Actually, I've changed them. Have you got a pencil?' Chopper gave him a pen and he emended the script for him. 'There. We're supposed to drive up to the bridge where we meet young Dick driving his flock to market. It's the first time the two of us meet, and I'm all beastly and horrid to him.'

'You're not the only one,' Chopper noted as the dog bit Sleat's hand and the pop star yelped.

Suddenly there was a canine blur as the yapping animal raced across the bridge and hurled itself at the sheep. The sheep went flying in all directions, some slipping off the sides of the bridge into the stream a few feet below, the others racing off down the path with the excited collie in pursuit.

'I think we're going to have time for another coffee, somehow,' Chopper remarked philosophically. As the dog, half the sheep and both animal handlers had now disappeared from view, Philip could only agree. They wandered over to the refreshment table.

Two coffees later the sheep had been rounded up and placed in a temporary rope pen. The dog had been sent home.

'It's never happened before,' the animal handler insisted desperately. 'I can't think what got into him.'

'So temperamental, these canine stars,' Philip observed. 'One dog food commercial and they think they're the new Lassie.'

'Yeah, but what am I supposed to do?' Sleat whined, nursing his injured hand.

'Don't you have a reserve?' Terry demanded.

'No, he's my best animal,' the handler said miserably.

'Well, how long will it take you to get another one?'

'I don't have another one . . .'

Terry and various assistants went into a technical huddle.

'They've got to get me a dog,' Sleat moaned, gesturing angrily to his bouncers. 'It's the whole point of the scene.'

'You could have a sheep,' Philip suggested.

'Huh?'

'You could have a pet sheep instead.'

'Yeah,' said Chopper, 'you could call him Mutton Jeff.'

'Or Jumper.'

Sleat glowered at them, then stomped off in a sulk. He went back to where his car was parked and got in. Terry had to go and ask him to come back out again. He said he wasn't going to until he'd seen a doctor. The dog was probably rabid and he would need an injection.

Who was going to inject the dog then? Philip wondered.

Sleat got his way, of course. He was driven off in the black limo nursing his injured hand. As far as anyone else could tell, the skin had not even been broken.

'All right, everyone,' Terry said briskly, 'this is what we're going to do. We'll do the coach shots and fit the dog in later when we've got one. Hopefully we'll get it all fixed by the end of the morning. Philip, Chopper, could you take your positions, please?'

They returned to the coach. Reluctantly Philip climbed back in next to Shelley.

'Why, hiya again, honey,' the sex bomb simpered. 'I'm glad you're back, I've been kinda lonesome all here by my little self.'

Philip smiled weakly. Terry appeared at the window.

'Are you all right?' Philip asked. He looked exhausted.

'Nothing that a week's sleep wouldn't cure. We're going to do a master, OK? Chopper's going to drive the coach down to the bridge, then when he stops you stick your head out of the window. Just run through the lines, then we'll set up here and do the interior of the coach. Shelley, we won't actually need you for this shot, you can come down if you want, take a break.'

'It's OK, sugar,' Shelley answered, pressing her leg against Philip's, 'I'm kinda comfy in here . . .'

Philip wished he were.

Some ten excruciating minutes later they were ready. Terry shouted, 'Action!' and the coach began to rumble forward.

'Cut!' Wayne screamed. The coach stopped. Philip poked his head out of the window to see what was the matter.

'That's my job!' Wayne protested. 'I'm the one who gets to shout "Action!" That's the best bit! I want to do it!'

Terry apologised (he had thought that Wayne was asleep and was reluctant to wake him for anything so minor as a take), and everyone prepared to go for a second shot. A make-up girl ran up to give Philip's face a quick powder. The clapper loader snapped his board.

'And . . .' Wayne's voice rose to a crescendo. 'ACTION! Pretty good, huh?'

The coach moved off again. Philip waited for another interruption but none came. Chopper braked the coach on cue in front of the bridge. Philip angrily thrust his head out of the window.

'Why have we stopped?' he demanded, pushing his chin up to give the camera his best side.

''Tis a young lad up ahead,' Chopper responded, 'a-taking his sheep to market, this being a Wednesday.'

'Drive on!' said Philip impatiently. 'I haven't —'

'Cut!' screamed a shrill voice suddenly. 'Cut! Cut! Cut!'

'What the hell!' Philip stuttered, and then, when he saw who was causing the fuss, 'Oh my God, where did he spring from? . . .'

Grimly he pushed the coach door open and climbed down. The camera was just on the other side of the bridge, about twenty feet away, Wayne on his platform just behind and to the right. The strangely amphibian features of Harvey Goldman were thrust into the director's face.

'You can't let him do this to me! He's ruining my script!'

'Hey, cool it, High Priest,' said Wayne.

'For the last time!' Harve yelled, his face crimson with rage, 'I am not the fucking High Priest of Doom! I am the fucking writer of your fucking movie, you airhead!'

'Mm . . .' Wayne considered this for a moment. 'Would it cheer you up any if I let you sacrifice a sheep?'

'What?'

'Plenty of them around, I'm sure one could be spared.'

Terry stepped wearily between them. He lifted a megaphone to his lips.

'Take five, everybody, please.'

'Could I just say something?' said Philip tersely, butting in. Harve turned on him furiously.

'You butcher! You assassin! You Philistine!'

'Mm. Fifteen–love,' said Wayne.

'Please, Mr Goldman,' said Terry, 'what exactly is the problem here?'

'I've changed a few lines,' Philip explained, 'that's all.'

'That's all!' Harve looked as if he was about to explode. 'You have defaced my masterpiece, you murderer!'

Wayne whistled through his teeth.

'Thirty–love to the High Priest!'

'Oh, come off it!' said Philip, torn between tears and laughter. 'It's not exactly Shakespeare, is it? I mean, look at what I've changed in this scene: when the coach stops I'm supposed to say to Chopper, "What ails thee, driver?" I can't say that, I'm not Frankie Howerd. Then I'm supposed to call him an "infernal wretch" and order him to drive the "insolent varlet" out of my way. Look, if it was meant to be *Carry On Sticking Them Up* I could probably get away with it, but it isn't, is it?'

'Thirty–fifteen,' said Wayne. 'Fine shot from the Dungeon-master.'

'And another thing,' Philip continued decisively, 'I have *carte blanche* to rewrite my own lines, so will you please —'

'You have what?' Harve demanded, his pop-eyes and crater-mouth veritable caverns of disbelief.

'Why don't we discuss this later, gentlemen?' suggested Terry, the still small voice of calm. 'We've a hell of a lot to be getting on with.'

'I have *carte blanche* from Ken Kilmaine,' Philip repeated calmly. 'Without it, I said I'd walk off the set, and I mean it. Now, are you going to walk off, or am I?'

'I think you'd better go, Mr Goldman,' said Terry quietly. 'If you've got a problem you'd best see Mr Kilmaine. There's some nasty-looking cloud coming up and we'd better get this shot in the bag.'

'Accomplice!' Harve snarled. 'Quisling!'

With eye moistening and chin quivering he stormed off in the direction of the car park. He stopped once, looked back and shook his fist at them. 'Don't think you've heard the last of me, Fletcher. I'll get you for this!'

'Mm,' murmured Wayne appreciatively. 'I'd keep your phaser on stun, if I was you.'

'Thanks for the warning,' said Philip. 'Now can we get on with it?'

But they couldn't. The clouds came over much quicker than Terry had anticipated and brought with them a light shower. The equipment was covered with plastic sheeting and an early lunch-break ordained. Everyone piled into the minibuses and headed back to the car park.

There was a catering van at one end of the car park and next to it a sometime double-decker bus which had been converted into a portable dining area. But while everyone else headed that way Philip went back to his caravan. He didn't feel like eating. He only felt like complaining.

'I've never worked with such bloody amateurs!' he moaned to Denis, because Denis happened to be there.

'Careful you don't burst a blood vessel now,' Denis answered phlegmatically. 'Don't want to get ketchup over your cossie.'

'I'll get ketchup over Harvey bloody Goldman if he doesn't keep out of my way. What's he doing on set interrupting filming? I've never heard anything like it. I ask you —'

There was a knock at the door.

'Yes!' Philip snapped, irritated at being interrupted halfway to building up a head of steam.

Mandy Morgan tentatively put her head round the door. 'I'm terribly sorry,' she said shyly. 'I hope I'm not disturbing you.'

'Oh, no no no no!' said Philip hastily. 'Please, please come in.'

She did. She was looking very fresh and pretty in a décolleté peasant smock costume. Denis gave Philip a suggestive look which he ignored.

'I won't stay long, I've got to get back to make up,' Mandy said. She seemed hesitant. 'I hope you won't mind, but I wanted to ask you for your autograph.'

'My autograph?'

'Yes, I know it sounds a bit silly, but it's just that, well, you know I told you that I saw your Uncle Vanya in Chichester? I didn't tell you that my schoolfriend Jenny and I bought a programme between us and we came round to the stage door afterwards to get you to sign it because you were so wonderful, only our form mistress came and got us and said we had to get back on the coach, so we didn't get it, but when I told Jenny I was working with you she made me promise, absolutely made me swear that I would get your autograph, and the thing is that we're not actually working together for ages and ages, so I thought I'd come today, seeing as we are both here. Would you mind awfully giving it to me now?'

Denis gave him an even more suggestive look. Philip pointedly ignored him.

'Not at all,' he said graciously, taking the familiar old theatre programme and opening it at the page which contained his photograph. Rather an old photograph, he now remembered. He scribbled his name underneath and handed it back.

'Thanks very much.'

'Not at all. I'm touched. And very flattered that you still remember my performance.'

'Of course I remember. How could I ever forget?'

She smiled sweetly and made her excuses. When she had gone Denis gave a dirty chuckle. 'Ooh, like 'em young, do we?'

'None of your business.'

'Sounds like you do, then. Well, looks like you're in there.'

Philip, who had been thinking exactly the same thing, shooed him away irritably.

The rest of the day's filming was a wash-out. When the showers had passed they tried to shoot the coach crossing the bridge, only to discover that no one had bothered to measure its width and that it was much too narrow for wheeled traffic. Then they waited in vain for the animal handler to reappear. When it became evident that he would not, an assistant was detached to scour the park – a popular public walking area – for anything with four feet and a tail that looked as if it might prove suitable. He was not wildly successful, returning during the course of the afternoon with an unappealing mongrel, an epicene shampooed poodle, two Rottweilers and a dachshund, all of whom competed vigorously to see which could cock its leg over the most delicate piece of electrical equipment. None possessed the requisite star qualities, and as Sleat had not returned from the doctor's, the exercise had become academic anyway. After a while it began to rain again, this time heavily, and in the end Philip was dismissed while a full hour of daylight remained, an almost unconscionable sin. He went home feeling utterly exhausted by the unremitting inaction.

It got a lot worse over the next few weeks.

8

30 January. God, I must be bored to start writing in this tacky little diary again. Bored? I'm going out of my mind. Filming is boring at the best of times, and these are not they. Boring and exhausting. Three weeks in and five to go but we're so far behind schedule it's bound to overrun. That's an understatement. I begin to wonder seriously if this film will ever be finished. I fear for my sanity.

What's the time now? Seven o'clock. Seven in the morning, been here for an hour already, sitting in make-up and costume in the back of my trailer waiting for my call. Correction to above: our trailer. It turns out that I have to share with Bradley Pitman. We both kicked up a stink about it, especially me as I've got billing above the title. Cost-cutting, I imagine. What else in this outfit? As it happens, Bradley and I are hardly ever called together so it doesn't matter, and I don't really give a shit anyway, but you've got to be seen to act the prima donna, it's part of the deal. And give them an inch and they'll sell your arm and a leg for medical research. The most conservative Ruritanian court is not more bound by hierarchical precedent than a film set. One of the lapidary commandments: Lose thy place in the pecking order and thou shalt eat cake. Hence the fuss, though I think we did rather better than Miss Shelley Lamour, who, although obtaining a caravan marked 'pouting starlet, for the sole use of', rent the skies with screams more hideous than a Hammer soundtrack on discovering that said item had spent the last thirty years gently rusting on Brighton Beach and had more holes in its roof than Harvey Goldman boasts in his head. Harvey Goldman. My pen twitches even as I write the name. Another commandment: thou shalt name the unnameable at thy peril.

It is not generally considered normal for writers to hang around film sets, but nothing about this film is remotely normal. The ghastly little frog-man is making my miserable life intolerable, bitching to everyone about me behind my back and constantly interrupting filming with his inane protests. I am not the only target of his ire – poor Terry has suffered from having to point out that most of his endless stage directions are completely unfilmable – but I am his principal hate figure. Yesterday's argument was the silliest yet, and my fault, I suppose, because I wasn't even involved in the scene. But when the Redcoat sergeant whom Dick has just encountered in the village inn told our hero that he and his men were 'on their way to join His Majesty's armies fighting the Seven Years War' I could not forbear to point out that no one actually knew it would last for seven years while it was still going on. It's a bit like having Columbus say, 'I'll call you from New York'. When I said this, Harve did a splendid impression of a man whose larynx is about to explode. I don't think he finds my criticism constructive.

I have been complaining endlessly about him, to no avail. It's a waste of breath talking to Wayne, and our producer seems to have disappeared. On the rare occasions when the phone in Ken Kilmaine's office is answered and his secretary can stop filing her nails for long enough to speak to me, he is always in a meeting or on the other line. More often than not I just get an answerphone message informing me that he is abroad on business, obviously having taken Shaz with him for diversionary purposes. Requests for him to call back are never answered. In view of the fax which I received from Martha, all this is worrying.

I've been asking questions on the West Coast and it seems I'm not the only one: your friend Ken Kilmaine is in demand. I've got too many creditors of my own to sit in judgement, but a lot of people are surprised he's got this movie off the ground. Where's he got his finance from? I don't want to sound alarmist, but make sure he pays you on the nail.

There's been a certain amount of, let us say, polite surprise at some of the names you gave me. Nobody can recall the last time Wayne Schlesinger worked. I remember him being described as a promising newcomer years ago, but then he was thrown off the set midway thru his second feature after accusing the camera crew of being extraterrestrial spies. Most people I spoke to seemed to think he was in a clinic someplace.

So he's employed Harve Goldman, has he? Can't say I'm not surprised. I remember him from way back, he used to send me 'plays' when he was a college kid. I use the word advisedly. One was a stage adaptation of The Lord Of The Rings which he reckoned he could get down to sixteen hours playing-time with a cast of forty-seven. Thankfully the notion of copyright hadn't entered his ugly little head, so he was easy to shake off on that one. He last came to me with a proposal entitled – wait for it – Watergate, the musical. Unfortunately he's a spoilt little rich boy who doesn't have to work for a living, so he's got all the time in the world to churn out this crap. I always thought he'd end up in an asylum but he went to California to write for the movies instead. That way he saves on the medical bills.

I'm afraid Shelley Lamour is not as big a star as she thinks she is. She hasn't worked since Desire ended, and that's nearly five years now. Seems to have been involved a lot with Ken Kilmaine projects that haven't gotten off the ground. There are a lot of strange rumors about her private life. People are reluctant to hire her on account of her husband, whose hobby is rearranging other men's facial features. The word is, keep your distance.

Don't want to depress you too much, but I'm going to anyway: when I mentioned the above list to my friend in LA, she said, 'What kind of a movie are they making over there? I thought they already did The Addams Family.'

Kate called me last week. She was in town to discuss a new Broadway show. She's doing very well, says she's been offered

*another movie, but she wants to go back on stage. I think she
misses London. She asked after you, was pleased you were
working. I think she'd like to hear from you. Anything more you
need to know, don't hesitate to ask.*

I read the above, less last paragraph, to Bradley. I said I
couldn't work out why we were both here as we seemed far
too competent.

'Maybe because we're cheap,' he suggested.

'I'm not,' I said, so then we got talking about money. I
was embarrassed, he's on a pittance. Still, he said, he'd
been out of work for three months, he had debts, couldn't
afford to turn down a lousy offer. I didn't tell him I'd
been in exactly the same boat. I wondered if perhaps Ken
had left it so near to shooting before casting my part that
he was desperate, but it seems he only cast Brad a few days
before me. Commandment the third: The Producer thine
employer shalt move always in mysterious ways. Nobody
behaves sensibly with money in the film world anyway. If
they did, it wouldn't be the film world.

Of course I've been on to John non-stop about the
money. I'm supposed to be getting a weekly cheque but I
haven't had one yet. Naturally no one ever pays on time,
but John says that anything more than three weeks in arrears
is unacceptable. That limit has now been reached. He's
found out Mr Witt is a Swedish industrialist. He's never had
any involvement with movies before but he's absolutely
loaded. John is sure that Ken's finances are secure, but I
want the money in my pocket. Bradley hasn't received a
penny yet either . . .

It was lucky for me that Brad was in here yesterday when
I got the fax. I don't know what Shelley's game is, but by
God it terrifies me. She flirts with everyone, but so far she's
been doing most of her scenes with me, so I bear the brunt
of it. It would be difficult enough to concentrate anyway
without this ludicrously over-endowed sex bomb
wobbling her assets under my eyes at every opportunity,

but with old Wyatt Twerp hanging round it's actually physically dangerous. But yesterday she appeared in the caravan to suggest we did an extra bit of rehearsal together. Thank God Brad was on hand when Marve came storming in looking for her. There's somebody else who shouldn't be anywhere near the set of course, but when I protested to Terry he simply told me that if I wanted him to leave then I would have to ask him, because nobody else dared. He says he's Shelley's personal manager and claims the right to be present. Unfortunately he seems to have appointed himself minder to the frog-man, with whom he has struck up an unlikely friendship, I presume on the basis of their limited shared mental capacity. I've never known a situation like it, it's ludicrous. Between them I think Harve and Marve, the terrible twins, may be the death of me. Brad and Denis both reckon Shelley plays it up for the clifftop cowboy deliberately, that it's her way of getting kicks and attention. I can't wait to get through my scenes with her. Let Sleat handle it, at least he's got his bouncers to protect him.

What do his bouncers protect him from normally? The wrath of Equity? The revenge of dead actors rising from their graves to punish his sullen infringement of our art? Fortunately I only have a few scenes with him. Unfortunately most of them are still to come. Brad has most to do with him and he has not been complimentary: if he is to be believed (and from my own brief experience I should say that he is), our favourite crooner has been boldly going where not even others of his ilk have managed to go before; in short, he has plumbed such depths as would normally require a bathysphere to film him in. And not merely is he a terrible actor (who ever expected less?), he has also become a grade one coward and complete hypochondriac since being bitten by that dog the other week. I wonder if he contracted rabies after all. The dog, I mean. God, it's all so awful ... Though occasionally something of a depressive character I am not usually suicidally so. However, were I to be offered a draught of hemlock right now I might think twice . . .

Well, maybe not. I just saw Mandy through the window, fresh as a daisy despite the hour. A sight to stir the blood, and why not? Lechery? I defy lechery. Besides, everyone should have a hobby. Denis is convinced she has a crush on me. I feign disinterest but it is far from being the case. Meantime my ego is deliciously massaged. Unfortunately I haven't had a scene with her yet. I await impatiently the opportunity to launch a full-scale pursuit.

Strangely enough, Terry says the rushes don't look too bad. He says I'm coming out of it the best (such a nice man, I do like him) and what more can an actor ask for? I shall have to resign myself to not getting an Oscar nomination this time, but did I ever expect one? Lucre was my sole motive and I had better believe it. If things really don't look too bad (and I can't believe they look too good either), then it's no thanks to Wayne Schlesinger. But at least if he isn't a positive influence, then he isn't a negative one either. He just sits there mindlessly vegetating and lets Terry get on with it, for which relief much thanks. Terry has just quietly picked up the reins and got on with it, a real pro. Hardened film buffs might choke on their *cahiers* to hear it, but it is actually possible to make a serviceable film in certain circumstances without the guiding animus of a director at all. Whether it's any good will be another matter, but this one was never going to be that anyway. In fact, give me a decent cameraman and a clever editor in preference to an *auteur* any day. Shush! I merely whisper it. Were such thoughts to be uttered out loud the fabric of contemporary culture would be rent. I might even be indicted for heresy. Better to suffer in silence. Let bullshit thrive! They've got to fill the arts pages of the newspapers with something.

Enough of this wittering. I am to be summoned. I hear the cold protesting cough of the minibus engine. My camel sniffs the morning and is indifferent. Pale dawn flushes the horizon. The hour is nigh, and, as Wayne would have it, the hounds of doom are knocking at my door.

Oh shit . . .

'Coming!' said Philip, putting away the diary and checking himself in the mirror. The knocking was repeated. 'All right, I'm on my way . . .'

He opened the door, expecting to see only the third assistant. He was more than a little surprised to find Ken Kilmaine on his doorstep.

'Your answerphone said you were abroad on business,' Philip said suspiciously in answer to Ken's irritatingly jaunty early morning greeting.

'Just got back into Heathrow an hour ago, so I thought I'd pop in and see how things are going.'

'If you ever returned my phone calls you'd know,' Philip answered sharply. 'Really, the situation has become intolerable. Wayne's eccentricities I can just about cope with, but I cannot work with Harvey Goldman hanging round and kicking up a fuss every time I alter one of his literally unspeakable lines.'

'Now, Phi-lip!' Ken was probably attempting to sound extra mollifying, but the effect was so little different from his usual tone of voice that it barely registered. 'I think we should maybe try and compromise here a little, don't you? The script's not all that bad, you know.'

'Ken, the script is a pile of shit.'

The smile almost disappeared from Ken's lips.

'Everyone else manages.'

'That's their problem, Ken. Harve has decided that I am public enemy number one. Will you please keep him off the set and off my back? Terry keeps trying to get rid of him but he hasn't got the authority. You have got to do it.'

'Hey, Phi-lip, my man, mellow out! You've got to understand, this is a big number for Harve. It's the first movie he's ever scripted entirely on his own.'

'You don't say! Doesn't that tell you something about him, Ken?'

Before Ken could answer there was a knock on the door and Terry entered.

'I just came to tell Philip that we're going to do the robbery scene first,' he explained. 'We're having to do quite a bit of rescheduling at the moment.'

'So you're a long way behind?' Ken asked.

'I think it'll only come down to a few days and we'll be able to make it up, though it doesn't help having Harve throwing his daily tantrums . . .'

'Amen to that!' contributed Philip, who thought that his assessment was wildly optimistic.

Ken looked thoughtful and worried, as well he might.

'It seems like I'm going to have to get down to the set more often to check up on things,' he announced after a pause.

'And amen to that too!' declared Philip emphatically.

Ken murmured something about having a word with Harve. He promised that he would look in later. Denis came in to check up on Philip as the others left.

'Very smart today, Your Honour!' said Denis when he had appraised his costume. 'You can bang my gavel any time!'

Philip smiled thinly.

'Cheer up!' said Denis gaily. 'Actually I might have some good news for you . . .' He lowered his voice and leant in conspiratorially, even though they were alone. 'I think you might possibly just be seeing the teenciest weenciest bit less of both Harve and Marve, at least temporarily. I was in Shelley's caravan yesterday and I overheard Harve boasting about his western video collection. Marve got terribly excited. Surprise, surprise, anything with cowboys in is his favourite viewing. Anyway, it seems that Harve has brought some of his tapes with him and he can't wait to show them off. Shelley's got a video-recorder with her in the caravan so the two of them are planning some regular couch potato sessions. Harve's going to bring in his tapes tomorrow, so with any luck you'll be shot of them for a while.'

'Good,' said Philip, a little dubiously. 'Well, I'll keep my fingers crossed.'

His fingers had been fixed in that position for most of the last month. It hadn't done any good so far. At last the third assistant came to give him his call. He put his caravan key and wallet into a canvas bag which he always used for the purpose (for no old pro lets his valuables out of his sight when working) and tramped morosely outside.

He closed the door behind him and pulled his black cloak tightly about his shoulders. A chill wind gusted between the caravans and vehicles clustered in the car park and billowed through the loose folds of the garment, filling him out like the Sandeman port figure. Through the trees he could see the first glitter of light on the surface of the lake. Someone called his name above the choke-rich chug of the minibus engine, and he walked rapidly over the cold hard ground.

By the dim interior light he saw that the minibus was full. He nodded at the silhouettes of familiar faces and answered the muttered greetings with a grunt; the hour was too young for anything more effusive. One seat at the back was free and he fell into it as the vehicle began to move away. The twin headlamps picked their way through the trees. Needless to say, when they reached the morning location Harve and Marve were both in evidence.

The scene was a different part of the woods, the shot in question the occasion of the evil Judge Jeffreys' second encounter with the clean-living folk hero Dick, seen here, minus sheep, engaged in his new day job of robbing coaches. Sleat had encountered a few difficulties in preparing for the scene, it transpired.

One of the assistants was leading him very carefully by a rope bridle. The bridle was actually attached to a plodding cart-horse with an Eeyoreish look to whose back the pop star was clinging for dear life. Chopper was attempting to coax him into a sitting position.

'Come on now, he ain't gonna hurt you.'

Sleat was not reassured. He remained bent forward at an acute angle in the saddle, gripping the shaggy black mane in both hands. Somewhere behind him amongst the trees there was a sudden raucous gust of laughter.

'Quiet there!' Sleat hissed at the offending technicians. 'You're gonna make him bolt!'

Chopper rolled his eyes heavenwards.

'Look mate, a fucking stick of dynamite and he might just about break into a trot. Relax.'

Philip raised an eyebrow at Terry.

'Is that walking tin of cat meat meant to be Black Bess by any chance, legendary thoroughbred and immortal heroine of the famous midnight ride to York?'

'Only in the close-ups of Sleat,' he was reassured. 'Any time we see the horse it'll be a real one in the distance with Chopper on it. Magic of the movies, eh?'

They were on the edge of the open space in the park, where a mock-up village, or at least the façade of one, was in the final processes of construction. Later they would have to film the coach going through the bustling streets, but most of the shots involving extras would be compressed into the last few days to minimise costs, so for now they were just doing the stick-up. That was the hardest part of filming, the constant mental readjustment necessitated by doing every scene out of sequence. That, and the long hours and the tedium of waiting.

The day's shooting started more or less on schedule, which was something. Philip boarded the coach and was delighted to find that for today's scene Shelley was going to be sitting opposite, giving him room to breathe and more. He returned her simpering morning greeting good-naturedly.

Chopper turned the coach around on the edge of the open space and steered it to the top of another of the innumerable paths that led off through the woods. On the command he drove off towards where the camera was waiting. After about fifty yards they slowed down and stopped.

'Stand and deliver!' squeaked the weedy, muffled voice of Sleat.

'Cut!' shouted Terry.

'Hey, I'm supposed to say that!' Wayne protested. 'Cut!'

Philip put his head out of the window. Terry was turning the cart-horse's head towards the coach. 'You've got to sit up,' he told Sleat wearily. 'The camera's behind you. When we pull back on to you as the coach approaches, it looks like you've got indigestion.'

Perhaps he had. He was wearing a knotted handkerchief for a mask and most of his face was invisible, but the eyes seemed dull with misery. They prepared to go for a second take. As the coach could not reverse, Chopper had to take them down on to another path and then in a wide loop back to the open space.

'Could you stop a little quicker this time, please?' Terry requested through the megaphone when they were in position.

'Better brace yourself,' warned Philip. Shelley was facing the front of the coach. She giggled.

'Exciting, ain't it, honey?'

Philip smiled vaguely. When she poked her toes out from under the frilly hem of her gown and began playing footsie with him he pretended not to notice.

'Action!' Wayne called out in the distance, and then, less relevantly, 'Come and get it!'

The stage-coach lurched forward. It rapidly picked up pace.

'He's hacking it a bit,' Philip murmured, more to himself than to Shelley, all forms of contact with whom he was keen to minimise.

Philip just heard Sleat's feeble challenge over the rattle of the wheels, but not the words. The wheels locked suddenly and Philip was flung back hard against his lightly padded seat. Shelley was thrown on top of him.

He jerked instinctively forward, trying to push her off, but succeeded only in slipping off the front of the seat and wedging himself into the narrow floor space. With his ankles sticking into his bottom and his knees jammed against the seat in front it would have been difficult enough to rise anyway, but with Shelley smothering him it was impossible. She made not the slightest attempt to move.

'Why honey, this is real cosy,' she murmured languidly.

He would have answered in the negative, but his nose was sunk deep into her cleavage and all his efforts were engaged in trying to breathe. He was only intermittently successful. Gasping, he tried to heave her off, but in the absence of any assistance from her it was an impossible task.

Suddenly the door to the coach was yanked open and the voice he had been dreading thundered in his ears: 'What you think you doing down there to my baby, mister?'

'Ah, honey,' Shelley giggled, 'looks like we gone and got all stuck.'

Philip felt a meaty fist punch him none too lightly in the shoulder.

'What you doing down there, answer me, Pop?'

If I could get your wife's breasts out of my face I would, Philip mused. Fortunately Marve tucked an arm round her waist and lifted her out. From the other side of the coach Chopper appeared to help him down.

'Sorry about that, mate,' he apologised. 'I forgot you can't do a handbrake turn with only two-horsepower.'

Members of the crew came clustering round to see that he was all right. He was, until Marve appeared suddenly, grabbed him by the lapels and threw him back against the coach.

'You keep your grubby little paws to yourself in future, mister,' snarled the jealous cowboy, 'or you'll be in trouble, you hear?'

'Take your bloody hands off me!' Philip snapped, anger overcoming fear. 'This is intolerable, who the hell do you think you are?'

Chopper thrust his way between them. 'Back off mate,' he said coolly, giving Marve a dirty stare.

The cowboy was momentarily taken aback. 'You keep outta this!' he growled at length. 'This ain't none of your business.'

'Oh yeah?' The burly stuntman casually folded his arms. He gave Philip a nod. 'He happens to be a mate of mine. Mess with him and you mess with me, geddit?'

Marve's eyes narrowed threateningly. He waved a threatening fist at Chopper. 'You're asking for a smack in the face, mister.'

'What, from you?' Chopper scoffed. 'You overgrown tub of lard.'

Everyone had backed off the instant Marve had appeared. Now there was a near-stampede for the bushes. Only Terry remained behind.

'All right, chaps,' he said lamely. 'Let's calm down, shall we?'

But it was much too late for that.

Marve dropped his shoulder and hooked his fist at Chopper's head. It was a blow to fell the proverbial ox, but even Philip had seen him telegraph it, and if he had, then Chopper was there long before him. Marve's fist impressed the intrenchant air and before he could regain his balance Chopper was under his guard, jabbing expertly into his solar plexus. As Marve doubled up with a grunt the downward thrust of his face met the upward jerk of Chopper's knee, and Philip heard the curiously unrealistic sound of one hand smacking a cabbage. The blood, though, he presumed was real.

There was enough of it. As Marve lay stunned on his back in the dirt it flooded out of his nose and gushed all down his face and neck. Shelley screamed and flung herself on to the ground beside him, though Philip noted that she took care not to get anything on her dress.

'My poor baby, what you gone done to him?' She cradled Marve's head in her arms decorously, the Florence Nightingale shot. Marve's eyes rolled but he was still conscious, if groggy. When Chopper poked his shin with a toe Philip saw the pupils dilate with fear. It was unmistakable.

'Any more of your crap and I'll really hit you hard,' said Chopper coldly. 'Get the picture?'

It was an expert delivery, worthy of Bogart at his best. Chopper may have been only a bit-part player, but he knew his stuff. He stood his ground and kept his eyes unblinkingly on his assailant until Shelley and a few of the crew had helped him to his feet and escorted him back to his dune buggy, head held back and blood-soaked handkerchief pressed to his nose.

'It seems inadequate to say thanks,' said Philip offering him a cigarette, 'but I'll say it all the same.'

'My pleasure,' Chopper replied. 'I've been itching to do that since we started. I knew it was all puff, he just throws it about 'cos he's built like a brick shithouse, but underneath he's tough as meringues. I reckon my gran could sort him.'

One by one the crew came up discreetly to give Chopper their congratulations. Even Wayne was impressed.

'Your friend's a useful man to have around, Dungeon-master,' he confided to Philip. 'Do you think he's had any experience of dealing with alien life-forms?'

'You mean like Harvey Goldman?'

With Shelley gone the morning's shooting had to be re-scheduled again, but Marve's injuries turned out to be depressingly superficial and she was back again in the afternoon. She brought Ken Kilmaine with her. Ken had in tow Mr Witt, the moneybags.

'I expect he's just here checking to see his investment's all right,' Terry said when Philip pointed him out.

'What's he going to do when he finds it isn't?' Philip wanted to know. Just as they were about to begin work again Ken appeared and took him to one side.

'What's this I hear about you and Chopper ganging up on Marve?'

Philip laughed hollowly. Ken did not laugh with him. His smile was beginning to look fatally compromised.

'Look, Phi-lip, you can't go throwing your weight around, you know. It's upset Shelley. I'm going to have to give Chopper the chop.'

'Oh no you're not.' Philip jabbed his finger angrily into Ken's collar-bone. 'He goes and I go, you understand? I'm quite prepared to scream and kick up a fuss if you like, but with your financial friend standing over there I don't suppose that would be such a good idea, would it? It's up to you, Ken, but say the wrong thing and I shall walk straight off this set, do I make myself clear?'

'Hey!' Ken attempted to lay a calming hand on his shoulder. 'No need to resort to threats, now.'

'I wish that were so, Ken, but it patently isn't. If you were here doing your job properly then none of this need have happened. At least now you are here you can get rid of Kermit.'

'Who?'

'The frog-man, who'd you think? If Harvey Goldman buggers up another one of my scenes I shan't be responsible for my actions. And with your Mr Witt hanging round I'm not sure you'd like that very much.'

Philip strode off without waiting for a reply. He climbed into the coach and threw himself into his seat. When Shelley got in a little while later he stared pointedly out of the window. To his immense satisfaction he saw Ken in the distance leading Harvey Goldman away. Shelley seemed subdued.

'I am sorry my husband got the wrong end of the stick this morning,' she told him earnestly when at last she succeeded in catching his eye, 'but he can be mighty impetuous sometimes. That weren't no cause though for Chopper to start fisticuffs, was it now?'

Philip didn't answer, but she wittered on anyway, feebly justifying her fallen Goliath. He gritted his teeth and at last they began to get through the taxing afternoon schedule.

Ironically, everything went smoothly for once. Mr Witt stayed for most of the afternoon and Philip supposed that he must have received a quite misleading impression from what he'd seen. He noticed that Ken's smile was looking more than usually stretched.

While Sleat went off to practise on an allegedly more docile black horse they prepared to finish the day with some long shots of Philip hurtling by in the coach. He was sure that they could have been done by a double, but he was in costume and he was there and he was too tired to protest overmuch. Besides, he was due a whole day off tomorrow. Shelley was not required and in this instance she did not offer to remain behind. Philip reflected that Brad and Denis were probably right, that she wouldn't consider it worth her while flirting without Marve on hand to add some extra spice.

They relocated a few times and after a lengthy break were ready for the final shot of the day. They had exhausted several locations from different angles and were by now down a narrow straight path far from the main area of filming. Wearily, Philip trod out the butt of his cigarette and mounted the coach for the last time. Chopper tapped the roof and he tapped back to show that everything was OK. He lined his head up with the open window so that the camera, a hundred or so yards further on up the path, would catch him in profile as he passed. The coach pulled away.

They gathered pace. The path was uneven and the carriage shook. Philip had to cling on to the door-handle to make sure that his face remained in shot. They approached the camera position, Chopper slowing down as previously instructed.

Out of the corner of his eye he saw the people round the camera flash by. They would be panning on to the rear of the coach, filming it all the way down to the next bend a quarter of a mile on. Chopper cracked his whip and the horses accelerated. Philip sat back and tried to enjoy the ride.

Suddenly Chopper cried out. It was a cry of surprise and fear, so out of character that Philip sat bolt upright with shock. The coach veered dangerously to the side and he was thrown to the floor.

'Jump!' Chopper screamed.

Philip saw the flash of Chopper's cloak as it flew past the window. He made a grab for the door-handle but the coach was shaking so much he couldn't reach it. Trees flashed past crazily, he felt the coach swinging to the side, coming off the path and crashing into the undergrowth. And then they hit something.

The world turned upside-down. It happened in an instant, but the shock was so sudden that his brain seemed almost detached, quite calm, so that he had a feeling of experiencing the event frame by frame, each sickening roll, each gut-wrenching bone-crushing fall against the walls, the floor, the spinning roof. The sense of spinning carried on long after the coach had stopped, leaving him lying dazed in some impossible twisted position staring through the splintered square of window at an oddly angled sky. The spinning sensation was underscored by the squeaky turning of the rear wheel. Soon voices drowned out the noise.

They pulled him from the wreckage and laid him on the grass, his big black cloak wrapped twice about him. He was dazed but quite conscious.

'Are you all right?' Ken Kilmaine screamed eagerly in his ear.

'Don't ask fucking stupid questions,' said Terry crisply.

It was curious, though, he probably was all right. He ached a bit, but that was all.

'Anything broken?' Terry asked. He was on one side, Ken on the other, both helping Philip up. He didn't really need their help, so he let them go. He swayed a little, but he didn't fall.

'Never felt better in my life,' he answered weakly.

'Bloody miracle he got out of that in one piece,' someone said in a tone tinged with awe.

It was. The coach had finally smashed into a tree. It had fallen apart like a matchstick model. If he hadn't been jammed into the floor the impact would have hurled him into the bole of the tree. His neck would have snapped like a dry twig.

'I called an ambulance on the mobile phone,' someone said.

'I don't need an ambulance,' Philip muttered stubbornly.

'Chopper does,' said Terry quietly.

Apparently he had broken his arm. Philip wanted to laugh. Chopper was the one who had jumped clear and he had had the worst of it. Apart from bruises, minor cuts and shock Philip was fine.

'I still want you to go in the ambulance,' Terry was insisting.

He knew that he would have to go. He still felt too disoriented to protest overmuch anyway. It was weird, he supposed he must be in shock because what had just happened didn't seem real. On the contrary, it felt like a waking dream. All of a sudden his head began to swim and his knees collapsed.

When the ambulance came they made him lie on a stretcher. He found the piercing wail of the siren easily the most uncomfortable sensation of the day. He was surprised when the doctor said that he would have to stay in hospital overnight for observation, but the x-rays showed no hidden damage. Only now, with the concentrated medical attention, was the narrowness of his escape beginning to sink in, and suddenly he felt shaken and vulnerable. It was just as well that he had been due the next day off anyway.

He was discharged the following morning.

9

Philip went to bed as soon as he got home from the hospital, but his fitful attempts at sleep were interrupted by a constant stream of telephone calls enquiring after his health. Eventually he just turned off the phone, but no sooner had he fallen out of consciousness than the doorbell was rung insistently and he was obliged to answer it to a motorcycle messenger bearing a bouquet of flowers and a gift-wrapped bottle of Scotch. When he saw that the attached Get Well card bore the ubiquitous KenKil logo he tipped the flowers unceremoniously into the bin, but the gesture did little to assuage his irritation. The damage had been done and he was too restless now to sleep. He looked lingeringly at the Scotch but just about managed to restrain himself, though this time he did not pour the bottle away. He stowed it discreetly in his make-up bag, mentally labelling it 'in case of emergency only'. Then he got dressed again and went out for a walk.

It did him good. He'd spent too much time of late just sitting about. He had meant only to stroll gently round the Fields, but he was bored and had nothing to get back for, so he walked on down to Upper Street. The rest of the day stretched ahead unappetisingly. He'd been working such long hours recently that he'd forgotten what to do with his leisure time. Then he remembered the video shop.

He didn't have his membership card with him, but fortunately the assistant on duty was one of the regulars and he greeted him by name. Eagerly Philip scanned the shelves for some two hours' celluloid traffic to take his mind off things, the more trivial and escapist the better. He supposed that in a year or two some poor schmuck in his position might innocently take down the sleeve of *Midnight Rider*, but that was exactly the kind of thought he was trying to dispel and he banished it peremptorily.

The problem, as always, was dealing with the embarrassment of riches. This was a big shop and, faced with too great a choice, Philip always became hopelessly indecisive. He wandered aimlessly about, picking out dozens of possibilities and replacing all of them after unhelpful deliberation. His mind only half-engaged, he found himself staring at some intriguingly risqué slip-cases.

He glanced up to the sign above the shelves and saw that he was in the 'Adult' section. The layout of the shop was haphazard and he saw that 'Adult' was placed incongruously between 'Children's Classics' and 'Animations'. He was thinking that he could probably give all three a miss when a title on the bottom shelf caught his eye. He blinked and read it again to make sure that he hadn't suddenly gone dyslexic. He hadn't.

'Well I never!' he chuckled to himself, turning over the video case of *Dr Dildo and the Busty Bimbos* and reading the credits on the back.

Kenneth Kilmaine's name was there, sure enough, though in very small letters. The illustration on the front was a real throwback: the scantily clad girls looked like failed Abba lookalikes, and the man in a white coat standing between them had bouffant hair and sideburns down to his mouth. Philip would have been prepared to bet quite a lot that he was wearing flares under the white coat.

He tucked the video case under his arm and carried it over to the counter. The assistant seemed amused.

'Not your usual kind of thing, Mr Fletcher.'

Philip was pleased to agree.

'Just conducting a little private research,' he said. The assistant gave the impression that he had heard that one before.

'Well, you certainly picked a cult classic.'

'Is it really? I thought "bimbo" was a modern word?'

'Well, that's something for your researches, Mr Fletcher.'

'You don't by any chance have a copy of *Aliens Stole My Surfboard*, do you?'

'I've never heard of that one, I'm afraid.'

'Never mind. Just this one then, thanks.'

'I'll get it for you.'

He went off to the back of the shop to look for the tape. Philip picked a catalogue off the counter and idly flicked through it.

'Why, good afternoon, Mr Fletcher. What a surprise.'

The stentorian voice, booming mere inches behind his ear, made him jump. It certainly was a surprise. He stuttered his reply: 'Oh, hello there, Reverend Washington.'

The imposing cleric laid down the copy of The Gospel Collection Volume 3 which he had come to return and eyed Philip gravely.

'It is undoubtedly fortuitous that I have crossed your path, Mr Fletcher. The matter on which we spoke previously has not been satisfactorily resolved. Young George's head remains stuffed with nonsense and he claims that you have been encouraging him. Is it true, sir?'

Philip sighed helplessly.

'I haven't seen him for weeks, frankly I've been much too busy. I did give him a kind of tutorial, it's true, but my only aim was to dissuade him from proceeding further. I have to say this, though, Reverend: if he's determined, then placing obstacles in his way is only going to egg him on further. It really is none of my business, you know, but I recommend heartily that you leave him to his own devices.'

Philip could see that his words were falling on stony ground. The Reverend shook his head sagely.

'Wisdom brings grey hairs enough, Mr Fletcher. George is a child and young for his years. He lacks fibre, he needs counsel, yours and mine. Will you help him, then, from the vantage-point of your age and superior moral position?'

'Well, I —'

'Here we are then, Mr Fletcher,' declared the reappearing assistant, 'one copy of *Dr Dildo and the Busty Bimbos*. Would you like me to reserve you any other Dr Dildo films, there's quite a series, you know?'

'Um, er, no thanks . . .'

'Think you can get too much of a good thing, eh? Well, don't get carried away now!' The assistant chuckled happily to himself before turning to his other customer. 'Are you just returning this, sir?'

'I have Volume 4 on order.'

'Ah, right, I'll just go and see if it's in.'

Hastily Philip shoved his video into his pocket and scooted for the door.

'Must dash!' he mumbled. 'Nice to run into you.'

'Mr Fletcher!'

He had to stop. It was a voice which demanded to be obeyed.

'Um, yes?'

The Reverend Washington clasped his lapels and rocked back impressively on his heels. His magnificent voice effortlessly filled the room.

'Beware the deceits of the world, the flesh and the devil, Mr Fletcher. Beware them.'

'Oh er, right, I will. Thanks for the warning!'

Philip exited the shop in a cold sweat and raced back home as fast as his legs would carry him.

Mrs Thing was in the kitchen. He carried the video-recorder into his bedroom before going in to talk to her.

'No need to do the bedroom today,' he explained glibly when he had finished listening to Mr Tomascevski's routine health bulletin. 'I'm just going to have a little sleep actually; I'd be grateful if you didn't disturb me.'

He went back into the bedroom and inserted the newly hired video-tape into the machine. He plumped up his pillows and settled down to enjoy an afternoon of serious viewing.

In a way it was. Not being a devotee of blue movies he hadn't really known what to expect, but he supposed that it was legitimate to anticipate at least a mild degree of titillation. It was not forthcoming. The grainy quality of the film didn't help, but a perfect cut would have offered little improvement. In any case, the porn itself was scarcely any harder than anything in your average Sunday night BBC serial. It would have drawn no more than a tired murmur from the moral minority.

There was a story of sorts. Dr Dildo, played by a small, thin actor born to have sand kicked in his face, had a surgery with a very large couch in it. This turned out to be almost the sole location, which must have kept production costs to a minimum. The episodic plot involved a succession of nubile young women, all coming to Dr Dildo with intimate personal problems, which was where the couch came in. Dr Dildo, it seemed, had a novel approach to medical ethics, and a severely limited diagnostic range, for there appeared to be no condition worthy of the name which could not be cured by a vigorous dose of rogering. To be taken three times daily was his parting advice, a joke which began to wear a little thin after the umpteenth identical consultation. Philip found the whole thing about as erotic as a double hernia, but he watched it anyway. He had nothing better to do.

Midway through some routine grunting and grinding the phone rang. Philip lifted the bedside receiver indifferently.

'Hello? It's Mandy.'

Hastily he turned down the volume on the remote control.

'I wasn't on the set yesterday,' Mandy said, 'I only just heard about your accident. Are you all right?'

'I'm fine, thanks, amazingly enough. It was quite a lucky escape. But I'm afraid Chopper's luck ran out.'

'That's awful. Are they going to have to redo his scenes?'

'Yes, I suppose they'll have to recast, put us even more behind schedule. Aren't we working together at last tomorrow?'

'Only a tiny bit, we don't even get to speak to each other. I think we're doing our big scene in the studio next week. I'm quite nervous actually. Looking forward to it, though.'

'So am I.'

Nothing like a spot of bodice-ripping to stir the sludge in his veins.

'If you're really feeling nervous, why don't you come round to my trailer some time?' He dropped in casually. 'If it'll help any we can run through it a few times.'

'Really, would you do that?' She sounded genuinely delighted. 'I'd be ever so grateful.'

'I'd be happy to oblige, my dear. Come tomorrow morning if you like. We're bound to be running late.'

Sometimes it was so easy to be a regular guy.

He caught his reflection in the full-length mirror by the cupboard. He winked at himself knowingly.

'The charmer's back. How do you do it, old man?'

'Natural talent. What can I say? Perhaps I should write a book.'

'What? *The Philip Fletcher Guide to Deflowering Virgins?*'

'No, nothing so exclusive. There are too few left to deflower.'

'You must have been overdoing it.'

'Not me. Not lately, at any rate. On my recent record I'd walk away with a scholarship to a monastery.'

'Can't imagine you in a monastery somehow. Bad casting.'

'Maybe, but I could have got the part. There's been a serious dearth of female company in my life lately. Time to remedy the deficiency, I think.'

Suddenly the phone began to ring again, and at the same moment the front door buzzer sounded loudly.

'We are popular all of a sudden . . .' He picked up the bedside phone. 'Hang on a sec, please.'

He went into the living-room and lifted the intercom. He waved Mrs Thing back into the kitchen.

'I'll get it, Mrs Tomascevski . . . Fletcher Towers?'

'You what?' came the electrically distorted reply.

'Oh, it's you. All right, come up . . .'

He pressed the entry button and picked up the phone by the door.

'Philip? It's Chopper. How you doing?'

'I'm doing fine. You're the one who copped it.'

'I know, I know. Now, listen, mate – you on your own?'

'More or less. Why?'

'Look, you know I'm not the paranoid sort, nothing like that. It's about yesterday.'

'The accident?'

'Yeah, well, that's it. I harnessed that carriage myself, first thing in the morning like I always do. No way should it have come apart like that, no way.'

'Did it break?'

'No. At least I don't think so. If I hadn't sodding well buggered my arm up I could have checked, one look would have been enough, but it didn't feel like a break, it didn't snap, unlike my sodding arm. It just, like, came away in my hands, so the horses went one way and we went the other. And that ain't right.'

'I see . . .'

There was a knock on the door. Thoughtfully, Philip placed his hand over the receiver while he opened it. He carried the phone over into the corner.

'You're sure about this?'

'Well, I can't be one hundred per cent, as I say, but near as dammit. That geezer was hanging round, you know, when we broke at four o'clock.'

'You mean the cowboy?'

'Who else? He was skulking out the way, wouldn't show his face too near in case I kicked another bit of it in, but he was there while we was off getting a cuppa, with that other little twit who's always having the screaming habdabs.'

'You mean the frog in residence?'

'That's a good one, that is. Yeah, that's the geezer.'

'I see. And you seriously think the carriage could have been sabotaged.'

'I wouldn't say nothing in public, mate, but between you and me, as they say, I got my suspicions. There's something not right, I just got a feeling, but I couldn't say nothing 'cos there ain't no proof, you know what I mean?'

'Yes. Well, I'll just have to keep my eyes and ears open, nothing else for it.'

'I'd do that if I was you. If it was the cowboy I'll lay you odds it was me he was after, but I'd watch out just the same, he ain't what you'd call a reasonable feller.'

Philip assured him that he would take extra care. He replaced the receiver thoughtfully. His first, his natural reaction, had been to dismiss the allegations as far-fetched, but Chopper was a sensible man, hard-headed and not prone to hyperbole. In any case, he knew from experience that stranger things had happened. Many of them to him.

'Well, George . . . To what do I owe the honour of this visitation?'

'Me uncle's got the hump with you. He said I was never to see you again.'

'So naturally you came round at once. I don't think he's quite got the knack of dealing with you, has he?'

'What about me Shakespeare lessons then?'

'George, you're about as cut out for classical theatre as I am for disco dancing, so — '

'There you go again! It's always the same thing, innit? You ain't giving me a chance, no one ever gives me a chance — '

'Yes, yes, George, please – we've had all this before and I'm feeling ever so slightly fragile today. Where are you going?'

George was marching purposefully across the room towards the bookcase. He snatched the Collected Works off the top shelf.

'Which bit was it? I can't find it . . .'

Again, and very much despite himself, Philip found the sight of the juvenile delinquent earnestly scanning through the Bard endearing. He felt himself soften.

'All right . . . Perhaps we should try something a little bit more up your street . . .'

It was obvious that George was not to be deterred easily. It occurred to Philip that there might be a better way of making him aware of his own deficiencies.

'Do you know what an improvisation is?'

'No.'

'It's a made-up scene. You have a character and a situation but you don't have a script. You have to use your ingenuity and wit to write your own script as you go along. You have to know when to speak and when to listen and it's very demanding. It's not a style of working which I enjoy, but it does have its uses. I would like you to play a scene with me now. Then perhaps we'll see if you have any talent. Do you understand what I'm saying?'

'Think so.'

'Good. Now, do you remember what you said to me the first time we met?'

'No.'

'You said "'kin 'ell" and ran away. At that point I hit you with a whisky bottle, a pity in a way because the scene had possibilities. Let's give it another go, shall we? Right, you go to the door. Go on, I don't have all day. I will position myself in the middle of the room by the sofa. Thus. Now I will give you your character. Your name is Philip Fletcher. You are a famous classical actor, in fact one of the best in the country, and why you are not currently giving your Lear or Othello to the adoring public is a mystery bordering on a national scandal, but we'll let that pass. It is late morning and you have recently risen after a night of serious over-indulgence. You have been out to the shops and are now returning home. You live alone and are not therefore expecting to find anybody in your flat. Now, in your own time, go out to the top of the stairs, turn around and come back in again, miming putting your key in the lock if you like. The moment you appear in here the exercise will begin.'

'I'm not –'

'Ah – ah! Don't say anything. Don't ask any questions. Just do it. Let instinct carry you. If you have any, it will.'

George hesitated. Philip dared hope that he might be on the point of surrender – a bloodless victory – but then there came an ominous stiffening of the frame and a mixed cocktail of defiance and determination that glistened in the eye. George turned and walked out of the front door, pulling it three-quarters shut behind him. Philip stationed himself by the sofa. He counted five.

The door was kicked open and George bounded in aggressively.

'What the fuck you doing here?'

'George . . .'

Philip put on his best schoolmasterly tone, letting him know he wasn't acting.

'George . . . two things: One, try to cut down on the pro-fanities, it upsets the viewers. Two, remember that you don't know that I'm here. You hurtled into the room like Chuck Norris on heat and came straight for me. You might perhaps think of registering just a *soupçon* of surprise first.'

'Oh yeah, I get it. Shall I start again?'

'It would be for the best . . .'

George went out again and Philip slightly altered his position. George made his second entrance and did a double-take that would have made a seasoned ham blush.

'Who the fu — bleedin' hell are you? What you doin' in my flat?'

'Ah, good evening, sir.' Philip smiled benignly. 'I trust you'll forgive me, I took the liberty of letting myself in. I'm Mr Washington from the local council.'

'But that's my na — . . . oh, I get it! Yeah, er, what you doing here?'

'Health and Safety Executive business, sir. It's a routine check-up, nothing to worry about.'

Philip tapped the nearest wall. He pointed to the sockets in the skirting board beneath.

'Have you got a licence for a multiple-plug extension?'

'You what?'

Philip gave the wall another tap.

'Very bad woodworm, I'm afraid. And – good heavens! is that the time? You'll have to excuse me, Mr Fletcher, I'm late already. I'll let you have a copy of my report first thing — '

'Hang on a sec!'

George moved smartly to block the door, upon which Philip had been advancing. There was a canny look in his eye. 'You got a warrant?'

'A warrant? I told you, sir, I'm a council employee, and under the provisions of the local government services act — '

'Bullshit, you're a fucking burglar, aren't you?'

'What an extraordinary allegation. Really, sir, your paranoia — '

George grabbed him suddenly by the arm.

'Cut the crap, you tosser, I'm nickin' you!'

'Unhand me at once! As a council employee it is I who have the power to arrest you, not the other way around.'

'Oh yeah? Well, get out of that!'

Philip yelped as George twisted his arm behind his back. He tried to break free but the young man's grip was firm. He made to backheel him in the shins, but George was quicker and his shoe scraped empty air. He lost his balance and fell, George crashing down on top of him. He felt his knee jabbing into his spine.

'Let me go!'

'Police! Police!'

'There's no need to get carried away, you're hurting me!'

'Shut up, or I'll smack you one.'

'Take your hands —'

'You ain't a council employee, you're a burglar, admit it!'

'Will you let go —'

'Confess! Confess or I'll beat the shit out of you!'

'You're already beating the shit out of me.'

'I'll – what the —'

Philip heard a tremendous thwack and George rolled off him, screaming. Philip crawled away, feeling dazed and shaken. Wild yells filled the air. He pulled himself up on to the arm of the sofa and gazed in some astonishment at the sight which greeted his eyes.

George was huddled into the corner attempting to shield his head with his hands. Mrs Tomascevski was beating him with a stiff-brushed broom.

'Take that, you bad man, you bad man!'

Philip let her carry on until he had got his breath back. Then he went over and gently relieved her of the broom. She seemed unimpressed.

'Why you stop me? He need damn good hiding.'

'Please, Mrs T, it wasn't for real. We were acting.'

'Acting?'

'That's right, we were playing a little scene.'

Mrs T gave an incredulous sneer.

'Him actor?'

'Of a sort, yes.'

Mrs T drew herself up proudly to her full height. She sniffed.

'He actor, I Pope!'

She turned on her heels and strode angrily back into the kitchen, banging the door behind her. Philip laid the broom against the wall.

'I thought she was gonna kill me!' George whined, slowly pulling himself up.

'No more than you deserved. There was no need to resort to violence.'

'I got a bit carried away, that's all. I was good though, wasn't I?'

'You mean as an all-in wrestler?'

'That ain't fair! I never done it before, I did my best.'

'Yes, I suppose so. You'll have to excuse me, I'm going to go and freshen up.'

He went through the bedroom and into the bathroom, where he combed his hair back into place, reknotted his tie and adjusted his neck, and dabbed at his flustered brow with a damp flannel. When he came out again George was standing in the bedroom doorway, an expression of utter bemusement on his face.

'What the effin' bleedin' hell is this?'

Philip glanced up distractedly. He had forgotten the video.

'Oh, that . . .' he said vaguely, registering out of the corner of his eye the fleshless thrusting buttocks of Dr Dildo. The eponymous hero was gallantly diagnosing his tenth busty blonde of the reel. 'Just filling in some of the holes in my education.'

George chuckled to himself.

'You got a dirty old raincoat then?'

'No, I have not.' Bristling with irritation, Philip strode over to the bed and snatched up the remote control. He pointed it at the tangle of quivering limbs on the screen. 'Now, if you don't mind, I've got plenty to be getting on with and I've . . . I've . . . Good God, I don't believe it . . .'

His arm fell limply to his side and the remote control slipped through his fingers. It fell with a dull thud to the floor at the same moment as he sank down weakly on to the side of the bed.

'What's up?' demanded George.

Philip ignored him. His attention was all on the video action. Not on the thin-shanked Hippocratic phoney on the couch, but on the busty blonde underneath him. And busty was a euphemism if ever he'd heard one.

The doctor's face was buried between her breasts. There was

room for a whole medical convention. Her head looked tiny in comparison, the cute, snub-nosed features so absurdly girlish as to seem almost surreal. The years had not withered her. Shelley Lamour hadn't changed a jot.

Philip picked the remote control up off the floor and turned the volume back on.

'Why, doctor!' her thin voice squealed on cue. 'Is that really your stethoscope down there or are you just pleased to see me?'

George snorted. 'Man, this is unreal . . .'

Philip was inclined to agree. He grabbed the slip-case and pored over the small print on the back looking for her name. It wasn't there. He looked up the date. She must have been a teen-ager when she'd done this. And her career had been downhill all the way since.

'At least it makes her look good in *Midnight Rider*,' Philip murmured aloud.

'You what?'

'Nothing . . .' He glanced up and eyed George wryly. 'Well, you did say you wanted an acting lesson.'

He nodded at the on-screen debauchery:

'Take a seat, and watch carefully. It may not be art, but by God that's what I call technique . . .'

10

Philip was sitting in his trailer killing time. It was mid-morning and he did not expect to be called for at least another hour. Bradley and Sleat were shooting a scene in the mock-up village and if Sleat was only half as bad as usual, then Philip might not even be needed till the afternoon. The waiting was getting to him.

Idly he pulled his binoculars from their brown leather case and trained them on the far side of the car park. They were his cricketing binoculars, veterans of the Test Match scene, a critical aid in the assessment of umpirical vagaries. And jolly useful, too, for keeping an eye on the bad guys.

He adjusted the focus and squinted at the right-hand window in Shelley Lamour's caravan. Yes, there they were, the backs of the two incongruous heads, side by side. Though the vast ten-gallon hat blocked out most of the window, it was just possible to catch a glimpse of the TV set to which they were both glued.

Harve and Marve were watching cowboy pictures, as apparently they had been for the whole of the previous day.

Although Philip remained sceptical about Chopper's conspiracy theory, it was comforting to know where they were. According to Denis, Harve had a 'literally limitless' collection of tapes, so they would have much to occupy themselves with. Feeling mildly cheered if far from complacent, Philip took a leisurely scan of the rest of the car park. It was a shame that he couldn't see Mandy's trailer, which was on the other side of the caterers' van. He was keeping his fingers crossed that she would drop by later: his end of the caravan contained a table and an awkward three-sided bench, but he and Bradley had agreed to fold down the table at the other end and spread out the double camp bed. It wasn't the most comfortable couch in the world but it would do for a bout of simulated bodice-ripping. His sweep complete, he returned his gaze in his own time to his enemies' corner of the camp.

They were still there. In fact, so immobile did they appear that they might have been dummies. Philip yawned and readjusted the binoculars. He panned along the caravan and peered in through the other window. Shelley Lamour was standing in it, looking at him.

For a moment he didn't think she'd seen him, but it was a vain hope: as his lenses came to rest on her she tossed back her golden curls and licked her lips. Then she gave him the benefit of her most suggestive wink and languidly flicked off the strap of her dress, baring her shoulder.

Hastily Philip slammed down his binoculars and slithered along the seat out of sight. With a trembling hand he grabbed the curtain and blocked out his window.

He would have to be a little more discreet in future, he decided sagely. The consequences of being caught snooping by the terrifying Marve did not bear thinking about.

He put the binoculars away in their case and stowed them under the table. He refolded his *Times* and returned to the half-completed crossword, that famous good old bored actor's stand-by. He was still trying to crack 4 across when there was a gentle rapping on the door.

A woman's knock if ever he'd heard one: he sidled out of his seat and quickly checked himself in the mirror before going over to the door. He wanted to look his best before molesting Mandy.

'Why, hello there . . .' He started speaking without looking. When he saw who it was, his voice trailed away and his smile thinned.

'Why, hello yourself, honey. Ain'tcha gonna invite me in then? It's kinda cold out here, you know.'

He cast a quick glance about the car park. There was no sign of her husband.

'Actually this isn't the most conven — '

But she was already climbing up the step and coming in. He just wasn't quick enough. He stepped back warily.

'My, it sure is cosy in here, ain't it?' cooed the blonde bombshell when he had closed the door.

'Ah, yes,' said Philip neutrally, backing off a little bit more to gain the extra yard, just in case. 'Um, to what do I owe the pleasure of this visit?'

Shelley pouted and wagged an admonitory finger at him. 'We just all gotta take our pleasures where we can, honey. And I sure ain't one to judge now, you know what I mean?'

Philip continued to eye her warily as she flounced over to the window.

'Why, look!' she exclaimed with theatrical exaggeration, flinging back the curtain and gesturing through the window. 'There's my baby! Cooee!'

She waved over towards her own caravan. Philip slunk away into Bradley's corner as Shelley called to him, 'Why don't you wave to Marve there now, honey? Do you see him?'

Philip didn't answer. Shelley noticed his binoculars case. 'Why, ain't these just cute!' she declared, taking out the binoculars and pressing them back to front to her eyes. 'Gee, you're all far away now, you know what I mean?'

Shelley broke into a fit of hysterical girlish giggling. Philip cringed.

'Actually I'm rather busy — '

'Oh, I can see that, honey,' she drawled, coming over towards him. He edged back but came into contact almost immediately with the end of the bed.

'We're not working together today, are we?' he asked airily, wondering how to make his excuses and leave. She obviously wasn't going to.

'Why, no, sugar, but all work and no play ain't my idea of fun, is it now?' She gave the binoculars a languid caress. 'It don't worry me none if you get turned on by an itty little bit of spying, Mister Philip Peeping Tom Fletcher. You can look now but you can't touch!'

Philip had no wish to do either. 'Sorry, I've got to be going,' he said brusquely.

'Why, you ain't going so soon now, are you?' she said, fluttering her eyelashes at him and coming even closer. 'What's the rush?'

Before he could reply there was a knock on the door. Before he could utter another word Shelley had hurled herself at him. 'Come in!' he heard her yell lustily as he crashed back sideways on to the bed with her on top of him, and then – a coy whisper in his ear: 'Why, Mr Fletcher, I think you're forgetting yourself . . .'

Desperately he forced her breasts out of his face and tried to rise. The effort defeated him. With dreadful resignation he turned his head towards the door.

'Oh. Hello there . . .'

He was red with embarrassment already. He felt himself turn maroon.

'I'm, I'm terribly sorry!' Mandy blurted out.

'What!' Shelley screamed in his ear.

At least she threw herself off him and he could breathe again. He clambered to his feet, straightening his disordered clothes. Shelley brushed past angrily, completely ignoring him, and thrust her nose at the window.

'Ah!' said Philip tamely, glancing at his watch. 'Nice of you to drop by, Mandy. Yes, we were going to go through that scene – '

'Another time, Philip,' she interrupted sharply. She was pale and her lip trembled. 'I'm very sorry to disturb you.'

She turned suddenly, ran down the step and out of the door.

'Mandy!' he called out uselessly. He winced at the crash of the door as she slammed it behind her. Shelley, still at the window, stamped her foot. 'Why, what's that darned fool up to!' she muttered furiously under her breath. 'Sitting there watching Cowboys and Injuns while I'm in here with another man!'

'Oh, shut up, you stupid bitch!' Philip groaned, giving the cupboard he was standing next to a savage kick. Shelley looked scandalised. 'Why, that ain't no way to talk to a lady, mister!'

'Well, remind me again next time I meet one.'

She snatched an ashtray off the table and hurled it at him. Philip ducked and hurled back a tirade of spontaneous abuse, but she was already storming out of the door, slamming it behind her even harder than Mandy had done. Philip strode up and down the narrow caravan swearing at the top of his voice and kicking the furniture.

A few minutes later, having just about managed to calm down, he glanced out and saw her through her caravan window, blocking the little of the TV screen that wasn't masked already by the ten-gallon hat. The hat swivelled in response to what she was saying and the meaty, ruddy face of its owner was turned unmistakably in his direction. Philip ran outside and hid himself for the next hour in the costume designer's van, having looked in vain for Mandy.

When finally his call came and he got on to set after lunch he was intensely miserable. As if doing this wretched awful film wasn't bad enough without having the threat of grievous bodily harm hanging over him! To make the intolerable worse, Mandy was very distant.

He didn't have a chance to patch things up with her before filming started. Not that he would have known what to say. He was aware that his version of the events she'd witnessed in his caravan was not going to sound convincing; indeed any explanation would come over as a lame excuse. How could he make her believe that Shelley had thought she was Marve, that she had thrown herself at him only to make her husband jealous? It was the kind of story an imbecile couldn't be expected to swallow. Mandy's coolness in the circumstances was doubly galling as it implied more than a dash of jealousy on her part. Philip felt consumed by frustration and irritation.

The afternoon's filming was taking place in the main street of the mock-up village, in front of the façade of the inn in which Philip had supposedly just failed to ravish the lovely Mandy. Sleat and Mandy had to run out of the front door together, then Philip was meant to dash out after and fire his pistol at them. As all villains in pictures are lousy shots, naturally he was going to miss. They would then cut away to a shot of Sleat's double pulling

Mandy's double up into the saddle and galloping away with her to safety. It all should have been immensely straightforward.

Two hours later they were still doing it. After a statutory tea-break they came back to attempt take twenty-one.

The actors had been called ready for the next scene, Dick's escape from the gallows. That meant Shelley was hanging around the fringes, and Philip was not best pleased to discover both Harve and Marve in attendance. They couldn't have run out of tapes already; Philip hoped to God that the video hadn't overheated and exploded. At least he had no physical contact with Shelley in the next scene, though as it was meant to be one of Sleat's big numbers it was going to be enough of a nightmare already. It was perhaps for that reason Ken Kilmaine was on hand, making one of his brief flying visits. Philip's satisfaction at finding the elusive producer present was tempered by his over-attentiveness towards Mandy. Philip felt a terrible surge of jealousy when he saw Ken idly lay his hand on her bare shoulder and murmur intimately in her ear. That she laughed at what he was saying and made no move to disengage herself only turned the green film in front of Philip's eyes opaque.

Angrily he staked out his position again, finding the mark which he had used in the previous twenty takes. There was a big window with shutters permanently thrown back midway up the façade and immediately beneath it a pole sticking out like a yard-arm from which Dick was to be hanged in the next scene (with Shelley decorously framed in the window above sobbing her eyes out). The rope was already attached to the pole, from which hung a painted inn sign bearing the legend 'The Spreadeagle Tavern', and Philip had been using the shadow of the noose for his mark. He adjusted it slightly to allow for the changed position of the sun.

He took up his position out of shot behind the inn door. The façade was a simple wooden flat, constructed solidly enough but none the less a little flimsy on the eye. The wind had been up earlier on, but wobbly scenery had been the least of their troubles.

'Let's hope it's twenty-first time lucky!' he said with forced pleasantness.

Mandy didn't answer. She pretended to be concentrating furiously.

'Shut up, everyone!' yelled the first assistant. 'We're going for a take now.'

Philip glanced across warily at Sleat. The pop star was standing on the other side of the door, in front of Mandy, also with a look of utter concentration on his face. As well he might have, Philip reflected. Though it hadn't done him any good so far. They awaited the director's muffled cry.

'I said, shut up!' the first assistant shouted angrily. 'We're rolling!'

Someone was clattering about just behind Philip. He couldn't see who it was because there was a solid wooden brace in the way, but the noises stopped.

'Action!' Wayne Schlesinger called out.

Sleat laboriously counted five on his fingers, grabbed Mandy by the hand and yanked her outside. This was usually the point at which he either a) fell over or b) pulled Mandy so hard that she fell over or c) managed both a) and b) simultaneously. It was a good thing he didn't have to walk and chew gum at the same time. Philip waited for the cry of 'Cut!'

It didn't come. He heard their faint footsteps receding. He should have been counting five himself; he was so used to them cocking it up that he hadn't been concentrating. He dashed out after them hurriedly.

As he came through the door they were just running past the camera, which was dead ahead of him. He noted his mark out of the corner of his eye and raced up to it. He snarled villainously for the benefit of the camera and flung up his right arm, levelling the flintlock pistol which props had given him. He pulled the trigger, there was the snap of a firing cap and a flicker of flame in the pan.

'Philip!'

The warning was frantic. It was Terry, screaming and waving desperately at something behind him. Everyone else was yelling too, even Wayne was half out of his wheelchair, gesticulating crazily. And Philip saw the shadow of the noose move.

Not only his mark but the whole edge of the façade beyond his feet was shifting. The shadows on the ground began to coalesce. He ran.

He was running towards the camera. His vision was blurred, all his senses overloaded, but he heard them shouting to him above the terror pounding through his ears, he could see them urging him towards them, like lifeguards to a drowning bather. He didn't dare look behind, but he had a terrible sense of movement in the air.

'Jump!' someone yelled.

Jump where? He was on the flat ground running, but he knew what they meant. He threw himself in a great dry belly-flop on to the earth.

There was a huge whoosh of air behind him, echoing the air his fall kicked out of his lungs. He felt it billow through his cloak and ruffle his hair. He pressed his face into the dirt and screwed his eyes tight shut as a thunderclap sounded in his ears.

His ears were still humming when they helped him up. He sat in a daze, his trembling chin supported on his knees as people fussed about him. They were asking him questions, but he couldn't hear them. His head ached. He stared dumbly at the mass of collapsed scenery.

Through the settling dust he saw the ribbed back of the set flat behind which he had awaited his cue a minute ago. One of the solid triangular braces had split on impact; the other stuck up in the air like a rude isosceles gesture. Somewhere underneath it all, buried under a ton of wood, was the little spot which he had taken for his mark.

He was still shaking twenty minutes later when they got him back to his caravan. No, he didn't need an ambulance this time, he insisted firmly, he just needed peace and quiet, a rest. They said they were going to get a doctor anyway, and he didn't argue, though he knew there was nothing for a doctor to look at. He had been lucky, again.

Again. He didn't like the sound of 'again'. He thought about it as they all reluctantly left off their fussing and prepared to leave him alone.

'This is if you need anything,' the second assistant said, putting down a portable phone on the table. 'Anything, anything at all. Just call me on my portable number, I've written it down.'

Philip thanked him and shooed him out with the others. He locked the caravan door, propped himself up in the corner on Bradley's couch and drew the curtains.

Through a crack in the material he could just see the end of Shelley's caravan. The TV set was off, the two heads were not at the window. Why had they been on set? Because Shelley had demanded Marve's presence, an exhibitionist in search of her audience? That was the innocent explanation, if innocent was the right word. What of the sinister explanation? Who had he heard clattering around backstage just before the take? Had the set just fallen over of its own accord, or had it been pushed?

There had been much talk of safety that morning. When the set had wobbled too much in the wind the carpenter had been called in, and he had insisted there was no risk of collapse. Philip had seen the heavy metal weights holding down the supporting struts at the back. It would take a Force Ten gale to knock that lot over, the carpenter had said. He had seemed confident and competent enough. Philip had seen no reason to doubt him.

Then why had the set fallen over? Why had he nearly been killed?

He drew a blanket up to his chin, settled back and closed his eyes. He didn't like to think about it, it made him feel sick inside. When he had lifted his face from the ground and spat the dirt out of his mouth the top of the fallen flat had been only inches from his feet. He had escaped by a whisker. Fractionally slower reactions and he wouldn't be here now.

He turned on his side, put his head under his blanket and shielded himself in an imaginary cocoon. His face was wet with perspiration, but he shivered. His mouth was dry.

This was the second accident to have befallen him. Chopper had been sure there was nothing wrong with the coach harness, just as the carpenter had been confident of his handiwork to-day. These were seasoned pros. People on a film set had to be, schedules were tight, efficiency was at a premium, incompetence could not be tolerated. Except on this picture.

Philip thought about who he would or would not trust to do their job properly. He had told Denis that he'd never worked with such a bunch of amateurs; he'd meant it: Sleat and Shelley, Wayne and Harve. Talk about Golden Turkeys, this lot of gilded poultry could take on all-comers. But the standards of those all around them were immeasurably higher. For three weeks now Philip had watched this particular technical crew at close quarters, with increasing admiration. If it hadn't been for their quiet competence the film would have long since been unsalvageable. It was inconceivable that any of their number could have been responsible for two near-fatal accidents.

Two near-fatal accidents . . . He mulled it over. Once might be misfortune, twice looked like worse than carelessness. His gut instinct told him that neither Chopper nor the carpenter had been at fault.

So who had been responsible?

'Well, I don't think we're going to need Sherlock Holmes to answer that one . . .'

He lifted aside the corner of the curtain again and peered across at Shelley's caravan. The terrible twins were back: there were the two heads side by side, the oversized stetson and the near-scaly hump of the frog-man's cranial dome, the pair of them sitting as if mesmerised before the cathode tube, their god. Philip imagined the smug looks on their faces. The pleasure of wiping them off would be immeasurable. But how?

He leant back and assumed a contemplative pose. What should he do? Go to the police?

'Like hell!'

Perhaps Mr Average in his place might have done so, but in all fairness to himself he knew that he could hardly be described as average, and in any case he had a near-pathological aversion to the sight of a blue uniform.

'What could I say to them, anyway? I think those two clowns over there have got it in for me? My dear chap, would you be so good as to throw them in the clink? What on earth would Mr

Plod say to that? I've hardly got what you might call evidence, have I? Let's think it through.'

He pushed open the cupboard door with his feet. There was a mirror inside. He stared intently into his reflection: 'All right ... so you think Harve and Marve are out to get you. Why?'

'Because Harve thinks I'm defiling his breathless prose and Marve thinks I'd like to defile his wife.'

'You think that's enough motive for attempted murder? And that's what it is; let's not beat about the bush here.'

'Perhaps not in any sane environment, but this is hardly that. Anyway, I'm not so sure ... where murder is concerned, the most trivial of motives may suffice.'

'Quite the little expert, are we?'

'Oh, I'd say I'm not without a certain expertise in the subject.'

Philip threw off his blanket and stood up. He lit a cigarette, inhaled deeply to dispel the inner cobwebs, and began to pace about the cramped caravan. He found it easier to think on his feet.

'So what now?'

'Take extra care and every precaution. Let's not wait for third time unlucky.'

'What are you going to do then? Hire a bodyguard? You'd look pretty bloody silly if it did turn out to be an accident.'

'Yes, but it's sensible to assume the worst. On the other hand, that being the case, it would be best not to alert them.'

'You mean they mustn't know that you know?'

'Precisely. I've nothing concrete to go on now. If I drive them underground I'll never dig anything out. No, no bodyguard. That's defensive thinking. Much better to attack in the circumstances.'

'But how?'

'Give me a bloody chance, that's what I'm trying to work out.'

There was a knock on his door. He stopped, glared at it and recommenced walking.

'Pre-emptive strike's what's needed,' he muttered under his breath. 'Nuclear deterrent sort of thingy. Hit them bloody hard before they get a chance to hit again. Knock 'em one between the eyeballs before they even know I'm on to them.'

There was another knock on the door.

'Oh, go away!'

'Philip?'

Hastily he ran to the door and unlocked it.

'Are you all right, Philip?' Mandy asked, looking up at him with her big, wide, stone-melting eyes. 'I hope you don't mind me coming by, I've been so worried about you.'

'Oh no, no not at all. Please come in.'

He offered her his hand and helped her up the narrow step. She handed him a styrofoam cup of coffee.

'I brought this for you, from the catering van. I thought you could probably do with it.'

He was touched. It was more than anyone else had thought of bringing him. He invited her to his corner and they sat down.

'Thanks,' he said. 'You've been very sweet to me already.'

She had been, the most solicitous of all those fussing over him after his narrow escape. If he hadn't been so dazed he might have been able to make up some lost ground. A second chance beckoned.

'How are you feeling?' she asked.

He shrugged gamely. 'Oh, you know . . . It's all been a bit of a shock.'

'I'll bet it has, you poor love.'

She took his hand and squeezed it. He continued giving her his most martyred and vulnerable look. He could see from her concerned reaction she was a sucker for it.

'A little peace and quiet and I'll be fine,' he said with brave restrained nobility. He allowed his eyes to fill with painful resignation.

God but I'm a bloody good actor! he thought admiringly to himself.

'If there's anything I can do for you, Philip,' she said earnestly, 'absolutely anything!'

'Really?' he said with a touch of perkiness. 'Anything at all? Well . . .' He looked as if he was trying to think of something;

and then he looked as if he just had. 'I'd love a little break, wouldn't you? Why don't you have dinner with me tomorrow night?'

Before she could answer there was a perfunctory knock on the door and Ken Kilmaine bounded in, his iron-on grin instantly in place. Philip cursed him roundly under his breath.

'Phi-lip! How you doing, my man?'

'I think he just needs a bit of rest,' said Mandy seriously, getting up to go. 'Perhaps we should leave him in peace.'

'Oh no no!' Philip protested urgently. 'I'm fine, honest!'

He took hold of her gently by the wrist. Ken eyed him shrewdly.

'You sure you're fine, Phi-lip? That looked like a pretty close shave back there.'

'Oh, I wasn't really worried!' Philip lied nonchalantly. 'I could always have done a Buster Keaton. You know, position myself under the window and just walk away afterwards.'

'Yeah, I saw the movie ... Wouldn't like to risk it myself. It could be pretty nasty.'

'It almost was.'

'Yeah.' Ken paused. He looked at him carefully. 'I've given the carpenter a bollocking. It won't happen again.'

'I'm pleased to hear it.'

'Yeah. Right. OK, then, that's all, I just wanted to check you were in one piece.'

'I seem to be, more or less. Thank you for asking.'

'Don't mention it. Cheerio, then. Oh, Mand!'

He was already on his way out. He stopped on the step, the old cockiness back in his voice. 'I checked the schedule, you are on call till seven tomorrow, aren't you? How's about if I send the car round to pick you up at half past, that all right?'

'Oh, yes,' she answered hesitantly.

'Great. I booked a table at that hotel down the road, the Rose Inn. I think you'll like it.'

He skipped out with his oily grin a veritable Torrey Canyon of slickness. Philip felt a sharp sudden gnawing in the pit of his stomach.

'Looks like dinner tomorrow is booked already,' he said with gritted teeth.

'Oh, yes.'

She was embarrassed. He tightened his grip on her wrist.

'Ouch! That hurts!'

He let her go. She took a step towards the door. He felt a savage surge of jealousy. He said suddenly:

'Did you sleep with him to get the part?'

She hit him hard. There were rings on her fingers, he felt them graze his cheek, force the water into his eyes. He didn't flinch.

'A hotel should be convenient. I expect he's got the honeymoon suite booked.'

Shock and anger filled her face. She raised her hand to strike him again.

'Go on,' he said, turning the other cheek. 'Try this side.'

She didn't. Instead, she looked at him with eyes bursting with pain.

'How dare you talk to me like that! How dare you!'

He met her hurt stare coolly.

'Well? Did you?'

'What's it to you? What do you care if I go out with Ken? He's been very good to me, very kind, that's all, and even though it's none of your business, no! No, I haven't slept with him. Yet!'

'Mandy!'

She was rushing for the door. She stopped, but wouldn't meet his eye. 'What does it matter to you anyway?' she demanded miserably. 'I know who you're interested in. I know what you're up to with Shelley.'

'Mandy, it's not what you think — '

'Oh, stop it! You bloody hypocrite! What do you care what happens to me?'

'I care a lot,' he said, but she had gone in as tearful and dramatic an exit as any actress could wish to make. The caravan shook after her fearful slamming of the door. Philip didn't think that the hinges could stand much more.

He couldn't stand that much more himself. He felt bloody awful. He lit a cigarette but nicotine didn't help. The devil came and sat upon his shoulder. His eye strayed to the make-up bag in the corner.

'Go on!' whispered his old forked friend. 'Treat yourself. You know it makes sense.'

'Go away. I don't want to listen to you.'

'You're not going to get rid of me that easily. You're one of my prime assets.'

'Angels and ministers of grace defend us!'

'It's their lunch hour.'

'Sod it, then . . .'

He opened up the bag and like a prize angler gently drew forth the bottle of Scotch which had arrived wearing the KenKil label. With a deft flick of the wrist he broke open the seal and poured out a generous measure into a conveniently placed glass. He swilled the pale liquid gently and held it to the light.

'Be thou a spirit of hell?'

He put the glass to his nose and inhaled deeply. It was the real stuff all right. He tipped back his head and slugged himself.

It was so good he could hardly believe it. Like a caress of raw silk to pleasure the throat; like sexual nectar . . . He thought he'd better have another just to check it was as good as he thought it was.

It was. Maybe even better. He went back into his corner and made himself comfortable. He hugged the bottle to him like a jealous lover.

'My problem in a nutshell . . .' he murmured wryly. 'Never was much good at dealing with the green-eyed monster.'

'Come off it. Do you really have to behave like such a complete prat? Tact, finesse, subtlety . . . is there no limit to your missing accomplishments? Don't you ever learn?'

'No. Look, I'm in a state of shock. I'm not feeling myself.'

'Whom – as the actress said – is kidding whom?'

'Oh God, God. How weary, stale, flat and unprofitable . . .'

He lifted his glass to the light again, turned it till the liquid glittered gold.

And let me the canakin clink, clink;
And let me the canakin clink.

'The liquor is not earthly. This will shake your shaking!'

'The devil damn me black!'

His head was swimming already. One more, he told himself,
no more than one. He had work to do.

He paused even as he put it to his lips. An icy fingernail
scratched lightly on his spine.

'It won't do, you know,' he muttered softly. 'It's just not
on.'

He put the lid back on the bottle and stowed it in his make-up
bag. With a pang of regret he tipped the contents of his glass
down the sink. He returned to his seat and thoughtfully lit
another cigarette.

'You're going to need your wits about you, old man. This is
no time to find yourself in a drunken heap on the floor. This is
Injun territory. Literally . . .'

With his finger he edged back the curtain. No cowboy hat
blocked the window. The TV screen was blank. As he watched,
the door to the caravan was opened and Harve and Marve came
down.

He reduced the gap in the curtains to a hair's-breadth, but they
did not glance in his direction. Instead, they headed over to the
far side of the car park and joined the queue for the caterers' bus.
Philip looked at his watch. Of course, it was tea-time. And even
sedentary cowboys have appetites. He glanced back to the caravan
and caught a glimpse of Shelley through the window. He dropped
the curtain back into place.

He played thoughtfully with his binoculars. He supposed that
once they had eaten they would return and resume their video-
watching. He thought about that, and about what he had just
seen. Was he just going to sit around and wait for another disaster
to happen? Or was he going to do something about it? He noted
the portable phone on the table. He had an idea.

Thoughts black, hands apt, drugs fit, and time agreeing.

He allowed himself a cunning smile. Not a bad idea at all, he thought darkly to himself. Not bad at all.

And he had had a few before now.

II

Anyone engaged in illicit activities had rules of thumb to guide them, Philip supposed. He had three: acute observation; rapid assessment; ruthless action. It took him a night and a morning to complete phases one and two. By lunchtime the next day he was ready to put phase three into operation.

He checked himself carefully in the cupboard mirror at Bradley's end of the caravan. Bradley wasn't called today, so he had the place to himself, a necessary precondition for his plans. The door was locked, the curtains drawn. The master of disguise required privacy.

He brushed the grey wig a little further forward over his forehead and carefully applied another coat of hairspray. It wouldn't do to show the join. He checked the eyebrows, moustache and unfashionable sideboards; all firmly glued. He examined his profiles, let his shoulders slip, his back hunch. He was a bit of a slouch, this fellow; perhaps a touch arthritic in the hip; a variation on his famous Firs (*The Cherry Orchard*, Bristol Old Vic) with a hint of Estragon (*Waiting for Godot*, Oxford Playhouse and national tour). Happy with his redesigned posture, he approached as close as he could to the mirror and scrutinised his face critically.

It was a thorough job, even if he said so himself. He put the character at a well-worn sixty, a little older than he'd first intended but well within his range. Still, he reflected appreciatively to himself, what wasn't?

The details on his face were particularly good. A bulbous nose, red cheeks latticed with the purple of broken capillaries – a fine stippling effect achieved with hard sponge and coloured powder; a Bacchic mechanical, with bad teeth, bad skin and yellow tobacco-stained fingers (Philip believed firmly that a job was not worth doing unless it was done meticulously). A pair of his special plain glass contact lenses banished all but the faintest echo of himself. He reckoned that a panel of judges would have been flint-hearted not to have awarded a perfect ten.

He practised his shuffling bowed walk up and down the caravan. The shoes were scuffed, the blue overalls (clean that morning in the surplus shop) lightly grubbified, the donkey jacket authentically Michael Foot. He tried out the voice: 'Express Services, miss. At your disposal.'

It said 'Express' on the breast-pocket of the overalls. Express what he didn't know, but nor would anyone else. He muttered the phrase over a few times, not quite content with his delivery: it was a little too like Parker to Lady Penelope and no actor worth his salt would court comparison with a *Thunderbirds* puppet, no matter how often a casual glance through the pages of *Spotlight* would seem to disprove this proposition.

Philip muttered his chosen phrases again and again, playing with the inflections, striking a balance between dodderiness and intelligibility. Now he thought he was sounding a little like Clive Dunn, but so long as he remembered not to append an appeal to Captain Mainwaring to every sentence, he thought that he would probably be all right. And in any case, he didn't suppose they got *Dad's Army* in Texas.

With an eye on his watch he repositioned himself carefully at his spying position. Through the tactical crack in the curtains he could see the door and strategically vital far window of the enemy base. The big white cowboy hat was in its accustomed place.

Everything was ready. The portable phone was on the table with his address book beside it open at the right page. When he moved his arm he could feel the weight of the video-cassette in his deep breast-pocket, nestling beside the much-folded black plastic refuse bag. He eased his binoculars from their case and laid them ready. The minutes passed. He wanted them to pass more quickly. He lit a cigarette, tried to calm his pre-performance nerves. It was always best to try and be doing something, activity could smother anxiety. He picked up the phone and dialled

George's number. No answer. He'd tried last night and got his uncle, which was no good at all, although he had been careful to disguise his voice. He would have to try again later. He put out his cigarette and checked his watch. Lunch-time was drawing near.

At almost exactly one o'clock the cowboy hat stirred. Carefully training his binoculars (the curtain and his position were so arranged as to make him invisible from the window where Shelley had spotted him), Philip watched as the little scene unfolded in every hoped-for detail. He felt a sudden adrenalin surge.

Marve was standing up, stretching. Harve was turning off the TV. They both disappeared from view.

A few seconds later the door was opened and they came out. In the moment before they shut the door Philip caught a glimpse of Shelley. He crossed his fingers. As long as she remained there to let him in he would be all right. He didn't think this cowgirl ate lunch.

He walked down to Bradley's end and arranged himself by the window there, in the position where he could best see into the caterers' bus. There wasn't much of a queue, they would be among the first. Even across the width of the car park he could smell the frying.

He saw them board the bus through his binoculars, the trays of food in their hands. He waited for them to sit, to begin their meal. When they were well and truly settled, he got up to go. He winked at himself in the cupboard mirror:

'Knock 'em dead!'

He opened the door carefully, stuck his head out and gave a quick glance to left and right. Nothing, either way. He darted out and cut across the rear of the caravans, keeping them between himself and the double-decker bus. He approached his objective from an oblique angle.

It took a sustained bout of knocking before Shelley answered her door. She did not take the intrusion kindly.

'I'm busy, mister. Why don't you come back later?'

'Sorry, miss, I gotter knock off now, won't take a minute, honest.'

She stared at him suspiciously, in fact so intently that for a moment he thought that he might have been rumbled. But there was no flicker of recognition in her eyes.

'Just who did you say you were, mister?'

Philip pointed to the logo over his breast-pocket.

'Express Cleaning Services. I won't be a tick, love, I just want to empty yer bin.'

Shelley shrugged. 'Gawd knows this place looks enough of a dump. You'd better come on in then, but make sure you're quick about it.'

Philip scrambled eagerly up the step – as rapidly as his arthritic hip would permit.

'Garbage can's under the sink,' said Shelley with a yawn, flopping lazily into her seat and picking up a magazine. She gestured vaguely towards the other end of the caravan. 'You might as well clean off some of that there junk, seeing as you're here. But mind you don't touch nothing you ain't ought to.'

'Oh, I won't, ma'am,' Philip lied effortlessly.

In his own time he walked down to the far end of the caravan, taking the black plastic sack out of his pocket. The table in front of the TV was filled with discarded cans, wrappers and food containers. Slowly – in keeping with his years – he began to scoop them into the bin-bag. He bent low and took a surreptitious upside-down glance through his legs. Shelley was immersed in her magazine.

As he pretended to tidy up in front of the video-recorder he gently nudged the Eject button, coughing to mask the faint whirr of the machine. There was no reaction from Shelley. With another light cough he took hold of the edge of the protruding video-cassette and removed it. A quick glance confirmed that the tape still had about a third left to run, which was perfect: they obviously weren't about to change over to another programme. He dropped it into his plastic bag in one smooth motion. Keeping his back to her, with one hand he transferred some rubbish from the table to the bag while with the other he removed the video-cassette from his pocket. With feigned clumsiness he knocked an empty drink can on to the floor.

'Silly old me!' he muttered with geriatric vagueness. 'Sorry 'bout that!'

He put on a considerable act of arthritic bending as he knelt to mask the recorder. A quick glance confirmed that Shelley's indifference to him was still absolute. A further cough hardly seemed necessary. He gave one, though, for the sake of thorough characterisation, at the same moment presenting the replacement cassette to the recorder, which opened its plastic lips greedily and sucked it into its maw.

Philip took his time regaining his feet. He put the last of the rubbish on the table into the bag and shuffled wearily towards the door.

'Hey, mister!' said Shelley sharply.

He paused, a little startled, at the door. Shelley pointed with irritation at the sink.

'I thought you came for the trash, mister.'

Philip gave a relieved chuckle. 'Right you are, miss. I'll be forgetting me own head next!'

Shelley clearly had no interest in his mental deficiencies. She carried on reading as he opened the cupboard under the sink and transferred the contents of the bin to his now bulging bag.

'Cheerio then, miss,' he called cheerfully from the door on his way out. 'Sorry to bovver you!'

He received no answer and he certainly wasn't going to wait around for one. He scuttled off with a perhaps exaggerated limp and retraced his steps to his own caravan, dropping off the useless refuse bag on the way. There were a few people about but no one appeared to register him, not that it would have mattered.

Hardly had he closed and locked his caravan door behind him than he was tearing off his wig and facial hair and undoing his overalls. He checked the double-decker bus through Bradley's window and confirmed that they were still eating. He wiped off most of his make-up, threw the donkey jacket, overalls and character shoes into the bottom of his cupboard, then settled down with his binoculars by Bradley's window. He was not kept waiting long.

There was a burst of activity in the double-decker and the

tell-tale white blur of the hat began to move. Philip returned to his own end of the caravan and took up position one. Now it all came down to a matter of timing. He picked up the phone, consulted his address book and rang the local police station.

'Quick! Come quick!' he yelped urgently into the phone before the man who answered it could finish speaking. 'There's been a serious incident, I think someone's going to be killed!'

'Calm down, sir,' said the policeman matter-of-factly. 'Can I ask who's calling?'

Philip took a deep breath. His version of the voice wasn't perfect but it was good enough:

'My name's Wayne Schlesinger, you may have heard of me. I'm working on the movie in Black Park. Please, officer, you've gotta come quick. There's no time for explanations, but believe me, there's a very serious incident taking place right now this very instant even as we speak and if you don't come soon someone's gonna be murdered — '

'All right, sir, if you could just give me the details — '

'For God's sake, man, there's no time for that! We're in the car park, get someone round here right away or it may be too late! Oh, no! It may be already! Please send help, I'm going to be cut off, we're in the car park, you've got that? Oh God, you've got to come — '

Philip hurled the phone down suddenly, cutting himself off in mid-sentence. He had worked himself up to a crescendo and there was nowhere further for him to go. Either the policeman bought it or he didn't; he could only hope. And if anyone tried to elicit an intelligible explanation from the real Wayne Schlesinger he could only wish them luck.

He peered through the crack in the curtains. Harve and Marve had left the bus and were crossing the car park. Philip took off his watch and laid it on the table. He hoped that he had left enough time, but there was no way of telling. The police station was nearby and the location well known (a local bobby had been in several times to liaise about security), but he knew that he was trusting a great deal to luck. In the circumstances there wasn't much more he could do than touch wood and cross his fingers.

Harve and Marve mounted the steps of Shelley's caravan and disappeared momentarily from view. A few seconds passed and then the white hat appeared in its customary place in front of the window. Through his binoculars Philip could just make out Harve standing by the video-recorder. Then he too came and sat down by the window.

The TV was on. Philip could just see the middle third of it, between the two heads. For a few seconds the screen was blank. Then a picture appeared. Philip hardly dared breathe as he concentrated on holding the binoculars steady.

A spindly, pasty-white torso filled the screen. The head on its shoulders was shaking from side to side, the features contorted in an expression of either pain or pleasure.

In the right foreground of his picture Philip saw the profile of Harve turn in towards Marve. He thought he detected a comically bemused expression. Though unskilled in lip-reading, he fancied he could follow the mouth movements saying something like:

'That's funny! What's this?'

There was no response from Marve. The ten-gallon hat remained rigidly still.

The picture on the TV screen changed to a long shot. Now it was apparent that the spindly man was administering enthusiastically to a large-breasted naked blonde who was bent face-down over a black couch. The camera moved in for a close-up of the woman's face, which was every bit as contorted as the man's.

Slowly the big white hat turned to the side, blocking out most of the view. Again Philip did his lip-reading act. In strong, demotic language Marve appeared to be asking for some kind of an explanation.

Philip could have filled him in. Dr Dildo was simply giving one of his famous prescriptions to Miss Shelley Lamour.

'Mm, talk of the devil,' Philip murmured to himself with considerable satisfaction.

For there she was, the soap queen herself, as large as life and filling up the rest of the window. Her mouth was working so furiously that this time Philip could not even begin to decipher the words. Although the light inside was not good, he did have the distinct impression that her face had turned a shade of over-ripe tomato. Suddenly the white hat rose and for a moment the massive shoulders of her husband completely blocked the view. And then the caravan began to shake.

At first Philip thought it was his hand trembling with excitement, but as he swept his binoculars along the caravan he realised that it really was moving violently up and down, almost as if it were at the epicentre of an earth tremor. It might have been his imagination, but Philip fancied that he heard a faint, distant cry of pain. He turned his attention back to the window.

Harve and Marve had disappeared from view. Shelley was there, though, both of her. On screen she was writhing about like a jelly wrestler under Dr Dildo. In real life she was preparing to throw a lamp-stand at the TV.

At almost exactly the same moment as she did so and the TV exploded, the door to the caravan was flung open and Harve tumbled out, followed by Marve who was yelling incoherently at the top of his voice. The racket brought people running from all directions, but none ran so fast as Harve. And with 250 pounds of steaming cowboy on his tail, Philip reflected, who could blame him?

Harve was running blindly in his direction (perhaps literally blindly, for he had lost his glasses at some stage during the recent eruptions). His arms were flailing wildly, sheer terror must have given his pudgy body wings. He hurtled past Philip's window and, for reasons best known to himself, threw himself at the door. Philip heard him clawing desperately at the other side.

'He's gonna kill me!' Harve screamed. 'You've gotta let me in!'

Fat chance, thought Philip snugly.

'Please!' Harve whined. 'Unlock the door, have mercy!'

Philip leant back casually and lit a cigarette.

'Really!' he tut-tutted under his breath. 'You're being very silly, you could have got away by now.'

He lifted back the corner of the curtain and glanced out of the window again. Marve's bull-like carcase almost filled the frame.

'Unfortunate choice of refuge, I'm afraid. Better luck next time . . .'

Harve uttered a piercing, dwindling scream, like a man plunging over an abyss, and Philip's own caravan began to shake. He heard the ominous smacking sound of knuckles striking flesh. He gave a semi-sympathetic wince.

'Mm, perhaps there won't be a next time. I wonder where the relief column's got to?'

As if on cue, he heard the sound of a siren coming down the lane. He gave a silent whoop for joy and punched the air. Then he walked down to the far end of the caravan, put an innocent expression on his face and stuck it out of the window.

'I say,' he said, putting on a bit of a Bertie Wooster act. 'What are you chaps up to?'

If they heard him they gave no indication, though Philip supposed that trampling elephants would not have impinged on poor Harve's consciousness. He was, in a manner of speaking, already being trampled by one anyway:

Harve, face and clothes torn and covered with mud, was being used as a trampoline by his erstwhile host.

'Please, Marve!' the helpless scribbler hissed between jackhammer blows from his size 12 feet. 'I don't know nothing about it, you gotta believe me!'

But alas for Harve, his credibility had been fatally undermined.

By now quite a crowd was gathering. Philip heard the siren drawing nearer. One of the third assistants, either braver or more foolish than the rest, dared to stand out from the crowd.

'Please, Mr Loudwater!' he declared with quavering voice. 'I think you'd better leave him alone now, please.'

Philip doubted that the effete Englishness of the appeal would have much effect, but just in case, Miss Shelley Lamour was on hand to forestall any weakening of her husband's resolve. She slammed her elbow into the third assistant's ribs and sent him sprawling. 'You just kick the shit out of that son of a bitch, Marve!' she screamed, shaking her fist at the practically inert body on the ground. 'Kick his ass to hell!'

'I sure will, honey!' the cowboy snarled between vicious toe pokes. 'Ain't gonna let nobody insult my baby.'

From the way Harve was slumped like a rag doll Philip didn't

167

suppose that he'd be insulting anybody for a while to come. But just to emphasise his point Marve seized the lifeless body by the lapels and began to bash the head into the ground.

Two policemen appeared in the crowd. They exchanged a quick glance and ran to Harve's assistance. One attempted to grab Marve by the shoulder.

Marve spun round furiously and punched him on the nose. The policeman was flung back against the side of the caravan.

Better and better! thought Philip gleefully.

The other policeman had produced a truncheon. He pointed it at the snarling cowboy:

'You're nicked, mate!'

The other policeman pulled himself up from the ground, wiping blood from his nose.

'Do you want to do the business or shall I?' his friend with the truncheon asked.

'My pleasure entirely,' said the other, producing a pair of handcuffs.

There followed a brief but entertaining exchange in which the law officer suggested that the cowboy might like to accompany him to the station and the cowboy suggested in return that he might like to stick his head up his butt. Policemen are very rarely amused by this kind of witty response and these two were no exception. A further request to come quietly was made for form's sake, elicited no response and led directly to a scuffle, in the course of which Marve aimed several wild blows which failed to connect, while the policeman with the truncheon hit him repeatedly over the head. Eventually the towering Texan toppled over and the bleeding policeman handcuffed him. It was so much like a Punch and Judy show that Philip, who held a ringside seat, felt like applauding. When the dust had settled and the bodies were being dragged away (an ambulance had been summoned for the hapless Harve) he reluctantly let the curtain fall back into place and returned to his own end of the caravan. He pulled the Scotch bottle from his make-up bag and poured himself a drink.

'Just a small one,' he said reassuringly to his reflection in the full-length mirror. 'A very small one.'

He couldn't begrudge himself that for a job so very well done. He knocked it back with immense satisfaction. He winked at the mirror.

'Two birds with one stone. Pretty bloody classic, I'd say.'

He sat back down in his place and reached for his address book and phone. This time George answered.

'I'm glad it's you,' Philip began. 'Is your uncle in?'

'No, he bleedin' well ain't!' George replied, none the less dropping his voice to a harsh whisper. 'He'll kill me if he finds out you rung. How'd you get our number, anyway?'

'The phone book.'

'Oh yeah, I hadn't thought of that . . .'

'No one ever does. George, I need your help, tonight.'

'Yeah? What's in it for me?'

'One of the things I like about you, George, is your admirable directness. How about fifty quid?'

'Fifty quid? What do you want me to nick?'

'Nothing.'

'Want me to do someone over, then?'

'George, you have the physique of an underfed chicken. If I want anyone "doing over", as you so quaintly put it, I shall recruit in more appropriate quarters. I want you in your chauffeur's cap tonight. Can you get the car?'

'Dunno.'

'Fifty smackers, Georgie boy. Two Shakespeares and a Nightingale.'

'Yeah, all right, but you gotta pay for the petrol.'

'It's a deal. I want you to meet me at half past seven outside the Crooked Billet — you know, that pub by the roundabout on the way to Kenneth Kilmaine's house. Wait in the car park.'

'That's in Iver, that's bloody miles away!'

'What do you expect for fifty quid?'

'Yeah, but I can't go out of London again — '

'You know, I was thinking today,' Philip cut in smoothly, 'I was thinking it must be about time we had another acting lesson. Wouldn't you agree?'

There was a longish pause while George thought about it.

'Yeah,' he said carefully when he had thought about it. 'Seven-thirty, all right. What if I can't get the motor?'

'Then I'm sure you'll be able to find a good local amateur dramatic society.'

Philip terminated the conversation abruptly. He turned the page of the address book and dialled again.

'KenKil Productions, can I help you?' demanded a familiar twangy voice in the mechanical tone of an airport announcement.

Philip cleared his throat. The man of a thousand faces – and voices – spoke: 'Er, is that Shaz?'

'Might be. Who wants to know?'

'Er, it's Steve here, on the set.'

'Oh yeah. How you doing, Steve?'

'Er, fine thanks . . .' Philip shrugged. As far as he was aware there was no one called Steve on the set. 'Look, Shaz, Mr Kilmaine asked me to give you a buzz. He says, can you come down here and meet him for dinner tonight.'

'Tonight? Oh, I dunno about that, Steve. Tonight's not really convenient, Ken knows that, I said I'd do me mum's hair.'

'Shaz, I know he'll be really upset. He's booked a table, and – I know I shouldn't tell you this, but he's ordered some flowers special.'

'Ah. Ain't that sweet. Where's he booked a table?'

'The Rose Inn.'

'Ooh, I really like that place! I had scampi and chips last time we went there!'

'And a prawn cocktail to start?'

'Here, how'd you know that?'

'Just a guess. Can I take that as a yes, then? He'll be ever so chuffed.'

'All right. I suppose.'

'He says, can you order a cab to bring you down.'

'Cheeky. Why can't he send the car?'

'He's given the chauffeur the night off. Will you meet him at the Rose Inn then, eight o'clock?'

'Yeah, I'll be there.'

'Oh, and Shaz – I got a message from Ken.'

'Yeah?'

'Wear the garter-belt.'

'Saucy!'

Philip put down the phone feeling exhausted. Even for him two Machiavellian schemes in one day was painting the lily. He hoped that he would have time for a quick lie-down before his afternoon call.

In the event he was only able to snatch a quick cat-nap, but it was enough to refortify him. He was actually called on time for a change because Shelley had disappeared – apparently she was attempting to fix bail for her husband – and they were skipping a scene. The destroyed set had been rebuilt overnight and Philip was summoned to complete the work so rudely interrupted the day before.

'I'm very sorry about yesterday,' he whispered in Mandy's ear before they went on. 'Please forgive me, I wasn't feeling myself.'

Her reaction was confused but not unkind. Perhaps she was mindful of the awful narrowness of his recent escape, or maybe it was just the irrepressible sweetness of her nature. Either way Philip did not press her. He certainly had no intention of bringing up the subject of her dinner date with Ken. He wanted to keep the *bombe surprise* on the menu secret.

Later, as shooting for the day finished and they prepared to go their separate ways, the second assistant informed him confidentially that Shelley's attempts to spring the Hulk had thus far proved unsuccessful. Furthermore, not only were the coppers planning to keep him chained up overnight, they were also intending to oppose bail in court the next morning, for Harvey Goldman was in a critical condition in hospital and more serious charges than assault and battery might very well be pending. All in all, Philip was able to reflect, it had been a pretty satisfying day's work. He trusted that the night's work would prove as rewarding.

He supposed that he would have to pay some sort of a fine for losing the video shop's copy of *Dr Dildo and the Busty Bimbos*.

12

The Rev. Washington's blue Ford was already in the car park when, after a brisk walk, Philip arrived outside the Crooked Billet at twenty-five past seven. George was listening to some frightful loud racket on the radio and did not notice his approach. He gave a startled gasp as the passenger door was pulled open and Philip slipped in smoothly beside him.

'What the . . .' George did not one but two double takes, a kind of quadraphonic over-reaction.

Philip turned off the radio. 'It's only me,' he said firmly.

George seemed reluctant to believe him. 'What you done to your hair?'

'It's a wig, George. A disguise.'

He turned the driving-mirror towards his face, checked himself out. It was the same grey wig he had used earlier, with a matching moustache. However, the only further detail this time was a pair of plain-lensed wire-framed spectacles. Tonight he would not require full-scale concealment; this was just to deflect a casual glance.

'You look fucking weird, mate,' George opined.

'And you suppose you don't? What a singular young man you are. Just drive, George. I'll give you directions.'

Ten minutes later they were parked across the road from the Rose Inn. Philip trained his binoculars on the large bay windows to the left, through which he could see much of the dining-room. The interior was too dark for a perfect view but it was tolerable.

Philip consulted his watch. 'I know the table was booked for seven-thirty. They're probably having a drink in the bar.'

'I don't blame them,' muttered George. 'You gonna tell me what this is about then?'

'No.'

At five to eight Philip began to get anxious. He wanted them to be sitting at a quiet candlelit table for two when Shaz showed up; if they were still at the bar it would not be nearly incriminating enough. Reluctantly – for his disguise was so very considerably below par – he concluded that a scouting mission was required. He told George to sit tight.

The Rose Inn turned out to have three bars. They were not in any of them. He bought a drink in the third one, waited a minute, then carried it casually through the other two. He marched boldly into the dining-room and when a waiter accosted him said he was looking for the cloakroom. While allowing himself to be redirected he carefully scrutinised every corner. Ken and Mandy were not in any of them. It was five past eight. He went out thoughtfully into the foyer and wondered which line to adopt next. Before he had come to a conclusion, Shaz swept in through the front door wearing a dress so short it barely covered her armpits. Philip ducked back discreetly into the nearest bar, keeping her just within eyeline and earshot. He heard her ask for Ken Kilmaine's table.

Philip saw the head waiter at his desk looking into the reservations book. The frown on his face was disquieting.

'Mr Kilmaine's table?' he repeated, tapping his finger against the page. 'I'm sorry, madam, but the reservation's been cancelled.'

'Eh?' Shaz looked at him blankly (no change there, thought Philip). 'You kidding or what?'

'No, madam,' the waiter repeated with that tone of effortless snootiness so prized by his ilk. 'Mr Kilmaine phoned to cancel his reservation this afternoon. I took the call myself.'

'What?' Shaz whined incredulously. 'I'm fed up with him always mucking me about like this. I could have done me mum's hair tonight, you know that?'

Without giving the waiter a chance to respond to this broadly rhetorical question, she turned smartly on her stilettos and trotted as fast as her tight little dress would allow to the door, muttering disconsolately, 'He's always doing this to me, the toe-rag, I bet me bleeding taxi's gone and all.'

But it hadn't – her one consolation of the evening. Through the bar window Philip saw her rush out into the road and hail down the minicab, which had just completed a laborious three-point turn. By the time he had got across to George's car the rear lamps of the cab were disappearing round the corner.

'Do you want me to follow that cab, then?' George demanded eagerly.

'No,' replied Philip through pursed lips. George looked crest-fallen. 'Just head back the way we came, please.'

'You still not gonna tell me what's going on?'

'That is correct. Drive, please.'

He wasn't sure what was going on himself. All he knew was that disaster loomed: somewhere Ken and Mandy were enacting the scene he had expected to witness in the Rose Inn. Somewhere, but where? His chief spoke-in-the-wheel had just buggered off, but if he didn't improvise another, if first he didn't find them, then how would the evening end? Appalling images stormed his private mental cinema: take one with the leering unscrupulous Ken and the pretty, ingenuous Mandy; gaining her trust with his slimy, seductive wiles, plying her with drink, then casually brushing his hand against her knee, then –

'Christ!'

He gripped the edge of the upholstery in a sudden paroxysm of jealousy. What doubly galled him was the certainty that in Ken's place he would have been working to exactly the same script.

'You all right?' demanded George.

'Yes!' Philip hissed. 'Just drive.'

But where to? He screwed up his eyes and thought hard. If Ken and he really were on the same wavelength (it gave him pause), then it was easy. What would he have done? What did he usually do? It didn't matter.

The realisation struck him suddenly. The restaurant scene was only a prologue and the location immaterial. The climax would be the bedroom scene.

'Turn left at the roundabout,' he instructed George tersely. 'We're going to Kilmaine's house.'

He looked at his watch. Wherever they were they could only just have started the meal, he ought to have enough time to think of something. He had always known that he might have to improvise anyway, that the sudden appearance of Shaz could have been insufficient to throw the oily Ken out of kilter, but at least there ought to have been a good chance of some fireworks. He had to think of something else to sabotage Ken's evening, and whatever it was it had better be bloody good. He took deep breaths, forced himself to concentrate. But after ten minutes' driving nothing illuminating had stirred in the panic-ridden recesses of his brain.

There was a pub opposite the entrance to Ken's house and Philip directed George to the far end of its car park. He rattled out his orders in a crisp military tone: 'Wait here. I may need you. Keep your head down.'

Philip crossed the road, stopped outside the entrance and casually lit a cigarette. After a moment he glanced up and took in the house at the end of the drive. Quite a few of the downstairs lights were on. A head bobbed in and out of view behind one of the kitchen windows on the left.

He ground out his barely smoked cigarette, checked that no one was looking, and slipped inside the entrance. He headed left, feeling his way along the line of the wall on the edge of the lawn. He could just see the outlines of the flowerbeds in the faint light spilling from the house.

He picked up a hedge and followed its bulky shadow almost up to the side of the house, from where he could see through a small window into part of the kitchen. The head he had seen earlier belonged to the Mrs Danvers character. It was bent over a tray, on to which she was arranging plates. She picked up the tray and carried it out into the hall, turning to the left as she went through the door. He moved stealthily across the lawn towards the back of the house, shadowing her.

He knew where she was going and he guessed what he would find when he got there, but the sight which greeted him when at last he peered through a crack in the dining-room curtains still made him shudder.

Ken and Mandy were at one end of the long table at which he had sat recovering from Marve's assault during the party. Candlelight played on their faces, and on the fluted glass which she was holding and he refilling with champagne. Philip heard the faint tinkle of her laugh and felt nauseous.

He watched Ken Kilmaine at work through a vert and gules haze. No wonder he'd cancelled the restaurant, this was a gift. Mrs Danvers was clearing their plates and preparing to offer them what looked like dessert. By God, they must have bolted it down! Either that or he'd got her there early, to finish the prologue quickly and get the decks stripped for action. While he'd been sitting like a lemon outside the Rose Inn the damage was already being done. That couldn't have been their first bottle, it was much too full, and look at her – Mandy – giggling like a schoolgirl as she knocked it back; a naughty, tipsy schoolgirl.

'Oh my God . . .'

He clapped his hands over his face. He could hardly bear even to peep through his fingers. He forced himself to watch as Ken finished filling her glass and drew his hand away slowly, trailing a finger and lightly caressing her wrist with the back of his nail. In the state she was in, she didn't even notice. A cup of tea and she'd be anybody's.

'Shit!' Philip barked.

He had to think clearly and fast: if they were on dessert already they wouldn't have long to go. What was next? Coffee followed by an invitation to see Ken's etchings? From the look of her that was about as subtle as he'd need to get. Perhaps he wouldn't even suggest an adjournment; he'd just ravish her over the After Eights. No, that wasn't his style. A man of his tastes would want to show off his water-bed, he'd want –

The water-bed . . . No, Philip told himself, don't be ridiculous. Yes, he answered back, why not? It was drastic action or bust . . .

Philip backed off grimly, felt his way along the hedge back out on to the lawn and into darkness and took in the dimensions of the house. He counted carefully along the upstairs windows, reconstructing the interior layout from memory. The second window from the end had to be Ken's bedroom. A terrible image seared his brain – Mandy half-drunk and semi-comatose upon the water-bed and Ken leering over her, a prescription from Dr Dildo in his hand . . .

Swallowing his jealous bile, he crept softly round the back of the house. He stopped outside the garden door which he remembered looking through at the party. It was very dark here, the only light was a dim one on the first-floor landing. A window fifteen feet above him was slightly open.

Suddenly he caught a movement out of the corner of his eye. He wheeled round, startled, and saw a human shape detach itself from the shadows mere feet away.

'Philip Fletcher, I presume,' whispered a hoarse, sepulchral voice.

Philip lashed out blindly. It was more of a nervous twitch than a blow of intent, but it connected and caused a terrified yelp.

''Ere! It's only me!'

He reached for the voice. His hand closed on the soft flesh of the throat and he squeezed hard. 'Do that again, George, and I'll break your fucking neck!' he hissed furiously.

He released his grip on the throat and George fell to his knees, coughing and spluttering. 'I was only joking,' he murmured feebly.

'Ha bloody ha,' Philip spat out angrily, just about resisting the temptation to administer a savage kicking. Instead, he grabbed him roughly by the collar and yanked him to his feet. 'I thought I told you to stay put.'

'Yeah, I know, I know,' said George, shrinking away. 'I got bored.'

'Oh, really? Well, poor you, I'll have to see how I can keep you entertained.'

Philip shrugged him off and turned his attention back to the house. It occurred to him that if George had been able to find him, then he might be visible from within, so he retreated a few steps back towards the greenhouses, pulling George along with him. He whispered into his ear, 'Seeing as you're here, you might as well make yourself useful. You see that open window on the first floor? Could you climb up into it?'

'Piece of piss.'

'I thought you might say that. Good. Now, listen carefully. When you've got through the window you'll see a narrow back staircase to your right. Come straight down and it will bring you to this door in front of us. I presume you'll be able to open it from the inside, but if not you'll have to try one of these ground-floor windows. Now, when you come to the door there's a corridor behind you, can you see? It leads to the dining-room and there are people in there, so you'll have to be very quiet. As far as I know, the only other person inside is in the kitchen on the other side of the house. Have you got all that?'

'Yeah. Why d'you want to get in there?'

'I really don't have time to answer that question now. Just don't screw up and there'll be another fifty quid in it for you. One more thing, you don't have a knife on you by any chance, do you?'

'What, are you gonna stick somebody?'

'You, if you keep asking bloody questions. Have you got a knife or haven't you?'

'Yeah. It's only a penknife, though. If you want to do some damage, you — '

'Just give me the sodding knife, George. Good. Thank you. Now get on with it.'

George crept off directly towards the house without replying. Philip pocketed the knife, reflecting that in the role of moral guardian he was so far failing to shine.

George disappeared from view amidst the shadows under the eaves. Philip crouched on the lawn and waited patiently. After a minute or so he heard a faint rustle by the corner of the house and a delicate scraping sound as a black amorphous shape detached itself from the even blacker background. The shape moved dimly up the wall and then along what must have been a narrow ledge. It stopped outside the open window, then disappeared inside in one fluent, rapid movement.

Another minute passed and the shape reappeared behind the glass panels of the garden door. Philip heard a click from inside as he crept across the grass towards it. The door was opened and he slipped inside.

'George, you're a genius.'

It was so dark inside that Philip couldn't actually see him, but he felt his presence. He glanced along the corridor and saw a spillage of light from under the dining-room door. He lowered his whisper still further: 'Get back to the car, please, and stay there this time. We may have to make a quick getaway. I'll need about five minutes.'

George slipped out wordlessly and Philip closed the door behind him. He paused, adjusting his eyes and ears. He felt his way along to the foot of the staircase.

He climbed the stairs one by one, on tiptoe. He could hear nothing through the thick dining-room door, but he had been caught out by a creaking floorboard on a previous illicit break-in and he was taking no chances. Once at the top of the stairs he went stealthily to the right. He stopped outside the door through which he had once heard Wayne Schlesinger's lunatic groans.

This time it wasn't locked. He pushed down the handle and stepped smartly inside. Heart thumping, he stood on the threshold of Ken's bedroom.

He had been debating whether or not to risk turning on the light, but there was no need. A dozen or so red candles, strategically dotted about, bathed the room in a subdued, ruddy glow. Those by the bedside illumined the fresh black satin sheets neatly turned back on the water-bed. A champagne bucket and two glasses stood within easy reach, under the largest of the grinning photographs. Philip stared grimly at his antagonist's fatuous portrait.

'You shameless goat,' he murmured, fighting to repress an instinctive twinge of admiration. 'Think you're pretty clever, don't you? Well, we'll soon see about that. Ha!'

He walked towards the water-bed, removing George's penknife from his pocket. He unclasped the blade and felt the point. It wasn't sharp, but it would do.

'Oh, yes, we'll see about that all right. I'd like to be a fly on the wall when you've got her blotto enough to follow you up here. Fling open the door thinking you're going to have your smarmy way with her on your disgustingly naff water-bed when suddenly, bingo! It's Noah's flood! Hope you've got life-jackets handy. Not going to be much room for your greasy manoeuvres with the Fire Brigade swarming all over the place and you knee-deep in H_2O ...'

With a savage smirk of self-satisfaction he knelt down and plunged the knife into the foot of the water-bed.

And the knife plunged straight back out again, leaving not the slightest impression.

He tried again, this time thrusting so forcefully that his entire fist was enfolded in the rubbery material. But when he withdrew it again, not so much as a spot of water dampened his knuckles.

He went and picked up a candle from the sideboard, knelt down again and examined the point of his attack. There wasn't a mark. He tried pushing in the tip of the knife slowly. Still not a tear. He swore crossly and tried the other blades.

After trying in vain for several minutes to twist the tip of the corkscrew into the bed he gave up, returning the knife to his pocket with some disgust. He reflected that if it was typical of latter-day stainless steel products, then it was impossible to feel sanguine about the future of the Boy Scout movement.

He glanced up and saw the grinning photograph of Ken Kilmaine. His eyes n   d.

'Not so fast, sunshine ...'

How did you fill a water-bed, anyway? There had to be a plug or something, like on a lilo. He got down on to his hands and knees and began a methodical inspection.

There was nothing in sight, no obvious plughole or plastic nipple. He peered round the back of the bed.

It wasn't quite flush to the wall, there was a little space. His hand closed around something hard and rectangular. He felt along the top and discovered a handle and catches. It was a brief-case. He returned his attention to the back of the bed and found it smooth. He got up to have a look round the other side.

As he thrust his hand through the gap between the bed and the wall he heard voices. He glanced up at the door and saw a sliver of light appear along the bottom. Ken Kilmaine's oleaginous laugh sounded somewhere out in the corridor.

Philip looked around desperately for a hiding-place. There was a door to his left, slightly ajar, through which he could see the edge of a bath. He took one faltering step towards it and stopped. No, he had bad memories of hiding in bathrooms. He looked again and saw a clothes cupboard. He didn't have particularly good memories of cupboards either, but at least this one looked roomy.

It wasn't really. A couple of suitcases occupied one end, and Philip had to squeeze in between shoes and assorted boxes in order to conceal himself fully. He was still settling down and had only just pulled the sliding-door to behind him when Ken Kilmaine slithered into the bedroom.

'Come on in, then,' Philip heard him murmur coaxingly. 'Do you want to see the rest of the house or don't you?'

Hardly daring to breathe, Philip perched himself precariously upon a pile of loose footwear. He peered out through the narrow crack he had left in the sliding-doors.

Mandy was standing uncertainly in the doorway. Ken wandered casually over to the top of the water-bed.

'Is this your bedroom, then?' Mandy asked hesitantly.

Philip cringed. He felt like a children's nurse witnessing the Slaughter of the Innocents.

'Sure is,' replied the vile seducer smoothly. Then, in an outrageous tone of surprise: 'Hey, look! Someone's left a bottle of champagne!'

Halle-bloody-lujah! Philip thought, grinding his teeth. What with having a few hundred pounds' worth of Gucci toe-caps sticking up his arse, his teeth were pretty much on edge anyway.

'Um, I think I've had enough to drink actually, thanks,' said Mandy quietly.

'Oh, come on!' answered Ken with a laugh. 'The night is young, my dear.'

Ken popped the champagne cork expertly. Reluctantly Mandy accepted the fizzing glass.

'Why don't you come on in, then?' Ken murmured softly in

her ear, moving in behind her shoulder. He posed for a moment like a vulture before dipping his lips suddenly towards her bare neck.

She stepped into the room just quickly enough to avoid his fleshy peck. His face split from ear to ear as he pushed the door shut with a flick of the wrist.

Philip squirmed. He didn't know how much more of this he could take.

'Why, you're not drinking your champagne,' Ken observed jokily.

'Um, no thanks, I really have had en —'

'Come on, come on . . . You've got to drink to this.' He lifted his own glass and clinked it against hers. 'To your glittering future as a movie star!'

She took a tiny sip. Ken put his glass down on the sideboard.

'What do you think of my water-bed?'

(Philip just about managed not to tell him.)

'Water-bed?' Mandy clearly hadn't seen it for what it was. 'Oh. Um, jolly nice.'

'Oh, yes, it is.' Ken sat down on the edge, sinking gently into the knife-proof material. He patted the space next to him. 'And amazingly comfortable too.'

Mandy laughed nervously. She pointed suddenly at the photograph over the bed.

'Nice picture!' she blurted out.

'Thanks,' said Ken without looking round. He patted the bed again. 'Why don't you sit down? Take the weight off your feet.'

Right, said Philip to himself, that's it! Sod the consequences, if Ken tried to lay a finger on her once more he'd be out of that cupboard and have his hands round the oily bastard's throat quicker than you could say Desdemona . . .

'Thanks, Ken,' said Mandy, 'it's been a lovely evening but I really think I should be going —'

'What are you talking about? It's not even nine o'clock!'

'I know, but I'm filming in the morning. I did tell you and you promised I could have a cab to take me home early —'

'But Mand . . .' Ken spread his hands in his favourite pseudo-conciliatory gesture. 'You haven't even finished your drink yet. Come and sit beside me, I want to talk to you. Just for a moment.'

'But —'

'I'm doing another film, Mand, straight after this one. There's a really juicy part in it, would suit you down to the ground. Come and sit down, let's discuss it . . .'

Philip had never heard anything so transparent in his life; why, it made *him* look subtle. He felt instinctively for the penknife in his pocket. It might be insufficient for puncturing rubber, but it would do for wiping the elastic grin off Ken's face.

Slowly, and with evident reluctance, Mandy went over, perching herself on the very edge of the bed. Ken gave her the full view of his shark-like teeth.

'There, that's better,' he said soothingly. 'I've got to go to Switzerland on Friday on business. Be back Sunday. Thought perhaps you might like to come with me. You could probably do with a break.'

Mandy blushed uncontrollably.

'I really, um . . .' she stammered. 'Look, if you want to talk about your film I think you'd better speak to my agent.'

She tried to get up but he grabbed her by the wrist and held her back. Champagne spilled from the glass she was still holding.

'Now look what I've done!' exclaimed Ken mock apologetically, taking the glass from her and putting it down on the floor. 'Clumsy old me!'

He produced a handkerchief and lingeringly rubbed her thigh, somewhat unnecessarily in view of the fact that the champagne had only splashed the bed.

Philip shivered with jealousy. The tiny penknife was gripped tight in his sweaty palm. Any moment now and he would spring out of the cupboard like an avenging demon.

'Thanks, um . . .' said Mandy, trying to push Ken's hand away. 'That's, er, all right.'

'Good,' he replied, leaving his hand exactly where it was. 'What do you think about Switzerland then?'

'But . . .' Mandy looked totally confused. 'But I'm filming on Saturday.'

'Then I'll change the schedule. I'm the man who calls the shots in this outfit, baby, and don't you forget it!'

And suddenly he made his move, like a snake striking in the grass.

It was no more subtle than anything that had preceded it. He simply grabbed her round the shoulders, threw her back on to the bed and leapt on top. What happened next, though, was quite unexpected.

Especially to Philip. His hand was already on the edge of the door, another second and his cover would have been blown to smithereens. Perhaps fortunately for Ken, his went first.

Mandy flung up her arm blindly to fend him off. He tried to force his mouth on to hers and she grabbed at his hair. He jerked back his head with a yelp and his wig came off cleanly in her hands.

There was a moment of stunned surprise and then Mandy burst into laughter.

At first it was little more than a giggle, a girlish titter masked by the back of her hand, but as the seconds passed and Ken's body remained frozen rigid while a succession of violent emotions erupted spasmodically across his face, her laughter became frankly hysterical. She rolled out from under him clutching her sides in apparent agony.

'I'm sorry. I'm so-so-sorry!' she spluttered, making an attempt to straighten her face. But when she looked at Ken and saw his expression of mixed outrage and embarrassment, the foxy eyebrows crossed in horror beneath the undreamt-of startling naked skull, it got too much for her and she doubled up so violently that she fell off the bed. A moment later she thrust her hand back up into view and waved the wig from side to side.

'Cooee!'

'Give-it-back!' stammered Ken furiously.

She avoided his wild grab, sat up against the wall and clutched the wig to her breast.

'No, you can't have it! I'm going to keep it for a pet. I'm going to call it Wally. Wally Wig . . .'

Ken made another wild lunge but she rolled out of his reach with her prize pressed close. She added:

'Or maybe Trevor Toupee . . .'

This time she laughed so loudly the floor shook, for which Philip at least was grateful: he was having great difficulty in controlling his own snickers.

'Give it back. NOW!' Ken screamed, his face alternately red and white with rage. He looked like a lobster in a cream sauce. With an egg on top.

She tried to turn away again, to shield the wig from his flailing hands, but she was too weak to resist. With a vicious jerk he pulled her round and snatched the crushed and somewhat battered rug from her grasp. He slammed it back down over his pate. For a moment she stopped laughing, then she pointed up at him weakly and started all over again: 'You've . . . got it on the wrong way round!'

Her mouth opened and shut in hysterical overdrive but no sound came out. She had no strength left in her. Her body shook helplessly with dry laughter.

Philip, stretched out upon his unlikely bed of designer leather and crocodile, sympathised. A terrible ache had spread out from his solar plexus and was engulfing him. His eyelids fluttered open and shut furiously in an attempt to control the flow of tears.

Ken snatched the lopsided rug off his head and stormed off furiously into the bathroom, slamming the door behind him. Philip breathed silent thanks that he had chosen an alternative place of concealment.

Slowly, painfully, Mandy dragged herself to her feet, still clutching her jellified ribs. She caught her reflection in a small mirror over the sideboard. 'God, I look a mess,' she murmured, wiping smudged make-up off her cheek.

It was all Philip could do to resist the temptation to rush out and give her a great big hug. Ken strode back in angrily with his wig set back properly and went straight to the phone. He didn't look at Mandy.

'What are you doing?' she asked, now sounding very embarrassed.

'Calling you a cab,' he answered tersely.

'Oh. Um, thanks . . .' She indicated the bathroom. 'Er, actually I think I'd like to go in there, please.'

He didn't respond. After a moment she slipped past him and went in anyway. Philip heard the sound of running water.

Ken ordered the taxi and banged the phone down again hard. He was obviously still very angry. With fists clenched and shoulders hunched he began to pace furiously up and down the room. He stopped suddenly.

A puzzled expression came on to his face. He walked over to the back of the bed, bending down slowly. Philip had to adjust his position in order to get a glimpse of what he was up to.

Ken sat down on the edge of the bed and picked something up off the floor. It was the candlestick which Philip had put down earlier in the course of his search for the plug-hole. He had forgotten about that.

The candle was still burning. Ken stood up again and carried it over thoughtfully to the sideboard, where it belonged. He put it down and turned back to face the room, staring suspiciously into the corners. Philip felt the hairs on his neck stand up as Ken seemed to stare straight at him, but he could have seen nothing through the narrow gap in the cupboard door. He walked back to the head of the bed, thrust his arm into the narrow gap by the wall and pulled out the briefcase which Philip had encountered earlier. He put the briefcase on to the bed, pressed the catches and flipped up the lid, glancing up towards the bathroom as he did so.

From where he was Philip could not see into the briefcase, but he noted the look of intense relief which crossed Ken's face as he checked the contents. He noted, too, the stealthiness with which he shut the case again and returned it to its position of concealment. When Mandy reappeared from the bathroom half a minute later he was standing with his hands behind his back next to the sideboard, apparently attempting to look casual.

'I've ordered your cab,' he said brusquely, still not quite meeting her eye. 'It'll be here soon. Come on, let's go down.'

Mandy didn't want to meet his eye either. Her freshly made-up face was averted, but her voice sounded sheepish enough.

'Thanks very much, Ken,' she said contritely. 'That's very kind of you, you've really been very — '

'Yes. Fine.' Ken cut her off curtly. 'Let's go.'

He held open the door for her. His face was still set rigid. He hadn't showed his teeth for at least five minutes, which Philip supposed must be some kind of record.

When they had gone Philip remained in the cupboard for another minute, ticking off the seconds in his head. Then he climbed out quietly and rearranged the squashed shoes on which he had been sitting. He crept over to the door and listened intently. The landing was deserted and the light had been turned off again, but he had the feeling that once Ken had got rid of Mandy he would come straight back up. He marched quickly over to the bed and pulled out the black briefcase. It was quite heavy and plainly full. He laid it down on the bed and pressed the catches. He lifted the lid. He whistled softly.

'Put money in thy purse . . .'

The briefcase was chock-full of fifty-pound notes, all neatly bundled in gummed paper bands. He skimmed his fingertips over the crisp virgin paper, attempting a mental calculation. The attempt defeated him. But it was a hell of a lot.

He closed the briefcase and put it back behind the bed. His head hummed with questions – buzz, buzz – but now was no time to try and answer them. He rechecked the cupboard to make sure he hadn't left any incriminating trace behind, then slipped out on to the landing.

He went quickly down the back staircase and out through the garden door, slipping the catch behind him. As he made his way round to the front of the house, headlamps appeared at the head of the drive and he ducked behind some bushes. He waited a few minutes until the cab had gone out again, Mandy's dark head just visible in the back. He darted out of the front entrance and ran across to the blue Ford in the car park.

'That was a long five minutes,' George remarked chippily.

Philip didn't answer. He pointed silently to the road and George knew to take his cue. He headed out as requested towards the motorway and didn't speak again till they were halfway to London.

Philip sat patiently in the front, putting two and two together, and coming up with about three and a half.

13

The talk in his caravan the next day was all of Harve and Marve. While Philip sat patiently waiting to be made up, Denis flitted around like a moth on over-drive.

'. . . And apparently Harve's in a much worse state than they thought at first, he's still on life-support in a coma, it's amazingly dramatic, and of course the magistrate had absolutely no intention of releasing Marve, so he's been remanded in custody for another twenty-four hours, because for all the police know it may be a murder charge by the weekend, and apparently one of the doctors said it was odds on that it would be, and even if Harve came round he said he'd probably be a walking vegetable — '

'Business as normal, you mean?'

'Don't, Philip. Ooh, you are awful. Now, where was I? I've quite lost my thread. Ah yes, and as for Shelley, well . . . she is in a tizzy, and did you know that apparently the police are thinking of charging her with aiding and abetting, because apparently she was egging Marve on the whole time and at one stage actually said — '

'No, I didn't know that, Denis. How very interesting . . .'

'Ooh, Philip, you're so dry! A proper little cream cracker!'

'Denis, have you ever considered a career in Trappism?'

But it took more than a dash of irony to staunch the flow of Denis. Philip was intensely relieved when eventually his call came.

Filming was out by the lake today, the scene where Dick has just rescued Celestia from her arranged marriage and is rowing across the castle moat to safety with the judge as hostage. The background castle would be painted in afterwards. It was meant to be a night scene, but the plan of action was to use day-for-night for the close-ups (the technique whereby a filter over the camera lens artificially darkens the picture) and then after darkness had actually fallen to take the long shots, the theory being that then it wouldn't matter if their faces were a little blurred. It seemed reasonable enough to Philip, but Sleat wasn't happy.

'I can't go out in that!' he whined, pointing at the small rowing-boat moored by the shore. 'It's got a hole.'

That was true, but the hole had a plug in it. This was to cater for the last stage direction in the scene, which had Dick pulling out his pistol and shooting a hole in the bottom of the boat to prevent anyone else using it. The boat would then be filmed quietly sinking.

'The plug's a hundred per cent secure,' the carpenter insisted. 'Look, there isn't a drop in the bottom of the boat, it's completely sealed. And you've got to remove this split pin and twist off the cap even to get at it.'

'What if there's a storm?' demanded the anxious pop star.

'A storm?' Terry repeated incredulously. 'This is a small lake in Buckinghamshire. Not the North Sea.'

Sleat was not convinced.

'Nothing's going to go wrong,' Terry continued, adopting a conciliatory tone. He pointed at the specially hired frogman, who was sitting on the bank putting on his flippers. 'In any case, Pete'll be in the water with you the whole time. Even if the unthinkable happened, Pete'd see you all right.'

'Unless the sharks got him first,' observed Philip gently.

'Sharks!' Sleat screamed. 'I ain't going in there if there's sharks!'

Terry shook his head reproachfully at Philip.

'I think he's having you on, actually. As I said, this is a quiet lake in Buckinghamshire. You don't tend to get a lot of sharks round here. Now, do you think we could get on with this, please. We've got a lot to do while it's still light.'

Sleat gave Philip one of his dagger-filled looks, but he went quietly, perhaps alerted by the widespread smirking of the crew to the foolishness of the figure he was cutting. As he got into the boat Shelley turned up and everyone stopped smirking anyway.

Philip was perhaps the only one present who didn't share the general sense of embarrassment.

'Philip, would you go and get tied up, please,' the second assistant asked. The props man was waiting to see to him.

'I'll leave the rope as loose as possible,' the props man explained, looping it half a dozen times round his body before securing his hands in front of him with a big knot. 'But it can't be too loose, it's got to look convincing.'

Philip wondered why. Nothing else did. He was particularly dreading the scene preceding this one (due to be filmed next week), where Sleat was meant to overpower and truss him up. He wasn't sure if he could act feeble enough to make it plausible. It would not have been overstating the case to suggest that so far Sleat's performance had been conspicuously lacking in the physical dimension.

When he had finished, the props man led Philip over to the boat and helped him into the bow beside Shelley. The reluctant pop star was opposite them in the stern, clinging to the sides for all he was worth. Pete the frogman pushed them gently away from the bank.

'Hey, be careful!' Sleat whimpered. 'It looks really deep . . .'

Philip raised an eyebrow. The water was currently lapping around Pete's knees.

'OK, that's far enough,' said the first assistant when they were six feet or so from the shore. 'Mark that spot, please, Pete. We'll go for a master. Can somebody wake Wayne?'

Pete dropped out of shot behind the boat, all but his head submerged. Wayne was dozing in his wheelchair. The third assistant shook him by the shoulder and whispered what was going on in his ear. The director sat up eagerly. As soon as the camera was running he shouted:

'ACTION!'

and immediately went back to sleep, happy.

'You'll never get away with this, Turpin!' Philip snarled Rathbonely.

'Pull harder, Dick!' squeaked Shelley, coming to life. 'The Redcoats are comin'!'

'Ugh!' gasped Sleat.

This exclamation was not in the script. Philip regarded him curiously, noting that he had turned green.

'I'm going to be seasick!' wailed the pop star.

And true to his word, he leant over the side and threw up over Pete's head.

Some two hours later they finally succeeded in getting the small scene into the can. It couldn't have been much good, but then at least, Philip supposed, it wouldn't stick out from the rest. In any case it was getting dark and they had to stop. Terry called a break and Philip was helped out of the boat and untied.

'Phi-lip!' A familiar and unwelcome voice greeted him. 'Everything going OK, my friend?'

'So-so,' Philip replied neutrally. The crew had gone by now, leaving the working lights on. Ken was a shadowy figure among the dusky trees.

'Just thought I'd check you're all right,' the producer continued. 'Everything going to schedule?'

'Hardly, but at least with our friend Harvey out of the way we might have a chance to make up for lost time.'

'Terrible business, eh? I'm afraid Marve's got a bit of a reputation for that kind of behaviour.'

'Then what was he doing here in the first place?'

'Phi-lip, my friend . . .'

He could barely see the face in the gloom but he could feel the strained smile.

'Phi-lip, if you've got a problem, let's talk.'

'You've been saying that for three weeks, Ken, it's a bit late now. In any case it's my break, and by God I need one. There's just one thing I'd like from you, Ken. Would you see that I get it, please?'

'And what's that, Phi-lip?'

'A cheque. Three, to be exact. There's a lot of money due to me and I'd like it.'

'Phi-lip, what's the fuss? You'll get your money.'

'Why haven't I had it already?'

'Hey, what's the big deal? Look, I'll tell you what I'll do.

What's today? Thursday. I promise you'll have a cheque first thing Monday morning, you've got my word on —'

'Why do I have to wait till Monday? Are you trying to tell me you've got no cash?'

'Phi-lip, it's not as if I can just go stick my mitt in the till, you know. Look, I'll even with you. There's a bit of a cash shortage at the moment – no problem, believe me, absolutely no problem at all, but the money's all coming from Europe, and there's all this stuff about international money transfers and exchange rates and that, but it's on its way, you've got my personal guarantee on that, and till then we're in exactly the same boat, my friend —'

'What do you mean?'

'I mean I don't have any money myself. Till I get the next cheque from Mr Witt I'm penniless. I don't have two beans to rub together, I wish I had!'

'Not two beans, eh? I see . . . but you'll have it by Monday?'

'Monday.'

'Fine. Now, if you'll excuse me, I'm going to have to get over to the cafeteria fast if I'm going to have time for a coffee and a sandwich.'

'Of course. Catch you later.'

They were on the other side of the lake from the car park, but Philip didn't bother to rush back. He wasn't hungry and he didn't even particularly want a coffee. What he wanted was the answers to some awkward questions, but as Ken was his sole potential source of enlightenment he figured that he was unlikely to get them. He would have liked to have asked him one thing, though, just to see the expression on his face:

'Ken, how does a man without two beans to rub together come to have a suitcase stuffed with fifty-pound notes hidden behind his bed?'

Of course, it was only to be expected that Ken was crooked; he was a film producer, the link was axiomatic. But precisely what kind of a fiddle was he on? It smelt like a roll-over to Philip: There could be another project he was working on which he hadn't finished; so he could be siphoning off funds from this picture and using them to finish the other, i.e. rolling them over. So many film producers did it that it was hardly considered unethical, but the problem was that once you'd started on the downward spiral it was difficult to stop the momentum. Now he would be needing to finance another movie just in order to put the missing moneys back into the budget of *Midnight Rider* before anyone noticed they were missing. And he would have to go on juggling more and more balls in the air until he reached the point where either the whole lot suddenly came crashing down or else he was lucky enough to score one hit big enough to pay off all the debts and return to square one. And on Ken's past record the latter was distinctly the lesser possibility.

Whatever was going on, Philip felt worried. To say that he didn't trust Ken Kilmaine would be an understatement of titanic proportions. It was pretty clear that the only cheque coming on Monday would be courtesy of the Flying Pig courier service. What could he do to get his money? Go on strike? That would alert everyone else, and Philip was sure that they were all in exactly the same position. He couldn't afford to risk sending everything up in flames by causing a general stampede. He would have to try a more personal angle. He would have to try . . .

. . . Blackmail. Yes, that was the word he'd been looking for, there was no getting around it. If Ken was trying to screw him, then the best solution was to screw him back. So he'd better get something on him. He could start with Martha in New York, a fax with a few pertinent questions, get her to root about and sniff out any other projects of his in the pipeline. With her connections she should be able to do that all right. Martha had once told him that he was pretty good at blackmail. He wondered what that nice Mr Witt would say if he knew Ken was hoarding huge amounts of cash . . .

It was completely dark by the time Philip got back on set an hour later, and the lighting men were adjusting the big arc lights they would have to work by. The rowing boat had been beached for the duration of the break and Ken Kilmaine was standing over the crew as they lifted it back into the water.

'Careful with that, now!' he said jokily. 'I've got to return it to the Serpentine tomorrow!'

'One knot or two?' the props man asked Philip, uncoiling his rope.

'One, I think,' Philip answered. 'In fact, would you make it pretty loose? This is going to be a long shot in the dark, no one'll see.'

'Sure,' the props man agreed. 'Look, if you pull your cloak tight how it was before, I'll just wrap the rope round a few times and you can hold the ends in your fists. No need to tie a knot at all.'

'Perfect. Thanks.'

Shelley was already in the boat when he got there and Ken was leaning over chatting to her.

'All trussed-up safely, Phi-lip? You look like a Christmas turkey!'

Ken helped him in. He winked at Shelley. 'Break a leg, darling!'

Shelley moved along to make room for him. They were almost on top of each other in the bow of the boat, but since Marve's incarceration she hadn't really bothered him. Philip vaguely sensed silent hostility. He felt like adding to it himself when Sleat climbed gingerly into the other end. He looked terrified.

'It'll be fine,' Terry was explaining gently. 'I promise. You won't be far from shore and it isn't deep. And Pete'll be with you the whole time anyway.'

Pete was sitting nearby in a grey rubber dinghy with an out-board motor. He gave Sleat a wary thumbs-up.

'OK, everyone!' Terry clapped his hands for attention. 'Let's get this shot in the bag. Shouldn't take long. Then we'll do the boat-sinking and we can pack up.'

Pete started his engine and manoeuvred his dinghy over. He tied a rope to the bow of the rowing-boat and towed them gently away from the shore. Despite some gentle wave turbulence Sleat managed to keep the contents of his stomach in place. Though he didn't stop complaining: 'We're too far out! We don't need to be this far from the shore! That water looks really deep!'

Philip glanced at the opaque black surface of the water. How could he tell?

'Relax in the boat!' Terry called out through his megaphone. 'We've got to rearrange the lighting. Take five. Sorry.'

The big arc lights on shore were turned off. The faces of his companions became indistinct blurs.

'Why don't they get us in?' demanded Sleat uneasily. 'It's cold out here.'

It was. Philip could hear Shelley shivering.

'I'd offer you my cloak,' he said gallantly, 'but my hands are tied . . .'

'I'll be OK, thanks.'

She didn't sound grateful for the offer; in fact her tone was tense and surly. He felt her lean forward, no doubt huddling into herself for warmth.

'Could I ask you two a question?' Philip said, trying to sound as friendly as possible.

'Yeah. What?' answered Sleat.

'About money. It's a delicate subject, I don't want to pry, but they seem to be taking their time about paying me. I just wondered if you'd experienced any problems yourselves.'

'Yeah, well, I don't interest myself in that side of things much,' Sleat replied. 'I leave that to my manager, but I'm not aware of any problems. We took a special deal, anyway. I'm not taking anything up front, just expenses and a percentage of net profits. A pretty generous percentage too, actually.'

'Really?'

'Oh yeah . . .' For someone who didn't take an interest in the subject he was surprisingly open about it. There was a complacent tone in his voice: 'It's a pretty incredible deal, actually. My manager's pulled off a bit of a coup.'

He was obviously waiting to be prodded further, but Philip missed his cue: he was momentarily too taken aback to provide it. Of course he had known Sleat was stupid but it hadn't occurred to him that his manager might share his mental disability. In the world of the creative accountants who controlled the purse-strings in the movie industry, 'net profits' were the statistical equivalents of 'pink elephants'. Sleat's manager was obviously as ignorant of the principles of film financing as his client was of acting; a rare double triumph.

'I see,' he said at length. 'What about you, Shelley?'

But before she could answer, Sleat uttered a plaintive yelp: 'Help! There's water in the boat!'

'Do calm down,' said Philip wearily. There was a smear of liquid in the bottom of any boat, but that was hardly surprising. 'For God's sake, sit still!'

Sleat was half on his feet, jabbering hysterically. The boat rocked from side to side and Shelley fell heavily against him. He slipped off their narrow bench and fell forward into the bottom of the boat, flinging out his bound hands clumsily to break his fall.

A nervous shock ran through him as he was plunged up to the wrists in freezing water.

'He's right, we're sinking!' Shelley screamed, grabbing at Philip for support. 'Help, we're sinking!'

There wasn't much doubt about it, really. Philip couldn't see a thing but he could feel the water rising, fast. He tried to shake off the rope that was hanging only loosely about him, but Shelley was clinging to his neck and he could hardly move.

'Help us!' she screamed, a cry echoed hysterically from the other end of the boat. 'Help us, somebody, we're going to drown!'

There was activity on shore. Their plight had been noticed at least. Over the cacophonous screechings in his ear Philip heard the buzz of Pete's outboard motor drawing near.

'Will you two bloody shut up!' he barked, trying simultaneously to free himself from the rope and Shelley. 'And sit down!'

But Sleat was jumping up and down in the bow like a jack-in-the-box. The boat veered crazily from side to side. Philip felt the water flood into his boots and soak his feet.

'Sit down or we *will* sink!' he shouted, but if Sleat heard he didn't respond. Philip swore and made a lunge for him, grabbing hold of his sleeve with his two fists. Sleat pushed him off and he fell back into the clutches of Shelley.

'Hold still, everyone!' shouted Pete from close by. 'Don't panic!'

The boat shook and Philip fell forward again. This time the water came up to his elbows. At least Shelley had momentarily let go of him.

He pushed himself up on to his haunches and reached for the side of the boat to steady himself. As his fingers closed on the planking a body thudded into him from the side. At the same moment the vessel gave another tremendous lurch and he toppled into the lake.

The waters closed instantly over his head and he plummeted straight down to the silt. The freezing darkness engulfed him.

His feet hit the bottom, he kicked and tried to push up to the surface. The waters were black and silent, he felt as if he was in a liquid tomb. His lungs were bursting already, as desperately he grasped upwards for the air.

His feet touched the bottom again. He wasn't going anywhere. His body was lead, why wouldn't it rise? He tried to strike out with his arms and found them pinioned to his side. He pushed and struggled and only then did he realise what he hadn't realised in the boat, that the rope ends hadn't been tied and he was holding them in his hands. He opened his fingers and the cords fell away. Now he thrust his arms up and the sodden weight of his cloak dragged them back. He clawed it off and his wig was thrown off with it. He rose at last, his lungs at the point of collapse, with awful-seeming slowness. His water-filled heavy boots slipped off his feet.

His head broke the surface and his racked lungs sucked in oxygen. He went under for the second time.

This time he seemed to sink as slowly as he had risen. The falling was so gentle, and the darkness and silence about him so absolute, that he felt suspended in the water and strangely detached. And in those brief stretched seconds he came to see inside his mind – as drowning men are supposed to – with sudden, brittle clarity.

He understood that it was no accident the boat had sunk. The water had not come over the sides, it had flooded up from beneath, from the plug which he had seen with his own eyes was secure and which therefore must have been tampered with. For the third time in a matter of days someone had tried to kill him.

His feet touched the bottom. That was strange, he had felt himself falling for minutes before, but this time it had lasted only seconds. The water wasn't deep at all. When he opened his eyes he could see nothing, but he guessed that he couldn't have been more than a foot or two out of his depth. He divested himself quite calmly of his velvet coat. He bent his knees and gave a good push. Without his heavy gear he ascended easily.

He came up for air for the second time and stayed up, vigorously treading the water. What he witnessed was a scene of pure chaos.

The boat was some twenty feet away and half-submerged. Either it had drifted or it had been pulled away by the rubber dinghy, which was alongside. Sleat and Shelley were both in the water. He couldn't see them but he could hear them, especially Sleat.

And he suspected that people as far away as Slough could probably hear them too: Philip had never heard such a racket, it was worse even than one of Sleat's alleged 'songs'. And there was pandemonium beyond them on the shore, where all the crew seemed to be vying with each other to produce the best headless chicken impersonation. Some of them at least were trying to get one of the big spotlights focused on the action, but the beam was flicking wildly all over the place.

Not very encouraging so far, Philip thought to himself. Somebody could drown out here . . .

Unfortunately it wasn't going to be Sleat. At that moment the spotlight settled at last on the dinghy and Philip saw that Pete had a firm grip on the pop star's collar, though it was not enough to make him lower the volume. Shelley was already in the dinghy beside the frogman.

'Where's Philip?' somebody stopped running about on shore long enough to ask. 'What's happened to Philip?'

Nice of you to ask, the object of their enquiries mused to himself . . .

Obviously they couldn't see him, but it might help if they looked a little harder. More lights were coming into play on shore, he could see them all right, but the half-dozen or so bodies he glimpsed wading into the shallows – and the dinghy was almost at the bank already – were intent only on giving Sleat and Shelley a hand.

Suddenly the beam of the spotlight came tracking fast across the water. It seemed to stab at random into the black liquid mass and missed him by a matter of feet. When it reached the limit of its swift traverse it started to return.

I could always wave and shout, Philip told himself. What then?

Why, they'd come and rescue him of course, and take him back to shore. To the man who had just tried to kill him. The beam came skimming over the water.

He took a deep breath and slipped back under the water. Holding his eyes wide open, he looked up and saw the sheet blackness briefly stippled white. Then it had passed and he was alone again.

Alone in darkness and in silence: the water was cold but he had adjusted; he felt almost comfortable. Perhaps it was some deep, subconscious memory of the womb that made him feel secure; or perhaps merely the thought that no one knew where he was. He began to swim under water.

He went for more than half a minute before having to come up for air. Not bad for a chain-smoking semi-alcoholic wreck. All those lengths in Highbury Baths hadn't been for nothing.

He was far out from the shore now, probably near the centre of the lake. There were more lights on over by the cameras, where a score or so of people were tripping over each other trying to get Sleat and Shelley on to dry land. The grey dinghy, its hysterical load discharged, was heading back out into the lake, guided by the fitful stabbing of the spotlight. There was no sign of the rowing-boat. Some voices were calling his name.

He turned over and carried on swimming, this time keeping his head above water, for he was beyond the spotlight's range. The voices grew fainter. He couldn't see exactly where he was going, and it was hard work, but he knew the lake wasn't wide. After another minute he spied a pin-prick of light up ahead which must have come from the car park. He took it as his mark.

His feet touched the bottom again. He dimly discerned the shapes of trees in front. He used one that was growing right on the edge of the water to pull himself up by.

They were still calling for him on the far bank. The rubber dinghy was empty around the spot where the boat had gone down. Pete was no doubt under the water looking for his body. While on shore the man who had attempted to murder him would be thinking: third time lucky . . .

He shivered. He couldn't stand here thinking about it, he'd catch pneumonia. He didn't have time to pause anyway, the police and ambulance would have been called by now, soon the area would be swarming. The car park was less than a hundred yards away, the light he had seen from afar now shining out vividly from within one of the caravans. He jogged towards it as rapidly as he could pick his way through the trees.

There was no one around his caravan, which was in darkness. He fished the key out of the canvas bag in his deep trouser-pocket, opened the door carefully and slipped in, locking it again behind him. He checked the windows. There was some movement down the far end of the car park, but there was no sign of life nearer. In any case, no one was going to come looking for him here. Why should they have done when he was meant to be ten feet under water?

He found his towel in the dark, peeled off his clothes and rubbed himself down. He opened the clothes cupboard where he hung his costume every night and the narrow strip-light inside came on. It shouldn't have been visible from outside but it was a risk he had to run. He put on the clean socks and underpants which he had laid out ready for after the shoot. He unpacked the carrier-bag at the bottom of the cupboard.

He changed into the 'Express Services' overalls, donkey jacket and boots. If they did come snooping in his caravan they weren't going to notice these clothes missing; no one knew they were here. He was going to have to take one or two items which might be missed, but then again, why should anyone be checking?

He put his wet costume shirt and breeches into the empty

carrier-bag and stuffed in his make-up bag on top. There was just room for the portable phone down the side. He laid the now bulging bag by the door and gave the floor a quick wipe with the towel, to remove any puddles. That would have to suffice; he had a lot to do tonight. He looked at his watch, which he had worn under his frilly cuff, but it had stopped – so much for the waterproof guarantee. Whatever the time was, it was time to be going.

He picked up the carrier-bag and slipped out of the caravan into the nearest dense patch of shadow. He headed off through the woods in a wide loop towards the road, and as he reached it he heard the approaching wail of sirens. He hid as police cars and ambulances flashed past, and when they had gone climbed over the wooden fence and trotted up to the main road, a dual carriageway that ran west into Slough, east towards Uxbridge. He pulled his wallet from the bottom of the canvas bag and found that he had four damp twenty-pound notes and a fiver. He offered the fiver to the driver of the first bus that came along, a 457 which took him all the way to Slough railway station.

He bought a single ticket to Paddington and while he was waiting for the train phoned George. A woman answered, presumably his aunt, and told him George was out and wasn't expected back for a couple of hours. Philip declined to leave a message. The train came in just a few minutes late. It was a quarter to eight.

14

The fourth time Philip rang George's number, the aunt got cross with him.

'I told you, mister, I don't know where he is. Why don't you leave a message?'

But how could he do that, when he wasn't even supposed to be walking the planet?

He was standing on the corner of Highbury Grove looking across at Lansbury House, the unprepossessing block of flats in which the eclectic Washingtons had their abode. It was cold, he wanted to get home, find some warmer clothes. He stamped his feet and rubbed his hands briskly.

'Come on, George, where the hell are you?'

He needed him. In fact, of all the people in the world whom he had ever met in the course of his entire life George was the only one who could be the remotest use to him right now. He smiled ruefully at the thought. Fate was a tricky customer.

It was a little after nine. The InterCity train had taken little more than twenty minutes to get from Slough to Paddington, the taxi to Highbury the same again. He had hauled himself out of the lake less than three hours ago. Why should he be in such a hurry, did it make any difference?

'Like hell . . .'

It made all the difference in the world. If he was going to strike back, then the iron needed to be not so much hot as incandescent white. He thought he had a pretty good idea of what was going on, though not of why, and it was that which he had to find out. And that was where George came in. Or would come in the moment he . . .

Two black youths brushed past his shoulder. He was startled, he hadn't heard them coming. For a moment his heart leapt into his mouth, but then he saw that neither of their faces – impish and cocky though they were – was the one he sought. They stopped a little further along the pavement and glanced back in his direction, though ignoring him.

'Where's he got to, then?' one demanded of the other. The other pointed suddenly.

'There he is. Here, George! Cheers, mate!'

'See you tomorrow,' said the other, waving vaguely. The two of them then turned and continued walking up Highbury Grove.

Philip turned the other way. A small familiar figure was bobbing jauntily towards him, stuffing his face from a bag of chips as he walked. He didn't look up from his feast as he passed Philip by.

'George!' Philip hissed.

George spun round guiltily. It was an expression which came naturally.

'What you doing, jumping out at me like that?' he demanded indignantly, at the same instant shovelling in another handful of greasy carbohydrates.

'Keep your voice down,' Philip answered softly. 'I'm in trouble, I need your help.'

George gave an exaggerated sigh. 'What is it with you, mate? Things you ask me to do, I dunno. Why you wearing that gear? That ain't your style.'

'George, someone's trying to kill me.'

George stopped munching his chips for a moment. He looked at Philip shrewdly.

'It's not that Polish bird, is it?'

'What?'

'She's weird, that one. Bleeding nutter.'

'George, Mrs Tomascevski has a number of eccentricities but homicidal mania is not among them. Look, I don't have time to explain now, but I need you very badly and if you help me out you will receive not merely my eternal gratitude but also a very substantial reward. Now, I don't propose to stand here on the street corner all night, so please listen very carefully. Not only has someone tried to kill me tonight but he is under the impression that he has succeeded. And so is everyone else. You are the only person in the world who knows that I am still alive. Under no circumstances must you admit to having seen me, much less spoken to me. Discretion, George, I want your lips zipped shut. Now what I want you to do is get your uncle's car and meet me outside my flat in half an hour. Got that? Don't come up, don't even ring the bell. What's the time?'

'Quarter past nine.'

'Good, I'll come down and meet you in the street at nine forty-five. I will have need of your professional services.'

'What professional services?'

'Don't be coy, George. Please be fully equipped, there may be an alarm system.'

'We ain't going down to Iver again, are we?'

'No, into town.'

'What if I can't get the car?'

'Then steal it. Don't forget, there's a great deal in it for you.'

'Yeah? What?'

'I will promise to get you into drama school.'

'You what?'

'That's right. Provided everything goes according to plan, I swear that I will get you into a reputable training establishment and I will pay all your application fees and audition expenses. I am not without influence in the profession. My name as referee should ease your passage considerably.'

'I thought you said I couldn't act?'

'George, drama schools are full of people who can't act, you'll feel quite at home. Now, look, there's no time to waste. I expect you at a quarter to ten. Is it a deal?'

By way of answer George extended the greasy paper bag in his hand:

'Have a chip.'

It was one offer Philip could live without. With a stern reminder of the necessity for discretion he left George and hurried home across Highbury Fields.

He checked that no one was about to witness his entry, then entered his house quietly, tiptoeing through the communal hall. Once inside his own door he went straight to the kitchen and rooted around in the drawers for a torch. He had two, and mercifully both sets of batteries were functioning. He put both torches into his pocket, one to act as a spare. Then he went quickly through the flat and discreetly drew all the curtains. He returned to the kitchen and put his wet costume clothes into the tumble-dryer, setting it on maximum blast for half an hour. He supposed that if a neighbour were to put his ear to the door, then the machine might just be audible, but none of his neighbours was really the sort.

He took his make-up bag into the bedroom and fished around with the aid of his torch in his wardrobe. When he had found everything he needed, he picked up his alarm clock and took everything into the bathroom. With the door safely closed, he turned on the light above the mirror. Again, if any of his neighbours happened to be prowling on the roof it was conceivable that they might see a reflection in the skylight, but the risk was negligible and, in any case, unavoidable: an artiste of his quality needed light to work by.

He checked out his wig collection. There were a dozen, carefully collected over the last three years to replace the store he had so foolishly burnt. Most were dark, to suit his colouring, but there was only one which would serve in the present case. He took it carefully off its block and subjected it to a thorough examination. The condition seemed excellent. He put it on loosely and checked his profiles and rear-view by deft manipulation of the mirror on the wall cabinet. It hadn't been designed as an Afro, but at night the close black curls would pass. Just in case, he pulled a loose black woollen hat on over it. Now it was perfect. He opened his tin of Negro No. 1, wet a sponge and began to black up.

'And why not?' he asked himself in the mirror, returning his thin smile with interest. 'If I'm to disappear for a while, then the more radical the transformation the better. And in George's company what could be more natural?'

'You'd better be careful there. You've never worked with an accomplice before, and he's only a lad.'

'Yes, but an ambitious one. And he perceives me as his guide and mentor. He knows how stark will be the consequences of failure. He may well turn out to be the most dependable side-kick since that happy day when Batman first stumbled upon his Robin.'

'But don't you feel a twinge of conscience at corrupting one so young?'

'My dear, protest not overmuch. Recall only the circumstances of our first meeting. Who is corrupting who?'

It was a moot point. His reflection considered carefully upon it and nodded its measured accord. He finished daubing his face and throat with pancake.

'Don't forget the neck and hands.'

'Give me a chance.'

He finished with the sponge and got to work on the eyes, keeping one of them on his clock at all times and going as fast as possible. He selected his darkest plain glass contact lenses and put the wig back on, this time securing it with tape. He tucked a few stray hairs away and touched up his lips. He looked away, then back again suddenly into the mirror, starting dramatically: 'I took by the throat the circumcised dog / And smote him thus . . .'

Not bad, he acknowledged to himself judiciously. Not as good as the Rev. Cornelius Washington might have been, perhaps, but not bad at all. The make-up wasn't flawless, but good enough for a night shoot. He consulted the clock again. He had five minutes.

'Good. Time to think.'

There was a bottle of Scotch in his make-up bag. He took a swig, just one, it cleared the brain. He lit a cigarette and sat down on the edge of the bath. He went through his plan of action in his head.

'Take a deep breath. Relax. Think it through.'

He had thought it through during his travels tonight, by bus, train and taxi, but it was something else to have a few quiet minutes of contemplation in his own home. He always liked to be able to talk his problems through in front of the mirror; he liked to be on familiar territory.

'Right, let's go through it one more time. It wasn't the terrible twins after all, was it, either singly or in tandem? One's in hospital, one's in nick. Who else was present at all three "accidents"? Why should any of the crew have it in for me? And poor Wayne is hardly capable. No, it's someone cunning, devious, ruthless. Now, who answers that description?'

'Well, if you're going to use adjectives like that, then the field begins to narrow. Odd, isn't it, how many film producers one knows to whom they might apply?'

'But why would Ken Kilmaine have it in for you?'

'Thereby hangs a tale. Before I can answer that question I'll need replies to a few others. Like, what's a man who claims extreme poverty doing with, what? – a hundred grand at least, I'd say, stuffed in a suitcase and hidden under his bed?'

'Maybe he doesn't trust banks.'

'More likely the banks don't trust him. The whole operation stank from day one. Why did I ever get mixed up in it?'

'Greed.'

'There is that. But once you get in so far, as the man observed, it becomes as tedious to return as to go o'er. I think it's high time we found out exactly what kind of a business operation our Mr Kilmaine is running. With a little help from our friends.'

It was a quarter to ten. He pulled on a sweater and put a pair of gloves into one of the deep pockets of his donkey jacket along with the torches. Taking his make-up bag (minus Scotch bottle) for retouching purposes, he crept softly out of the house. A red car was sitting across the road, with the engine idling and George behind the wheel, eyes closed and head moving from side to side to the beat of the radio.

'This isn't your uncle's,' Philip observed as he got into the passenger seat. He turned off the radio.

'Nah,' George answered with a yawn. 'Couldn't get the Escort, borrowed this from a mate, goes like a – AAGH!'

George's shriek stung Philip's ears. The young man leapt as if electrically charged out of his seat and slammed his skull into the roof. He slumped back in a dazed heap and stared dumbly at Philip with his jaw practically propped against his navel.

'What the . . .' was all he was able to say, his voice a strangled whisper.

'Please keep your voice down,' said Philip calmly. He turned the driving-mirror towards his face and just caught a glimpse of himself before the interior car light went off. 'I don't look bad, do I?'

'You look – ' George began, but words still failed him. After a few moments' reflection he pulled himself up into a more comfortable position and stared rigidly ahead. Finally he murmured, 'You're weird, mate.'

'So you keep telling me. Now can you head for town, please? We're going to Soho.'

He directed George to Highbury Corner and Upper Street. It was the route by which the taxi had taken him the night of his first fateful encounter with Ken Kilmaine. They passed the spot where he had ripped up Kate's postcard.

'Got a girlfriend?' he asked conversationally.

'Might have.'

'George, you really must get out of this habit of treating every question you're asked as if it's part of a police interrogation. I was only going to offer some advice.'

'Yeah? Like what?'

'Stay single. It's much for the best. Turn right here.'

Traffic was light in the centre of town but car parking spaces were at the usual premium. George's attitude was cavalier, but the last thing Philip wanted was to return to the car later and find it clamped. He made George drive around until they found a vacant meter near Golden Square. He stowed his make-up bag out of sight on the floor.

They walked along Glasshouse Street into Wardour Street. Philip held his head up boldly; no one paid him any attention. They cut through a narrow alley into Dean Street.

'And here we are,' he said, stopping outside the KenKil offices. He checked that no one was looking, then skipped up the steps and tried the plate-glass doors. They were locked. He pressed the dozen or so intercom buttons on the wall more or less simultaneously. Two of them were answered.

'Express Cleaning Services,' he muttered into the speaker. A light went on in a glass panel above, through which a camera lens scrutinised him. He lifted up his sweater and pointed to the logo on his breast, repeating the phrase like a mantra: 'Express Cleaning Serv — '

The release buzzer sounded before he had finished speaking. The light in the glass panel went off as the door opened with a click. Philip held the door open and summoned George within.

'What you need me for, then?' George asked.

'Keep quiet. People are working in the building.'

They ignored the lift and took the stairs, three flights up to the KenKil offices. No one was on the landing. Philip indicated the door with the crossed Ks plate.

'Can you get in there?'

George examined the lock. He shrugged.

'Ordinary Yale. Piece of piss. Is there an alarm?'

'I don't know. If there is, will you be able to disable it?'

'Yeah, but it'll go off once the door is opened, there'll be contact pads, you see. I'll have about twenty, thirty seconds to get to the alarm. If I don't cut the wire in time people in the building might hear, not to mention the cops if it's — '

'You have to cut the wire, do you?'

'Unless you've got a key.'

'I see. I was hoping we could get in undetected, but maybe it won't matter. Might be a good thing to put the wind up him. Any way of checking if there is an alarm?'

'Sure. Come with me.'

George walked down to the end of the corridor and gently opened the window. He put his head outside and summoned Philip to join him.

'Look.' They were at the back of the building. Although it was dark, Philip could see the outline of a box set in the wall a couple of yards away. George patted his pockets and Philip heard a metal clink. 'I'll nobble it, all right?'

George nonchalantly swung his legs over the parapet. For a moment Philip thought he was about to witness a daring example of vertical cat burglary, but apparently George had stepped on to the fire escape. Philip kept his eyes peeled for any sign of trouble.

The fire escape was a black iron ladder. George swung up a couple of rungs and levered a screwdriver in under the box. When he had loosened it to his satisfaction he put away the screwdriver and produced what looked like an aerosol spray. He inserted the nozzle into the gap he'd made and squeezed. Some kind of foam substance dribbled down the back of his hand.

He finished with the aerosol, glanced around to confirm there was still no one about, and came back inside. Philip closed the window.

'I take it that wasn't anti-perspirant you were using.'

'Cavity insulation gear. Get it from any builders' merchant. Won't work on the electric models, though, so what you have to do is —'

'All right, George, you can do the lecture later. Let's get into the office.'

They went back to the door and George reached again into what must have been the deepest inside pocket in the entire Milletts range. He took out a long thin key.

'I can't believe you buy equipment like that over the counter,' Philip observed.

'Depends who you know, dunnit?'

He inserted the long key into the lock and jiggled it delicately. Philip heard a faint click. He readied his torch.

'That's it,' said George, taking off his right glove for long enough to withdraw a pair of wire clippers from the ubiquitous inner pocket. 'Got to find that alarm quick.'

George opened the door and they stepped smartly inside. Immediately an intermittent electric pulse began to sound from the other side of the room. Philip's torch picked out a slim metal cabinet set in the far wall. George crossed to it, and yanked open the door. He bent down swiftly and snipped a wire. The electric pulse ceased immediately. He produced a small torch of his own and examined the display-board. Philip joined him.

'Is that it?' he asked.

'Got to check for a line monitor.'

'A what?'

'It's like a second alarm that tells you if the circuit's been broken. If the system's plugged in direct to a security firm or the cops they'll still know there's been a break-in.'

'Now you tell me!'

'Yeah, well, I don't know, do I? I got to get the panel off, have a butcher's, but it ain't exactly state-of-the-art this system, there's a —'

'How long have we got if the worst comes to the worst?'

'I don't know, ten minutes, it depends —'

'I'll get cracking then. I'll be next door, tell me as soon as you know.'

He went through into the inner office. The desk was covered with papers and files but he didn't expect to find anything important in plain view. He went straight to the safe in the corner.

He shone his torch on to the combination lock and operated the vital statistics in sequence, 38–26–36. Unless Ken had just changed his secretary that should be all there was to it. He turned the handle.

The safe swung open smoothly. He pointed his torch inside. There was a thick file on the top shelf, nothing else that looked interesting. He carried the file over to Ken's desk. George appeared in the doorway.

'Done this sort of thing before?' he asked suspiciously. 'It's OK, there ain't no monitor. No one knows we're here.'

'Will you go next door and keep your eyes and ears open, just in case? I'll be a little while here.'

He went through the file methodically. Everything in it related to the film. There were copies of all the contracts and some of them made interesting reading. Even more interesting were the bank statements and telexes. He carried the file next door and flicked through the big appointments diary on Shaz's desk. He jotted some dates down on a scrap of paper. Then he turned on the photocopying machine.

'What you doing?' George wanted to know.

'Collecting information. There's too much to take in all at

once and I don't propose to spend all night in here. I don't want him to know the safe's been broken into – let him sweat. Let's try and make it look like a common-or-garden breaking and entering. Have a look around and see if there's anything worth nicking.'

George went into the inner office to investigate. He returned with a video-recorder tucked under his arm. He joined Philip at the photocopier.

'You doing the lot, or what?'

'Just a few more. I hope the machine's fully loaded.'

George shone his torch at the pile of papers already collected in the plastic tray. He gave a little snort: 'Ha! Least they got insurance.'

Philip removed the policy document which he had just copied and laid a letter from the offices of Mr Witt on the glass in its place.

'It's not that sort of insurance, George. It's for the film.'

'What, in case someone nicks the camera?'

'More in case some mishap befalls one of the actors.'

'You mean one of the actors like you?'

'Spot on, George, although it appears to be more complicated than that. There, that'll do. I'll just return these to the safe and then we'll be off.'

He put the copies into his pocket and carried the originals back next door. He replaced the file where he had found it and relocked the safe. He rejoined George and the two of them slipped quietly out into the corridor. The whole operation had taken less than fifteen minutes.

'I don't fancy walking around with a stolen video-recorder,' he whispered as they crept down the stairs. 'Give it to me. If you go and bring the car round I'll wait here.'

George nodded and went on ahead of him. Philip put the recorder down in the darkest corner of the lobby and waited nonchalantly, ready to put on his Express Services act if challenged. He wasn't. When the red car pulled up outside ten minutes later he sneaked out and into the passenger seat in one fluent movement.

'Thank God for that!' he declared, putting the video-recorder down on the floor next to his make-up bag. 'Home, please, James.'

'Shit!' George swore angrily. He stepped suddenly on the accelerator and Philip was thrown back into his seat. Almost immediately another car pulled out in front and the sudden pressure on the brakes almost threw him into the dashboard.

'Steady on! I haven't got my seat belt on yet.'

'Sod that, mate. We're being followed.'

Philip glanced back through the rear window. A police motorcycle was about fifty yards behind them.

'I thought he was on me tail,' George mumbled, keeping his eye on the mirror as they started moving again. 'Saw me getting into the car. The bastard!'

'You may be wrong. Take a left here.'

'All right. Is he still there?'

'Yes. All right. Left again.'

They turned into Frith Street. When Philip looked again the policeman was still following them, though he was keeping his distance.

'Damn! Why the hell's he following us?'

'Don't need no reason, do they?' George answered bitterly. 'Now you know what it's like. See a black face in a motor, they always think you nicked it.'

'I see.' Philip laughed uneasily. 'Well, at least he's wrong about that, isn't he?'

George didn't answer. They stopped at the junction of Soho Square. The white fairing behind drew nearer.

'George!'

'Yeah, well . . .' George shifted in his seat uneasily. His eyes were glumly on his wing mirror. 'You said if you can't get a car, steal one.'

'WHAT?'

'All right, keep your hair on. Me uncle wouldn't let me have the Escort, so I just, like, borrowed this one. You said it was urgent.'

'Yes, I know, but – Christ, what are you doing?'

With a squeal of tyres the car roared suddenly into Soho Square. The rear of the car veered crazily across the road as they raced round the first corner.

'Doing a runner! What's it look like I'm doing?'

Philip cast a desperate glance over his shoulder and just caught a glimpse of the police bike before it disappeared from view. Another car had pulled out in front of it and George had chosen that moment for his charge.

'Shit!' George screamed, slamming on his brakes. Philip was flung forward again as George banged violently on his horn. 'You stupid bastard!'

A taxi had stopped in front of them without signalling to disgorge its passengers. The road was blocked. George kept the horn pressed down.

'Stop it, George, you're making it worse!'

Oh yeah! the thought flashed up in his mind, how much worse can it get? Here he was, allegedly dead, sitting in disguise with a known delinquent in a stolen vehicle with a hot video-recorder at his feet. The police bike would be round that corner in seconds. He might as well be waiting with his wrists held out meekly for the handcuffs.

He yanked George's hand away from the horn and gave the wrist a savage twist.

'Ow! That hurt!'

'It was meant to. Don't argue, do exactly what I tell you. Park the car behind the taxi.'

'What the — '

'Do it. NOW!'

George did as he was told, swinging the car in expertly flush to the kerb. Philip snatched his make-up bag off the floor and pulled out a handful of grease-sticks. He dropped all but one back into the bag and began to apply it furiously to his eyes, twisting round the driving-mirror to work by.

'What the bleedin' hell you doin'?' George demanded, thunderstruck. 'The taxi's going now, we can make a run — '

'We wouldn't have a chance,' Philip snapped, applying the grease stick to his mouth. He adjusted the mirror and saw the police bike swing into view. It was heading towards them fast.

'Look at me, George!'

George looked. It was a lousy make-up job, he knew, but the best he could manage in the circumstances. He slapped the grease-stick into his hand.

'See what I've done? Copy it. Exactly the same. Use the mirror, don't argue, just do it. Remember that improvisation we did the other day? This time it's for real. Just use your brains, and get a move on!'

The motorbike had stopped behind them. The policeman was just swinging his leg over the saddle. Philip took a deep breath, then flung open the door and jumped briskly out.

'Come on, Dai old chap, we haven't got all day!' he called out heartily, in his best old trouper's voice.

The policeman glanced round on hearing his voice and pulled up stone-dead in the act of setting his bike on its stand.

'Good evening, officer!' trumpeted Philip gaily. This is it, he thought, no time for fainthearts now, it's knock 'em dead in the aisles or I'm blown to buggery! He launched himself into overdrive: 'Can I be of assistance in any way, officer? Always glad to help our gallant lads in blue! I say – we're not parked on a double yellow line, are we? Gosh, I do hope not! We're in the most frantic hurry, you see, been looking frantically for a parking space, doing a special late night benefit at the Dominion, don't you know, and we're on in – good heavens! Is that the time? I say, Dai, do get a move on, it's curtain up in twenty minutes!'

Philip tut-tutted and pulled an exasperated face for the policeman's benefit. The policeman did not react. Not a muscle twitched. He might have been carved in basalt.

The passenger door was thrown open and George climbed out. Philip mouthed a silent prayer, took another deep breath, and turned to face him.

Hallelujah! his brain screamed inwardly. The boy's a natural!

Like his own, it was hardly the best make-up job in the world, but in the dim light of the street-lamps it was adequate enough. Two neat white circles ringed his eyes, while a rather more untidy oval patch enclosed his mouth. Philip laughed, a touch hysterically.

'Good old Dai! Late as always!'

The policeman's mouth opened ever so slightly, as if indicating he might be about to speak, but if so, he quickly thought better of it. Philip sympathised: he didn't suppose that police training procedures covered the correct method of apprehending a pair of black and white minstrels. Philip decided not to give him a chance to work it out for himself:

'Campdown ladies sing this song, doo dah, doo dah!' he burst out singing, in his best bass voice.

The policeman appeared to have stopped breathing. George looked scarcely more animate.

'Come on then, Dai, snap snap!' Philip roared, clapping his hands together briskly. 'We'll miss our call. Oops, mustn't forget my make-up, it's in the car! There ... lovely talking to you, officer, please excuse us, we must dash. Oh – if you get off early by any chance, do drop by at the box office (Dominion, just over there!), I'll tell them to leave you a ticket – say you're a friend of Dai's!'

He grabbed George by the shoulders and propelled him forcefully in the direction of Oxford Street.

'Whatever you do,' he muttered under his breath, 'don't look back.'

Philip launched into a voluble and somewhat erratic vocal limber. He could not help but notice that a number of passers-by had stopped dead in their tracks and were staring at him. He marched on stubbornly, head held high and booming at the top of his voice:

''Ole man river, that 'ole man river ...'

He felt George's sharp physical wince.

'... He just keep rollin' along!'

They turned the corner into Oxford Street and strode boldly on towards Tottenham Court Road. At least, Philip did.

'Shut up, can't you!' George groaned despairingly out of the corner of his mouth. 'I feel enough of a berk without you drawin' attention to us!'

'George, two black and white minstrels striding arm-in-arm down Oxford Street are going to be noticed regardless of how much noise they make. Just keep your eyes fixed straight ahead and ignore them.'

'That copper's still watching, you know.'

'I thought I told you not to look back. Is he following us?'

'Nah, he's just, like, standing on the corner.'

'Good – excuse me, madam.'

A bemused woman stepped back out of the way. As they approached the junction of Tottenham Court Road a passing drunk made a rude comment, but for the most part any eye which Philip happened to catch was turned instantly in the other direction. The English mortal dread of being seen consorting with strangers cleared a path all along the pavement. They turned the corner.

'Is he following us?' Philip demanded.

'No.'

'We'll take this taxi.'

It was probably a good thing the cab was stuck in traffic; he doubted it would have stopped for them otherwise. As it was, the driver at first refused to open the door.

'Please,' Philip said urgently. 'We're going to a surprise fancy dress birthday party in Highbury. We're very late.'

The driver relented. He released the door-catch and they climbed in gratefully. The cab pulled away into the northbound traffic stream, past the front of the Dominion Theatre.

'No sign of him,' said George, looking out of the rear window. 'We got away with it. I don't believe it.'

Philip slumped back into his seat and breathed out slowly, like a deflating balloon. He was drenched with sweat and he could sense his make-up running; he felt thoroughly enervated.

'That,' he said softly, 'was what I would call a *coup de théâtre*. Phew!'

They turned right into the Marylebone Road. George was staring at the floor. He shook his head thoughtfully. 'I ain't sure I'm cut out to be an actor.'

The cab stopped at a red light. The driver cleared his throat, the time-honoured preface to an up-to-the-minute opinion check. He half-turned round in his seat:

'You know, I had one of them black and white minstrels in the back of me cab once . . .'

15

It was raining when the cab reached Highbury Corner, and the streets were mercifully empty. When he had paid off the cab, Philip let his sponge fill with some of the fortuitous rain-water, after which he and George stood together beneath a tree on Highbury Fields wiping the make-up from each other's faces. They made little impression on the splodges of white grease – Philip advised his young accomplice to raid his aunt's cold cream when he got home. He thanked him again for his invaluable help, and for the umpteenth time impressed upon him the need for absolute silence and discretion. He did not waste his time in making appeals to loyalty or any other abstract concept: the carrot he dangled was of the variety labelled 'self-interest'. If George really was intent on drama school, then Philip was his only man; he was unlikely to get in anywhere on merit.

Philip crossed the Fields and approached his home stealthily. Once he had sneaked back into his flat he immured himself again in the bathroom, the only place in which he dared to put on the lights. Though worried by the noisome antiquity of the plumbing, he decided that his need for a bath outweighed the need for caution – when he removed his wig he found his hair stiff with a Medusan lacquer of sweat and lake-bed muck. In the circumstances the requirements of hygiene were pre-eminent. He turned on the taps and while waiting for the tub to fill, leafed through the papers he had filched from Ken's office. They repaid his close attention.

He lay in the bath with his flannel draped over his freshly scrubbed head and tried to relax. He recalled the evening's events and couldn't resist laughing aloud:

'The expression on that policeman's face! It was like something out of Ben Travers . . .'

When he had finished chuckling to himself he gave an expansive yawn. He felt bone-tired after his night's exertions, the hot water was comforting. And it was a damned sight better than being at the bottom of a freezing lake.

He sat up suddenly, splashing water on to the floor. He tore the flannel off his face and tossed it angrily towards his feet.

'He tried to kill me tonight, and he bloody nearly succeeded . . .'

He glanced over at the pile of papers sitting on his bathroom chair.

'Bloody nearly . . .'

The identity of the culprit could no longer be in doubt. Who else had been present at all three incidents? Who else stood to gain from his demise? He reached out a dripping hand and carefully lifted up the top paper between finger and thumb.

'A bit corny this plot, Ken old love. Just because you make crap films you don't have to live them as well, you know. Swiss bank accounts, dodgy insurance policies, you've got a hell of a nerve if you think you can get away with a scam like that. But then, that is one thing you do have a hell of a lot of, isn't it? If I were casting I'd have to pick you for the Artful Dodger. You should have been my number one suspect all along; strange how sometimes you can stare the obvious in the face and miss it. But then again, you're slippery as a greased eel. Does take something to live on your wits, I know. In a way I ought to admire you, as one pro to another. But I don't. I just despise you . . .'

He unhooked the plug-chain with his toe and climbed out of the bath. He stood dripping on to the mat, staring at his steamy reflection in the mirror. His eyes were hard, expressionless. He smiled thinly, with his mouth only.

'I'm afraid you picked on the wrong fall-guy this time, Ken old boy. You have scotch'd the snake, not killed it. Too bad you're not going to get another opportunity. It's my turn now. It's only fair.'

He put on his towelling robe and sat down on the edge of the bath. He looked through the sheaf of bank statements among the papers. They bore the logo of the Canton Union bank, Zurich.

'So you're off to Switzerland again tomorrow, are you? Told Mandy you'd be going in the evening. With that little bundle of greenbacks in your briefcase. That gives me a few hours to play with. A few hours for you to sweat in. I wonder what you'll be thinking when you discover your office has been turned over. You'll be worried about this little lot, you'd be a fool not to be. I'll keep you guessing for a while. Keep you off-balance. Do you perceive how I give line? Never hit a man when he's down. Wait till he's not looking, then kick him in the groin. You can't say you don't deserve it, you double-damned smiling villain. Oh, that one can smile and be a villain. Still, I suppose I shouldn't take it too personally. Mustn't let emotion complicate the issues. And what are the issues, pray? Why, that's easy enough: death and money. Your death and my money.'

He lit a cigarette and smoked it to the butt, inhaling deeply as if trying to draw in inspiration. When he had finished he lit a second from the remains of the first. He tapped the sheaf of papers with the back of his nail.

'You promised me a hundred grand, Kenny my boy. It's all here, in the contracts. Never intended to pay me though, did you? Not a sausage. Not a penny. Not a very good idea, my friend.'

He blew smoke at himself in the mirror, misting his reflection.

'Steady on, that's practically an act of *lèse-majesté*.'

'My apologies, Sir Philip.'

'Less of the lip, old boy, let's get back to the details. How do you propose to separate the man from his loot? You've done enough cat-burgling for one night, haven't you?'

'I agree. Even if the money's still in his bedroom, which is by no means certain, at this time of night he'll be there as well. It's too risky.'

'Glad to hear a note of realism at last. How, then?'

'Blackmail, of course.'

'You sure you've got enough on him?'

'You're joking! The man's another Maxwell!'

'Ha! I think he'd be flattered.'

'Yes, you're right. No, Kenny's a hick, he's not a big league player. It's very crude all this stuff, you know, that's probably why he had to come to Britain. He's obviously done it before and he may have run out of stiffs in the States to con; it's not the kind of routine anyone's going to fall for twice.'

'All right, but what if he agrees to give you the money? He's not going to take it lying down, is he?'

'No.'

'In fact, if he was prepared to nobble you before, think how much more cause he'll have now. You going to wear a bullet-proof vest, then?'

'Not a bad idea; a pity I don't have one. No, I shall just apply the old movie-making maxim: screw all others as they are screwing you, only preferably screw them first, before the same thought even occurs to them.'

'Sounds just like the good old days to me.'

'Indeed. The good old bad old days . . .'

'And have you worked out a plan?'

'It's coming. I have the location and I have the method. They are both apt. The rest is detail.'

'The rest is silence. Are you sure you're up to it? This is heavy duty.'

'What do you mean, am I up to it? Have you forgotten that you're in the presence of one of the most successful murderers in British criminal history?'

'That was a little while ago.'

'Riding a bicycle, old man, it's like riding a bicycle. Once learnt, never forgot.'

'I'm not sure it's the analogy I'd choose, but I take your point. And you've motive enough.'

'Oh yes, I have cause. And will, and strength and means to do it.'

'Good. Then let it work . . .'

He turned out the light and went into his bedroom, where he rummaged in the wardrobe with the aid of his torch. He picked out a suitable collection of old clothes and laid them ready with his make-up for the morning. He reckoned that he would need an hour or so to prepare. He set his alarm clock for six, tucked it under his pillow to muffle the noise, and got into bed. Despite his tiredness he took some time to get to sleep. His head was full of schemes.

He awoke to a cold, dark, unwelcoming morning. No change there at least, he thought, remembering all the dismal dawns he had witnessed in the past few weeks. He dressed in his pre-selected old clothes. At least there would be no gruesome filming today, although the location at Black Park featured heavily in his plans. He approved of symmetry in all things.

He thought about the scene in Black Park while he sat in the bathroom applying his make-up. He presumed they would have been up all night, trawling the lake for his body. The lake wasn't large, he wondered at what stage they would become suspicious and give up. He thought that they would probably have to keep at it for the rest of the day. He wondered if the story had leaked out yet.

Of course it had! There couldn't be any filming, what else would the cast and crew have to do but talk? Fax and telephone lines must have been humming through the night. The press might be an added complication, but in view of his own parlous situation he couldn't afford to delay his plans. If Ken Kilmaine was spooked prematurely, his trip to Zurich might be a one-way job.

It might anyway. Philip imagined a series of crisis meetings. The backers would be asking questions. How skilled would Ken be at deflecting them? Pretty skilled, if past performance was anything to go by. He had, after all, inveigled everybody in to begin with, Philip included. He imagined how the meetings would go, Ken joining in with the general scratchings-of-head and worried frowns, appearing to search desperately for a solution. But there wasn't one, as he well knew. A film which stalls halfway through shooting, with an unusable because unfinishable major performance in the can, is simply unredeemable. Now, if the film had been nearly complete, then they might have been able to stitch something up, using a double and an actor with an approximate voice for dubbing purposes. Alternatively, had they been near the beginning of shooting, then they could have done an emergency recasting job, but for the project to collapse at the midway point presented insurmountable difficulties, not least because of the contractual unavailability of Sleat from the end of the next month. Philip probably knew the details better than anyone, Ken excepted; he was in possession of photocopies of all the contracts.

Sleat's was the most interesting: as Philip had suspected after their brief conversation in the boat, it could very well have served as the role-model for a course in how-not-to-draw-up-a-movie-contract. But fascinating as it was, it took on an extra dimension when read in conjunction with a couple of faxes from the offices of Mr Witt, for the gentleman in question (Mr Witt-less as Philip now thought of him) appeared to be under the impression that the pop star had only agreed to sell his services in return for a very considerable six-figure sum in advance. Quite a lot of other invoices failed to match up to actual payments and most of the expense claims looked fanciful to say the least. The money transfers from Witt-less's office in Brussels, the trips to Switzerland and the hefty deposits of not unadjacent sums in the Zurich account formed a pattern which a congenital idiot could not have failed to notice. And financially illiterate as he so very nearly was, Philip Fletcher managed to notice it too.

It took him half an hour to apply his make-up. It was a rather less startling job than last night's, but none the less quite radical. It was another of his famous old men.

He had always been good at old men, ever since he had been cast to play Firs in Bristol at the age of twenty-eight. That performance was one of his finest memories, and although he no longer had the original wig and whiskers, the new grey hairs which he combed lovingly into place suggested at least a hint of his former triumph. He was older now, and the bags and lines which he had once etched on to his youthful face did not, alas, have to be worked up entirely from scratch, but the end-result still looked sufficiently unlike him to warrant the deferral of abandoned hope. He checked himself in the full-length mirror in the bedroom. In his tatty old black coat and frayed trousers he gave off an air of genteel dereliction. He gave himself the thumbs-up:

'Suit the action to the word, and the word to the action. Come in, Ken Kilmaine, your time is up . . .'

He went into the kitchen and made himself a large pot of coffee and a jam sandwich, which was about all there was in the house. When he had finished his scanty breakfast he took his judge costume out of the drier and put it into a stout carrier-bag, along with the portable phone, his two torches, his alarm clock, his emergency make-up kit and a thermos containing the rest of the coffee. It was going to be a long day.

He went rapidly through the house covering up signs of his presence. It was possible that the police might think of some reason for wanting to snoop around his flat, and he didn't want to arouse suspicion. Displaying the same caution, he sneaked out of the house while it was still just dark, though he knew full well that none of his neighbours was likely to spot him at such an early hour.

He walked briskly across the Fields to the tube station, stopping only to buy an armful of newspapers from the kiosk outside. He scanned through them eagerly on the journey to Piccadilly Circus.

He had made as many front pages as if he'd just won an Oscar – it was impossible not to feel gratified. And the things they'd said about him! Appended to all the details about the accident and the search for his body was a set of quotes from his peers to make even a hardened egomaniac blush. And underneath his thick coat of make-up, Philip blushed. People out there really did like him!

'Sally Field, eat your heart out,' he murmured as the train pulled out of Holborn.

The only sour notes came from a director who gushed a little overmuch about his extraordinary talents (if you felt like that about me, why didn't you ever employ me when I was alive, you little bastard? Philip thought) and one of the sillier tabloid theatre critics (the term was relative), who described him merely as an actor of 'the middle order'.

'Hope your life insurance is up to date, luvvie,' he breathed as they passed through Covent Garden. He thought that he might yet come to terms with being dead. He wondered how long he'd have to remain missing before any of them ran his obituary. And what they'd say if he wrote in afterwards to offer corrections.

He was still snickering to himself as the train stopped at Leicester Square. A few of the other passengers gave him sidelong glances, but a bit of loopiness quite fitted in with his characterisation, so he didn't mind. He carried on giggling and mumbling to himself on the short haul to Piccadilly Circus. He turned over the front page of the *Daily Mail* as the train slowed down, looking for the promised bit of 'contd page 2'.

'Well, bugger me!' he yelped involuntarily, twitching convulsively in his seat and spilling newspapers all over the floor.

It was probably just as well that he'd done a bit of spadework in the harmless eccentricities department. All the other passengers studiously ignored him as he snatched up his scattered papers and lunged for the door, catching it only just in time.

He stood on the platform as the train pulled away, feverishly reading and rereading the little paragraph. It was the photo above which had caught his attention:

'Kate Webster – "terribly upset"', the caption said.

There was more. The reporter had obviously got to her with the news first, and it had been a shock. She had sounded 'tearful and horrified', it said. Philip Fletcher's loss was a 'cruel blow' and a 'senseless waste', it said. (Go on! he thought – more!) And she was flying 'straight back to England', it said.

Philip preened. He hadn't felt this self-satisfied since leaving a note at the age of thirteen to say that he'd gone off to join the Foreign Legion and then hiding in the cellar while his mother and aunt wailed hysterically for half an hour in the living-room.

'Well, that'll learn you,' he said smugly, refolding the paper and putting it into his carrier-bag along with the others. He left the tube station with a surprisingly jaunty step for one of his advanced years.

He found a perfect spot in Dean Street in which to wait, a little alley whose entrance was more or less opposite the KenKil offices. He sat down on a conveniently placed cardboard box and prepared for a long wait. At least he had plenty of reading matter to be going on with.

The delectable Shaz finally rolled up at about a quarter to ten. The police were there fifteen minutes later. Ken Kilmaine took another hour.

He leapt out of the back of his chauffeur-driven Mercedes even before it had stopped moving and took the three steps up to the front door in one bound. Philip caught only the briefest glimpse of his face, but the look of sweaty fluster gave him enormous satisfaction.

He got up, dusted himself down and picked up his bulging carrier-bag. Now he had to find a quiet spot.

Of course, there is no such thing in central London in daytime, but an untenanted corner of Soho Square suited his purposes well enough. He settled himself down against a tree and took out his portable phone. Ken had been in his office for ten minutes now, long enough to know the worst.

Philip dialled the office number. It was engaged. He tried the second line. This time it rang. In fact it rang and rang and rang. He was beginning to feel a little anxious when finally it was answered.

'Yeah, whaddya want?' demanded an edgy-sounding Shaz, deploying her full range of receptionist's skills.

'I vant to speak to Herr Kilmaine,' said Philip thickly, employing his best BBC general-purpose Nazi.

'He's busy, he ain't got — '

'Tell him zat I am calling from ze Canton Union Bank in Zurich, I think zat he vill vant to talk viz me, it is most urgent, thank you, *Fraülein*.'

It was not the kind of voice to brook any argument. While Shaz went off to find her master, Philip took a quick look around the Square. A motorcycle messenger sitting on a bench was staring in his direction, but he glanced away quickly when Philip leered manically at him. He had the portable phone wrapped loosely in a newspaper, so he supposed that he looked just like any other common-or-garden nutter communing with today's *Daily Telegraph*. London was full of them.

'Ken Kilmaine speaking,' said a familiar voice tersely. Philip pressed his mouth very close to the receiver.

'Hello, Ken, me old china,' he said, slipping into his none-too-subtle cor-luv-a-duck Bailiffs' Men routine (*Aladdin*, Bournemouth, 1978).

'Who the hell is this?' Ken snapped back, without a hint of his usual stick-on charm.

'Ah, don't say you don't remember me, Ken me old mate. I'm cut to the bone!'

'Christ, you're not another sodding reporter, are you?'

'No such luck, not for you at any rate, my son. I'm just someone who happens to be in possession of certain information concerning the disappearance of one Philip Fletcher. Or should I say – murder!'

He left the tiniest of pauses. Ken's failure to make an instant response told him everything he needed to know. He continued quickly, not giving him a chance to recover.

'That's right, Kenny my boy, there may be some as thinks it was just a boating accident, but you and me know better, don't we? What would your insurers say, I wonder, if they knew just who it was who'd pulled the plug on our chum Phi-lip?'

'Look, who the –'

'Not so fast, sunshine, it's me who's asking the questions, and you ain't heard nothing yet. What about that little bank account you've got in Zurich, then? Insurers know about that too, do you think? And that nice Mr Witt? And the Inland Revenue, let's not be forgetting the little grey men with calculators. I expect Her Majesty's Inspectorate of Taxes would be very interested in a copy of some of these charming little bank statements like what I have a fistful of right here and now in front of me at this very moment in time. About time you changed the combination on that safe of yours – 38–26–36 – don't you agree, Kenny?'

'I said, who the hell are you?'

The voice was shocked and quiet. Philip laughed softly.

'Now, you don't really suppose I'd be telling you that, do you? Let's just say this – I'm not a greedy man.'

There was another pause at the other end. The voice when it spoke again was cooler and more in control.

'What do you want?'

'A hundred K.'

'A hundred thou . . . you have got to be joking, I can't get hold of that sort of dosh, be realist – '

'Oh, Kenny, don't disappoint me! What's in that black suitcase you keep hidden under your bed, then? Monopoly money?'

The pause this time was interminable. Philip was glad that he wasn't paying the phone bill.

'OK,' Ken managed eventually, his voice colourless and practically inaudible. 'What do you – '

'I'll call you later with the details,' Philip interrupted smoothly. 'Be on this number at between four and five o'clock this afternoon.'

'But – '

'No buts, matey boy, or when you check in at Heathrow tonight you won't get a boarding pass and a trolley for the Duty Frees. It'll be the Fraud Squad with a pair of off-the-peg bracelets for you, my lad!'

Philip threw down the phone (and the *Telegraph*) without giving him a chance to reply.

'And now,' he said, rubbing his hands together like the Demon King (also *Aladdin*, Salisbury, earlier vintage), 'let it come down . . .'

He picked up his carrier-bag and headed back to Piccadilly Circus, where he bought a one-way ticket to Uxbridge. He had less than five pounds left in his pocket. If things didn't work out, he was going to have trouble getting home.

He was in Black Park by lunch-time, courtesy of tube and bus. As he had suspected, the whole lake and car park area were cordoned off, but the open space, containing the mock-village set, was still accessible. He approached it the long way round through the trees and settled down in a secluded spot amongst the undergrowth. With the car park closed there were few people about anyway, but a succession of heavy showers in the early afternoon must have dispersed all but the hardiest walkers. Sometime round about two o'clock he noticed that the whole open-space area was completely deserted. He made his way rapidly over to the village, to the spot where he had almost been killed.

The façade of the Spreadeagle Tavern had been repaired and re-erected. He checked around the back first and saw that the braces were reinforced with extra metal weights. He lifted a few up and replaced them. They were almost too heavy for him. In other circumstances he would have found that comforting.

He marched round to the front and carefully measured the façade with his eyes. The big glassless open window with the shutters pinned back was dead in the middle, about fifteen feet up, the pole with the gallows rope sticking out a foot below. The rope was looped about the pole, tied up safely out of harm's way. He went back to the rear of the flat, climbed the narrow steps up to the window and unhooked the rope. He let out all of the slack, until the noose was coiled up on the ground below.

He went back down and unpicked the noose. He paced out the area in front of the façade. When he had made his calculations he dug his heels in to make a mark and left the tip of the rope next to it. It was just long enough.

He double-checked around the back again, made some further adjustments and carried one of the smaller weights out to his mark. He tucked the end of the rope underneath it. Satisfied that everything was in place, he returned to his secluded spot in the woods.

At half past four he dialled Ken's number. Ken answered personally.

'Got the readies, me old matey?'

'Yeah, but what — '

'Ken, Ken, Ken! You really must get out of the habit of asking so many questions. Now listen, and listen good, I'm gonna say this once only: be at the film set in Black Park outside the Spreadeagle Tavern at six o'clock. Have the money in your black briefcase, and you'll get all your documents back. Got that? Oh, and come alone, any sign of company and I'm scarpering.'

'Look, I don't — '

'Just be there, Kenny my boy, or you might as well go straight round to the nick and book yourself in for thirty years. See you at six, Kenny. Don't be late.'

He put down the phone. He didn't see how Ken could afford to be late, not if he wanted to catch that plane. A lot would depend on traffic, though, he'd be heading out on the M4 during the worst of the rush-hour. He was unlikely to be early. It would be dark by six.

It would be dark, quiet and secluded. A dangerous place to be. Philip hoped he knew what he was doing. It was a bit late now if he didn't.

Another heavy shower had started. Philip sat hunched uncomfortably under a tree, water dripping off his wig. It was just as well there was nobody about, he could feel his make-up streaking. At least it would be dark soon.

In fact it was almost dark now. He took the opportunity to skirt round the edge of the woods and have a look out over the lake. There were some lights in the car park but none round the shore. He wondered if they had officially given up searching for him. He returned to the village to make his final preparations.

He put his carrier-bag down behind the tavern façade and took out the two torches and his white frilly costume shirt. He walked out front to his mark and tied the sleeve of the shirt very loosely to the end of the rope. Then he laid the small torch down beside the metal weight and turned it on, the beam pointing upwards. Carefully he covered the torch with the shirt, weighing the corners down with some pebbles in case of a breeze. It was a clumsy device, he knew, but he would need the shirt for later and it was simpler to work with the materials to hand. He retreated to the doorway, the big torch off but at the ready, and waited.

He watched patiently as darkness finished falling. It was a cloudy, squally sort of evening, and well before six everything was enveloped in pitch. He thought he could just see the faintest cloudy glow spilling out from underneath the shirt, but he may have imagined it. He could no longer see to read his clock. But it must have been almost on the dot of the hour when Ken Kilmaine turned up.

Philip saw the thin beam of his torch approaching from the direction of the lake. He didn't suppose that he had used the car park, but the road ran nearby in that direction, so it was the logical quarter from which to expect him. Philip climbed up the steps to the first-floor window and waited for the torch to draw nearer. It seemed to take an age.

'Hello?' Ken whispered hoarsely from out in the middle of the street. 'Anybody there?'

Philip reached out for the pole and gave the rope a tug. The shirt slipped off and the glow of the small torch became visible.

'Where are you?' Ken demanded edgily, flashing his own torch wildly all over the place. He failed to pick out Philip, who was peering round the side of the window.

'Walk towards the light!' he commanded firmly.

Ken turned the torch towards his voice, but Philip ducked his head back in time.

'Try to shine that on me again and that's it, matey,' he said crisply. 'I'll be out of here quicker than you can say Swiss bank account . . . now turn off your torch and walk up to the light.'

Ken did as he was told. His silhouette materialised out of the darkness. Quickly Philip climbed down the steps and repositioned himself in the doorway.

'Where's the money?'

Ken indicated his briefcase.

'Put it down next to the light and open it towards me.'

Ken knelt and unclicked the catches. He lifted the lid.

'Now step back and keep your hands by your sides where I can see them.'

Philip knew all the best B-movie lines.

He turned on his torch and shone it into the briefcase as he walked over. He knelt down and thumbed through a wad at random. It looked real enough.

'Who are you?' Ken demanded.

'Tut tut!' Philip aimed his torch on to him, forcing Ken to

raise a shielding hand. 'You are inquisitive, aren't you? Move round – over there . . .'

He indicated where he wanted him to go with the beam, a little nearer the base of the tavern flat. By now his own feet were close to the metal weight, the end of the rope with the shirt attached was inches from his toes. He had everything as he wanted it; he had Ken exactly where he wanted him.

Go on! he told himself. Now do it!

But Ken was standing there docilely enough. He wasn't going anywhere in a hurry. And Philip's curiosity was burning a hole inside him.

'It's me who's going to ask the questions, Kenny, and you who's going to answer them. Let's start with an easy one: how many times have you done this before?'

'What do you mean?'

'You know very well what I mean. How many movies have you deliberately screwed up – and how many backers have you screwed along the way?'

Ken hesitated. Philip shone the torch directly into his eyes, keeping up the pressure.

'I don't know . . .' he answered, flapping his hand at the torch-beam as if trying to push it away. 'Five or six. It's never got this far before.'

'How far does it usually get, then?'

'Just to pre-production. Get hold of the right sort of mug to deal with and sometimes you can get a hefty slice out of them without any more than a two-page treatment. Usually you need a script, though, to get any decent development money.'

'And that's when you say "We'll need another hundred K up front", only if you've got a mug like Harvey Goldman on tap he'll do it for half of that and the rest goes into your back-pocket?'

'That's right. Only a mug like Harvey Goldman's a lot cheaper than that.' There was a hint of cockiness in Ken's voice; even now he wanted to show off.

Philip smiled grimly. 'And of course someone like Wayne Schlesinger comes pretty cheap too. It's clever, Ken. Ninety-nine movies out of a hundred never get made, but not usually for want of trying. I can see that you could make a pretty good living from just pocketing the development money. But why did you take it so much further this time?'

'I didn't intend to. Only Mr Witt and his friends were a bit sharper than any of the others I'd dealt with. Or maybe I just got careless. In any case, I'd only worked the racket in the States before, I wasn't used to Europe. I was a bit casual with some of my expenses, Witt kept wanting to see results. I had to start booking locations, studios, even actors, just so he could see some action, and he kept checking up on me too. No one had ever done that before, the slimy bastard even had a tail on me for a couple of weeks.'

'You don't say?' Philip murmured with heavy irony. Slime, he assumed, was in the eye of the beholder. 'How did you manage to snare old Witt? He's no fool with money, they say.'

'Oh yeah? Don't you believe it!' Ken's voice was full of contempt; he was clearly warming to his theme. 'I've seen it happen dozens of times before. You get some punter who's bright as a button and shrewd as they come, and the moment you mention "movies" to him he goes bananas. And just when you think the world's run out of mugs another one always comes along. If you think about it, it stands to reason: I mean, no one sensible would ever have anything to do with making movies, it's all pot luck and bullshit, look at Hollywood – no one knows what the hell they're doing, but they think if they keep running fast enough no one'll notice. It's all about keeping balls in the air, and that's what it is, a load of balls.'

'So why have you failed to dazzle Mr Witt?'

'I haven't. Oh, he's been as big a sucker for it as any of them. You know, showbiz parties, dinner with Shelley Lamour, he lapped it up. That's usually all they want, set 'em up with an actress or two and their feet don't touch the ground. Only Witt wasn't interested in leg-over. Can you believe it – a Swede who never gets laid! You know, he goes everywhere with that ugly little daughter of his? Miserable Scandinavian git.'

'Maybe you should stop using a faded has-been like Shelley Lamour as your bait. So Witt refused to just go away quietly when you accidentally-on-purpose failed to get a deal off the ground and wanted to know where the money had gone. Don't tell me the creative accountants have met their match?'

'Yeah, well, not so you'd notice . . . anyway, eventually he said that if I didn't start filming within a month he'd pull the rug out from under me, and he'd want to know where every penny had gone. As I'd nicked everything I hadn't spent, that wasn't on now, was it?'

'I take your point. Why did you pick on Philip Fletcher as your fall-guy?'

'Because he was there. I had Shelley to give it respectability, and then I had Wayne and Harvey and that pop singer wally who I always thought would back out of anything at the last minute anyway. In short I'd hired a bunch of dickheads, couldn't shoot their way out of a paper bag, let alone a sodding film. I thought if I got enough dickheads together it'd all be bound to fall apart, I couldn't believe it when I heard about Fletcher, thought he'd been made in heaven for me. Wasn't my fault that the bastard went and dried out before we started filming, was it?'

'I think you made a big mistake there,' Philip told him coolly. 'Fletcher's a real old pro.'

'Yeah, well I was just trying to load as many dice in my favour as I could. I thought between that lot of weirdos one of them had to foul up.'

'But when they didn't, you decided to give a helping hand. Why did you go for Fletcher?'

'I had to. Sleat was too expensive to insure, the papers I sent to Witt were fakes. Anyway, Sleat had his bodyguards round him the whole time. Fletcher was vulnerable, I thought Marve was gonna make mincemeat of him.'

'So that was the plan, was it, the set-up with Marve and Shelley?'

'You don't make plans where Marve's concerned; he's so thick it'd be a waste of time. But you've only got to let any bloke within three feet of Shelley and it's like a red rag to a bull. I done it before, it works a treat. But then the stupid bastard goes and duffs old Harve up. Shelley shouldn't have let it happen.'

'So Marve's reputation for busting up other men is down to you, is it? But usually you get him to work on the punters before anything's got off the ground, only Mr Witt wouldn't play ball. Is that all there is to it?'

'More or less.'

'So this time you aimed to turn Marve loose on Fletcher?'

'Yeah. He didn't have to kill him, you understand. Six months in plaster would have done fine. It's a pity what happened to Wayne didn't happen to him. Would have saved a lot of bother. You work in Witt's office, don't you?'

'Eh?' Philip shrugged. 'What makes you say that?'

'No one else apart from my secretary has access to this kind of information, and she's as thick as Marve. She's well pissed off with me at the moment, she is. Was it her told you I had the dosh in my briefcase?'

'Whoa there, I thought I was asking the questions. So let me get this straight: with the film folding due to circumstances beyond your control, you're planning to cash in your insurance policy and use it to fill in the gaps in your dodgy paperwork. Sounds risky to me, but I'm sure you know what you're doing. Now I've got a technical question for you: how did you get that boat to sink? The other accidents were easy to arrange, but the plug in the boat looked secure when it left the shore. How did you manage to tamper with it?'

'He didn't,' said a cool woman's voice out of the darkness behind him.

The hairs on Philip's nape stood up like a wire brush. He started to turn automatically, but barely had he begun to move when something hard and metallic was jabbed into his spine.

'Hold it right there, mister, this thing is loaded and I ain't kidding.'

Well, of course she knew the B-movie dialogue too; she'd been in enough of them herself.

'Christ, Shelley!' Ken swore through gritted teeth. 'You took your time!'

Philip felt his head swim. Over the blood thundering in his head he heard the sex-bomb's low, throaty laugh.

'Never fear, the cavalry's here.'

She thrust her gun harder into his lower back.

'Hands up, mister, and don't move a muscle. Ken, frisk him.'

Philip put his hands above his head, though he felt so enervated he hardly had strength to raise them. Ken came over and searched him roughly.

'Christ, Shelley, never do that to me again. I was shitting bricks.'

'I had to be sure he was on his own, honey.'

'And is he?'

'Yup. There ain't nobody here but him . . .'

She punctuated her words by tapping the point of her gun against his back. There was still a touch of the familiar folksy drawl in her voice, but there was an underlying hardness which Philip hadn't heard before. Perhaps, he acknowledged ruefully to himself, she was a better actress than he had given her credit for.

'He's clean,' Ken said when he had finished patting him down. The photocopied papers were pulled from his inside pocket. Ken snatched the torch out of his hand. 'Right, let's have a look at what we've got!'

Philip winced as the torchlight stabbed his eyes, but it was turned away as abruptly.

'Jesus wept!' Ken gasped. 'What an ugly sonofabitch!'

Philip did not usually think of himself in those terms. He supposed that his make-up must have run rather more badly than he had realised.

'Yuck!' Ken muttered, flashing the light briefly back on and off his face. 'He looks like the bloody elephant man!'

'Don't be stupid,' Shelley snarled, giving Philip another poke. 'Who are you, mister?'

'I'm Sean Kilmaine, Ken's long-lost half-brother.'

'Like hell!' declared Ken indignantly. 'I'm an only child!'

'Shut up!' snapped Shelley. 'Can't you see he's making a fool of you?'

She came round in front of him and thrust the gun into the pit of his stomach.

'Put the torch on him again.'

Philip tried to turn away as Ken shone the light at him, but Shelley grasped his face with her spare hand and held it in place. Her fingers were strong and her grip hard.

'This ain't no long-lost relative, you imbecile,' she snarled. 'Why, you're as stupid as that half-witted husband of mine.'

She sank her fingers into his hair and with one savage jerk ripped off his wig. There was a moment's silence, then Ken gasped in disbelief:

'You . . .'

Philip couldn't see him, but he could imagine him standing there, like one of the conspirators before the unmasked Count of Monte Cristo, jaw agape and pointed finger trembling.

'Yes, that's right,' Philip answered as lightly as he was able. 'It's only little old me.'

'I don't believe it!' Ken squawked, his voice bursting with panic. 'What are we gonna do?'

'Same as we were going to do before,' Shelley answered with steely calm.

'What?' Ken yelped, aghast. 'You can't shoot him here!'

'I'm not gonna shoot him here, you idiot,' she snapped. 'Keep your voice down and get a grip on yourself.'

'What a trusting and amiable partnership you two must have,' Philip tossed in casually.

'You keep your opinions to yourself, mister,' Shelley commanded.

'But we can't just carry on as if nothing's happened!' Ken pleaded desperately. 'It's not just some nobody trying to screw us like we thought. Look who it is, for God's sake!'

'Yeah, I'm looking,' Shelley replied. 'I'm looking at a man everyone thinks is already dead . . .'

There was a pause, then Philip heard the long, low whistle as Ken sucked in his breath. He had got it.

'The brains as well as the beauty of the outfit,' Philip acknowledged with a show of gallantry, inclining his head towards her. 'At least I understand how you got the boat to sink.'

He could just about see her now she was in front of him. Ken was a little behind her shoulder and a slight spill from the torch touched on the blonde tresses and pale face. He was glad really that he couldn't see the face – if the eyes were half as cold as he imagined them, he might have been unnerved.

'Why, a gentleman to the last,' she answered with a sneer. 'I figured Ken's game early on, and I don't like being used, mister. That damnfool husband of mine used me, tricking me into marriage by making me believe that bull about all his oil millions. Only oil that dumb hick ever owned was for greasing his six-gun . . .'

Like oil it was all flowing out of her now: the words gushed as if breaking through a dam of repressed bitterness. He was only half-listening, the rest of his brain was desperately engaged in trying to think what to do next. It wasn't easy.

'. . . I spent my life with bullshitters, so when a guy like Ken here comes along I spot him a mile off –' (there was a mild whimper of protest from behind which she ignored) '– but when I saw him coming on with his first con I thought, hell, I'd like a piece of that, why not? Folks have always been using me, so I just been doing a piece of using back. I'm good, huh? You've gotta admit that.'

'Oh, I do,' Philip answered. 'You're very good.'

A real pro, in fact. The dumb blonde act had certainly taken him in, and countless others before him, as he now realised. Ken may have been the instigator, but in a situation like this hers was the cool head, and she was the one to fear.

She was the one with the gun.

'Not bad for a faded has-been, huh?' she sneered. 'All right, I ain't gonna stand here yakking all night. Ken, tie him up.'

'Tie him up!' repeated Ken incredulously. 'What with?'

'Don't be dumb. There's a rope by his feet, can't you see? And give me your torch.'

Ken handed her Philip's torch and took his own out of his pocket. He was well covered now. For a moment Ken's body passed in front of the gun, but he didn't dare run, he wouldn't have had a dog's chance. He knew somehow that she could use the gun, that when it came to it she would be the one pulling the trigger and not him, and that there wasn't a molecule of compunction in her. And in any case the odds were better where he was, if only he could keep his nerve.

He was calmer now. His legs still felt a little weak, but the fog in his brain had cleared. That was good. He knew that there might only be a split second in which to act, and that if he missed it they wouldn't hold the final curtain.

'The rope's attached to something,' Ken mumbled grumpily, pulling the loosely tied shirt off the end and giving it a tug.

It may have been his imagination but Philip thought he heard a trembling in the wood and canvas frame of the façade. Ken dropped the rope.

'I'll go and untie it.'

Ken shone his torch at the façade, picking out the other end of the rope looped round the pole. Philip knew the moment had come.

'Oh, please!' he whimpered hysterically. 'Please don't shoot me, please!'

He flung his face into his hands and burst into tears.

'Knock it off!' growled Shelley.

Philip sank to his knees and stretched out his hands imploringly.

'Spare me, I beg you! I won't tell anyone, I promise. Let me live and I'll do anything you say . . .'

His face fell forward into the dirt. His body was racked with sobs.

'Shut up, you wimp,' Ken protested with disgust. 'Die like a man, can't you?'

Philip turned his cheek and blinked the water out of his eyes. Ken was standing about six feet from the base of the flat, pointing his torch upwards. Philip edged his body closer to the metal weight, his mark. His right fist closed around the end of the rope.

'I'll have to go up around the back to unhook it,' Ken complained. 'Do we really need to bother? He's so pathetic he's not going to cause trouble.'

'Famous last words . . .' said Philip.

He knelt up and pulled on the rope with all his strength.

'Hey, what you doing?' Ken demanded.

He had seen the rope go taut. Philip was pulling with all his strength. For a moment it didn't seem to be enough, but then the rope suddenly went slack.

Ken and Shelley were shouting, either at him or at each other, he couldn't tell. He hunched himself up into a ball and waited what seemed an age.

'Shelley! The wall!'

Ken's torch flashed across the moving mass of scenery. It was falling so slowly it looked like something out of a cinema shot. He dropped his torch and ran.

'You bastard!' Shelley said simply.

Ken's screams were drowned by the crash of scenery. The noise rolled over Philip in waves from all sides, threatening to burst his ear-drums. His eyes and lungs filled with dust. He flinched as something hard winged his leg, but he kept himself screwed up tight. The earth beneath him shook.

His ears were humming long after the noise had stopped. He raised his head slowly, painfully, choking and gasping for air. He struggled to his feet in a daze.

His shoe brushed against the metal weight, his mark. There was a whole row of the things over by the base of the façade, lying where he had put them after loosening the supporting braces. The black briefcase and the small torch lay next to the mark, on a patch of ground six feet square. The window had fallen exactly over them, his calculations had been flawlessly accurate. Buster Keaton would have been proud of him.

The air was still thick with dust, exactly as he remembered it from last time. He shone the small torch around and saw that one of the struts had broken exactly as before, though the façade itself had not fallen flat this time. Instead it had split and there were jagged tears in the warped wood. That was how it had been meant to look, after the 'accident', with him buried underneath it. Only Ken and Shelley had taken his place.

Ken was somewhere near the base, under a hump of twisted wood and canvas. Shelley was rather nearer.

She hadn't tried to run, she had stayed where she was, inches from the sanctuary of the window square, if only she had known it. Her right arm was visible, the hand extended forlornly towards him as if begging to be rescued. The gun had slipped from her fingers. It was a neat black revolver. He picked it up and found that it was warm.

'My God, she tried to shoot me! The bitch!'

He snapped open the chamber to confirm it. One of the cartridges had been fired.

'Oh no, my leg . . .'

He shone the torch on it anxiously and saw that the calf had been grazed. There was a lot of blood, but it wasn't deep. The bullet had only nicked him, she must have been thrown off her aim by the collapsing scenery. She wouldn't have missed at that range otherwise.

Philip stood gaping at the gun and the lifeless hand which had fired it at him. He couldn't believe how lucky he'd been. He felt the merest twinge of regret: Miss Shelley Lamour had been a worthy foil. He trembled so violently he could hardly put the gun away in his pocket.

'Pull yourself together!' he said urgently. 'Got to get moving . . .'

The noise of the crashing set had been tremendous. In the stillness of the night it must have carried for miles, and although the police had given up searching the lake for the night, he was sure that they must have left at least a patrol or two behind. They might be on the spot within minutes.

He snatched up the black briefcase and shone the torch on to the ground to check that he hadn't left any tell-tale signs. He had – several: not only the frilly white shirt but also the grey wig which Shelley had snatched off his head and which was sticking out from under the edge of the window.

He picked them up and stumbled over to the base of the wreckage, from where he retrieved his carrier-bag. Pausing only to stuff the shirt and the wig into the bag, he headed off briskly in the direction of the road, the small torch showing the way. His big torch was somewhere under the flat, but there was no point in worrying about that. There was nothing to connect it with him anyway.

It took him ten minutes or so to negotiate his way through the trees and the dense undergrowth. He wanted to be away as quickly as possible, but he was forced to stop for long enough to remove the remnants of his make-up, which he had to do without benefit of a mirror. He could only apply the cold cream liberally and hope. When he had done what he thought was a reasonable job he reapplied the grey wig, pulled up his collar and muffled his face with his scarf, and walked down the road to catch a bus.

When he returned from Slough by the same bus an hour later, the air was thick with the sound of sirens.

WORLD EXCLUSIVE!

STAR DISCHARGED

'It's great to be alive!' says 'lucky' Philip.

Actor Philip Fletcher, whose sensational disappearance rocked the nation, discharged himself from hospital today only forty-eight hours after being discovered alive and well.

A smiling Philip, pictured here with pretty nurse Jackie Williams, twenty-two, described himself as feeling fitter than he'd ever felt before, adding, 'It's great to be alive!' He was discovered in a barn on the property of local farmer Bill Merton nearly thirty-six hours after he had gone missing following a boating accident on nearby Black Park lake, during the filming of *Midnight Rider*. Philip still cannot remember exactly what happened.

BEN GUNN

'I'm afraid my mind's a complete blank,' said the star of TV's *Sir Walter Raleigh*, scratching his head. 'I remember swimming for my life but nothing after that. The police think I must have somehow dragged myself out of the lake and wandered round in a daze before stumbling into the barn and passing out. Luckily for me there was plenty of straw handy or I'd probably have died of hypothermia! I'm very lucky Mr Merton found me in time – he must have thought I was Ben Gunn! – and I'd like to express my gratitude to him, the police, and the doctors and nurses at the hospital for saving my life. But I know that I'll never be able to thank them enough.'

TRAGIC LOSS

Mr Fletcher was shocked to learn of the tragic deaths of his co-star Shelley Lamour (Montana Madigan in *Desire*) and his producer Kenneth Kilmaine, as reported first and exclusively in this paper last Friday. 'It's a terrible loss,' he said, visibly shaken and fighting to control his emotions. 'I really feel as if the whole film was jinxed. First Harvey, then me and now this. It's unbelievable.' Mr Fletcher was referring to scriptwriter Harvey Goldman who is himself recovering in hospital after being assaulted by Miss Lamour's husband, Mr Marvin Loudwater, who is reportedly devastated by his wife's death. Mr Goldman was said to be in a comfortable condition yesterday evening.

POLICE BAFFLED

The police are still baffled by the deaths of Mr Kilmaine and Miss Lamour, who were crushed to death by falling scenery. Mr Fletcher confirmed that it was not the first accident involving the set.

'We just don't understand what they were doing there,' said Chief Inspector Nick Becker, who is leading the investigation. 'We are ruling nothing out at this stage.'

FRAUD SQUAD

Chief Inspector Becker refused to comment on press speculation that Mr Kilmaine's death may have been suicide and that Miss Lamour perished while trying to save him. However, he did confirm that as a result of papers found in Mr Kilmaine's possession the Fraud Squad have been called in to investigate serious financial irregularities in Mr Kilmaine's film production company. 'It's one hell of a can of worms,' said a source who did not wish to be identified. 'I shouldn't be surprised if we're looking at a major scandal here.'

An early episode of *Desire* featuring Miss Shelley Lamour is to be shown as a tribute tonight. Turn to our TV guide, page 24, and you too can enter our Spot the Star competition!

16

George came to collect Philip from hospital in his uncle's car. He was surprised when Philip asked him to drive first to Slough station, but he knew him well enough by now not to ask questions. Nor did he quiz him about the black briefcase with which he returned from his trip to the left-luggage lockers. All he asked, very politely, was for a time when it would be convenient for him to come and collect the references he had been promised. Philip told him to bring round his drama school application forms later in the afternoon.

They stopped at an off-licence on the way and the first thing Philip did on reaching home was to put the bottle of champagne which he had just purchased into the freezer. He then went and listened to his messages (only one was of any interest) while flicking through the Yellow Pages for a florist. When he had found one who promised same-day delivery he rang through with a long and detailed order.

He took the champagne out of the freezer (barely chilled but it would do), stacked it in the ice bucket and took it, a glass and the black briefcase into the bathroom. He opened the briefcase and tore off all the paper sleeves on the bundles of fifty-pound notes. Then he scattered the money all around the bath.

He opened the champagne, kicked off his shoes and jumped into the bath.

Philip was asleep in the bath when the phone rang. He rose stiffly, shedding flakes of money like dead skin, and went through to the bedroom to answer it.

'Philip?' said Mandy shyly.

There was something about the unaffected coyness of her tone which really got to him. He lit a cigarette to steady his nerves.

'Oh, Philip, thank you for the flowers, they're so beautiful!'

'Not at all. Thank you for yours.'

'Oh, but they were nothing in comparison. Anyway, you had dozens in hospital. You could hardly have noticed mine.'

It was true his room had looked like an outpost of Kew Gardens. But he had given her bouquet pride of place.

'How are you feeling, Philip? I can still hardly believe I'm talking to you after what happened. It's a miracle!'

He told her how perfectly well he felt, putting on his modest game-for-anything act which he did so well. His quiet courage thrilled her. His own brilliance astounded him.

'All those terrible things that happened!' she said, shocked and earnest. 'It's just awful! Poor Shelley. And poor Ken. The things they're saying about him, they can't be true, can they?'

'I'm afraid they are. It seems he was a pretty unscrupulous crook.'

'But all that work we put into the film, it's such a waste.'

'Yes,' Philip answered neutrally. 'I hope you haven't suffered financially.'

'Well, I'm owed money, of course, we all are, but I've got another job, did you know that?'

'No.'

'Oh yes, I start in a month's time. It's one of the leads in a three-part American mini-series. It's just come up out of the blue, I've been really lucky.'

'How wonderful. I think this calls for a celebration. What are you doing tonight?'

'Tonight? Well, I – nothing! What did you have in mind?'

'In all conscience I couldn't possibly offer you less than a champagne dinner. Only – I'm still feeling just a touch on the weak side . . . would you mind awfully coming here?'

'What, and pick you up?'

'No, I was thinking we could eat in. I'm actually rather a good cook, if a little rusty.'

'But I don't want to be any trouble – '

'No trouble at all. Yes, I'll get something in, that'll be much cosier. Shall we say eight o'clock? You've got the address.'

'Well, if you're sure it's no trouble – '

'Of course I'm sure. I look forward to it.'

'So do I. See you at eight.'

When he had finished on the phone Philip made a quick recce of the flat. It was in urgent need of Thing-like ministrations. He tidied vigorously for half an hour, then sat down and wrote out a shopping list. When George rang the buzzer he went out to meet him in the hall. He waved the shopping list and a couple of fifty-pound notes in George's face.

'While I'm filling in your forms, would you be an angel and pop down to the shops for me? You can keep the change.'

George offered no protest. True to his part of the bargain, Philip went back to his desk and earnestly composed specious encomiums to his young friend's dramatic abilities. There were half a dozen of them, all aimed at the best schools. With the recommendation of one of the finest actors in the country behind him, George damned well ought to be able to get into one of them. When he had finished he went into the bathroom for some loose change to cover the audition expenses. The phone rang as he came back into the bedroom.

'Is that . . . Philip Fletcher?' said a girl's voice hesitantly. 'It's Jackie Williams, from the hospital.'

'Jackie! My dear, how are you?'

'I – well, I'm . . . I just wanted to say thank you so much for the flowers, they're really amazing.'

'Nowhere near as amazing as you! It's just a very small token of thanks, for all your care and attention. I don't know what I'd have done without you.'

'But it's so sweet of you . . . I don't know what to say.'

'Then say nothing at all. Honestly, it's the least I could do. You know – I say, I've just had a thought. Now I'm up and about again I really feel like celebrating. Funnily enough I've got to come back down to your neck of the woods tomorrow to sort a few things out. You're not free by any chance tomorrow evening, are you?'

'Tomorrow? Well, I'm on duty till eight – '

'Perfect! I can come and pick you up at the hospital. I think the very least I can do after all you've done for me is to buy you a champagne dinner. You live near Iver, don't you? I'll book a table at the Rose Inn.'

'Oh, but that's terribly expensive!'

'Please, please, no more protests, I won't hear another word. It'll be my treat and no more than you deserve. It'll be lovely to see you again, Jackie.'

'Well, I – I, yes . . . that sounds wonderful.'

'Then I'll see you tomorrow at eight. Look forward to it.'

Philip replaced the receiver neatly on the bedside table. His critical eye on overtime, he fastidiously tucked in a corner of the freshly changed sheet. Then he went next door and rearranged the dining furniture.

George returned with two bulging shopping bags. They unpacked them in the kitchen.

'What's these things, then?'

'Asparagus.'

'How'd you cook 'em, then?'

'You boil them for four hours in scalding water. Pass me the candles, will you?'

Philip arranged the candles on the dining-table and lit them to check the effect. He drew the curtains.

'Somethin' wrong with the lights, then?'

'Candlelight is generally considered to possess aphrodisiacal qualities lacking in its electrical counterpart.'

'You what?'

'I thought you'd stopped doing that. Have you chosen your audition speeches yet?'

'Yeah, well, I thought I'd do that Romeo geezer again.'

'Yes, well, when you do "do" him, try and sound a little more enthusiastic, will you? Faint heart never won bugger-all, George. Take it from me. There.' Philip stood back from the table and admired his handiwork. He readjusted the fresh flowers in their vase. 'What do you think?'

'Got a bird coming round tonight, then?'

'George, your talents will be wasted in the theatre. You would make a natural consulting detective. Excuse me, I have to answer the phone — '

He went into the bedroom to take the call.

'Philip?'

He was rather surprised, he didn't know why. He had been expecting her, after all.

'Philip, it's Kate.'

'I know, darling. I haven't forgotten the sound of your voice already. Thanks for the answerphone message. I was going to call you later. How are you?'

'How am I? I don't think that's the issue. How are *you*?'

'Oh, bearing up — '

'Come off it, Philip, don't give me any of your mock-heroic nonsense. I've heard the dying speech from *Hamlet* too often.'

'Thanks, I've missed you too.'

'Have you?'

Her tone was serious. He didn't know what to say. Fortunately she carried on speaking anyway. 'I never thought I'd say this — but I have missed you, Philip.'

'Oh?'

'Yes . . . Mind you, it doesn't mean that I've stopped thinking you're a vain, selfish, egotistical, egomaniacal, ridiculously self-satisfied arrogant self-destructive infuriating bastard, but then again, nobody's perfect. I've got to go back to the States on Friday. Any chance of seeing you before I go?'

'After that character reference I'm not sure my ego could stand it.'

'Your ego could stand a nuclear explosion. Are you free tomorrow?'

'Um, no, er, business meeting. Wednesday?'

'Fine. Should I make a reservation?'

'Why don't you come here? I'm still a dab hand in the kitchen. Unless you've forgotten the way.'

'All right. I look forward to it. And Philip — I'm glad you're alive. When they told me you were dead I — it was just awful.'

'Yes, I found it pretty awful too. I'll tell you all about it on Wednesday, come at eight. Oh, and Kate — one last thing.'

'Yes, Philip?'

'Thanks for the Christmas card.'

When he returned to the living-room, George was sitting in his chair, idly skimming through a book.

'You know somethin',' he said, glancing up from the page. 'You still ain't told me about what happened the day after we did the Soho job.'

'No, I have not, and I'll tell you something else; nor am I going to. We actors each have our parts to learn, George, and it's quite enough without having to bother with everyone else's. Now it's time for you to be going, I'm afraid, I've a busy schedule. Here are your forms, and here's the money for the fees. What's the book you're reading?'

'Anthology of verse, you said I gotta learn some poem.'

'Not "some poem", George, I told you to learn a Shakespearian sonnet, an essential tool for the aspiring verse-speaker. You won't find one in there; I'll sort out the right book for you tomorrow.'

'You gonna give me that lesson tomorrow, then?'

'Yes, yes, now shoo!'

When he had gone, Philip picked up the book and wandered back into the bathroom, flicking idly through the pages of densely packed poetry.

'I suppose I'd better clean this lot out,' he acknowledged reluctantly, looking into his money-bath. He glanced at his watch.

'Oh, plenty of time.'

He kicked off his shoes and climbed back in. He reclined on the bed of notes, stretched, and opened the book at random.

'Got to take it easy. Conserve my strength. At least I won't have to bother to move the dining-table back. Mm, I wonder what the spare sheet situation is. Can't afford half-measures. I've a reputation to live down to.'

He snapped shut the book on his chest and reclined gracefully. He smiled up at the ceiling and recited from memory.

> Then bring my bath and strew my bed
> As each kind night returns.
> I'll change a mistress till I'm dead
> And fate change me to worms . . .

'Bring my bath indeed!'

He ran his hand along the bottom and splashed some money about. He noticed his champagne glass by the soap dish. He raised it to the mirror.

'I'll purge, and leave sack, and live cleanly, as a nobleman should do.'

He took a sip. It was a little flat, but not unpleasant. He winked at his reflection.

'But not just yet . . .'